"You don't owe me an explanation."

"Don't I?" Beau's voice held a husky edge.

The boat rolled again, this time the hull creaking. This time Tuesday barely registered the motion. A body could only hold so much emotion. His cool gaze locked on her face.

"What do you want?" she whispered.

He leaned forward as if to stand, then snapped his head back.

"This." He grabbed her in his arms and his mouth found hers right as the boat rolled on another breaker. They went flying back onto the mattress.

His lips tasted like butterscotch, and he braced his weight, holding himself over her like a surprised shelter.

She also got an overwhelming feeling of safety…even as his kisses became more dangerous by the second.

"I can't be near you and not do this," he growled into her mouth.

ACCLAIM FOR LIA RILEY'S NOVELS

IT HAPPENED ON LOVE STREET

"Witty banter, sizzling chemistry, and a romance that captured my heart!"
— Jennifer Ryan, *New York Times* bestselling author

"In this thoroughly delightful novel, the sexual tension is steamy, the plot engaging, the characters always entertaining, the dialogue witty, and the situations often hilarious. This tale is certain to make readers smile, laugh outright, and sigh dreamily. In short, it has everything a reader is looking for in a romance."
— *BookPage*

"Big-city girl meets her match in a tiny Georgia town filled with quirky characters, legends, secrets, and puppies in Riley's Everland, Georgia, series debut. The stars . . . are skillfully done. The feud between the two towns and a buried treasure subplot make this laugh-out-loud funny."
— *RT Book Reviews*

"Thanks to friendly townspeople, crotchety Scrabble players at the dog park, and an irrepressible younger sister, even city dwellers will see the appeal of falling in love while stranded in a small Southern coastal town."

—*Publishers Weekly*

WITH EVERY BREATH

"In this emotionally charged contemporary the protagonists' personal struggles for self-worth and redemption develop into pulse-pounding adventure and breath-stopping romance. . . . This novel will delight [Riley's] fans and new readers alike."

—*Publishers Weekly*

UPSIDE DOWN

"Fresh, sexy, and romantic, *Upside Down* will leave you wanting more. I cannot wait for the next book. Lia Riley is an incredible new talent and not to be missed!"

—Kristen Callihan, award-winning author of the Darkest London series and *The Hook Up*

"*Upside Down* is a refreshing and heartfelt new adult contemporary romance."

—*USA Today*'s *Happy Ever After* blog

"Lia Riley turned my emotions upside down with this book! Fast paced, electric, and sweetly emotional!"

—Tracy Wolff, *New York Times* and *USA Today* bestselling author

The Corner of Forever and Always

PREVIOUSLY BY LIA RILEY

Off the Map

Upside Down

Sideswiped

Inside Out

Carry Me Home

Into My Arms

Wanderlust

With Every Breath

Everland, Georgia

It Happened on Love Street

The Corner of Forever and Always

An Everland, Georgia Novel

Lia Riley

FOREVER
New York Boston

Copyright © 2017 by Lia Riley
Excerpt from *It Happened on Love Street* copyright © 2017 by Lia Riley

Cover design by Elizabeth Turner.
Cover photography © Shutterstock.
Cover copyright © 2017 by Hachette Book Group, Inc.

Forever
Hachette Book Group
1290 Avenue of the Americas, New York, NY 10104
forever-romance.com
twitter.com/foreverromance

First edition: September 2017

Forever is an imprint of Grand Central Publishing. The Forever name and logo are trademarks of Hachette Book Group, Inc.

The publisher is not responsible for websites (or their content) that are not owned by the publisher.

The Hachette Speakers Bureau provides a wide range of authors for speaking events. To find out more, go to www.hachettespeakersbureau.com or call (866) 376-6591.

ISBNs: 978-1-4555-6872-7 (mass market); 978-1-4555-6871-0 (ebook)

Printed in the United States of America

OPM

10 9 8 7 6 5 4 3 2 1

To Bronte... I'm so proud that you've learned to read—way to go! Someday you can even read this book, but all in good time, big girl.

Acknowledgments

First up, big thanks to Michele "Emotion Whisperer" Bidelspach for always spotting authentic ways to deepen every story—you are such a talent, and it's an absolute pleasure to work with you. To Emily Sylvan Kim—I'm proud to call you both an agent and a friend. To PB&J—who have learned to yell in my ear when I'm drafting to get my attention...I'm a little deaf, but I love you. To Nick— you are my forever and always, and here's to another eleven years (and many more). To my writer friends who keep me sane each and every day—Jennifer Blackwood, Jennifer Ryan, Chanel Cleeton, A. J. Pine, Megan Erickson, Natalie Blitt, and Jules Barnard. To my readers—there are lots and lots of books in the world; thanks for picking up mine.

Fairy tales are more than true: not because they tell us that dragons exist, but because they tell us that dragons can be beaten.

—Neil Gaiman

The *Back Fence* Moderator Private Facebook Chat:

Phaedra1953: I was on my morning power walk—Doc said to drop fifteen pounds or start the blood pressure medication—when Mayor Marino flew by on that new motorcycle of his. We should make him our next *Back Fence* matchmaking project. It's nothing short of our Christian duty.

ScrabbleLuvR: Beau Marino is a boy, and you're a cougar—worse, a horny old saber-tooth. Although it is high time that the mayor got a second chance at happiness. What do y'all think about Pepper Knight's sister, the one with the funny name? She's pretty as a picture.

IdaMayI: If Beau's a boy, I'm a bikini model. Tuesday Knight will never do. Last week those two almost knocked down the sun-dae table at the Halfway Baptist Ice Cream Social, bickering over the best way to peel a banana. But not to worry. We'll find the per-fect princess for our prince. Lord knows he deserves a happy ever after.

Chapter One

Owning a pair of heels that went with everything was convenient, except when they blended into the background like chameleons.

"Where are my glass slippers?" Tuesday Knight scanned her bedroom. They could be hidden anywhere beneath the chaotic avalanche of maxi dresses, celebrity magazines, bohemian scarves, and Lindt chocolate ball foils.

Her twelve-year-old Boston terrier emerged from beneath the quilt piled at the end of her unmade bed.

"Any bright ideas?" Tuesday asked, shoving a loose bobby pin deeper into her French twist.

J. K. Growling spluttered a snort as a rooster crowed from deep beneath the mess. Tuesday hiked up the skirt of her fuchsia ball gown, kicking items left and right. That crow was her nine o'clock backup alarm, the one that meant "Leave now or you'll be late."

A vague memory started to take shape as she plucked her

iPhone from beneath a back issue of *Vanity Fair*. Last night, following a ten-hour shift as Happily Ever After Land's newest princess host, she'd collapsed on the couch—ears ringing from the carousel's Wurlitzer band organ—to play a game of Oregon Trail.

Of course!

She tore down the hall, skidding to a stop in the living room doorway, and punched the air. Sure enough, the glass—or rather, plastic—slippers, were propped atop a throw pillow. Right where she'd shucked them off after dying of dysentery at mile eight hundred and forty on that stupidly addictive phone app.

A rhinestone-encrusted tiara twinkled from atop the coffee table book *Broadway Musicals: The 99 Best Shows of All Time*. Tuesday plopped it on her head, adjusted her bodice over her nonexistent bosom, and shoved her feet into the smidge-too-tight heels. Good to go.

J. K. Growling peered around the corner with a bemused expression.

"It's not easy being a princess." Tuesday gave her a good-bye head pat. "But if the shoe fits…"

Opening the front door, she paused, struck, as usual, by Everland's quiet. Manhattan had been a noisy symphony of jackhammers, cab horns, loud neighbors, and police sirens. Here the coastal breeze rustled the hundred-year-old live oaks lining the shady street, dripping moss from thick, gnarled branches. A bird sang. A dog barked. A neighbor tuned a mandolin on a front porch swing.

Just another September morning in small-town Georgia.

Her orange car—Pumpkin—started on the third try, the gas light blinking on. Forehead, meet steering wheel. Her least favorite game was playing "How Low Can You Go" with her gas tank.

But there wasn't a choice. She didn't have enough funds in her checking account to afford a refuel, not after giving Lettie Sue, a park waitress, her last hundred bucks before tomorrow's payday.

Yesterday, the single mom had broken down in the staff room over her inability to cover next week's day care bill. Afterward, Tuesday had snuck to the snack bar to make an ATM withdrawal and had left an anonymous envelope in her coworker's locker.

She didn't regret giving the hardworking woman a single penny, but the impulsive decision couldn't derail her obligations. In twenty minutes she was hosting a field trip for Foster Friends, a local children's charity. If she didn't dilly-dally she'd have enough in the tank to get to work and home.

It Came Down to Fumes and a Prayer: The Tuesday Knight Story.

A sudden movement caught the corner of her eye. Her big sister, Pepper, and her sister's fiancé, Rhett, staggered from the house next door, a laughing tangle of limbs and leashes. Between them, the happy couple owned four dogs. At the start of summer Pepper had moved to Everland for an ill-fated legal clerkship. After losing her job on day one, she'd detoured into what had turned out to be the right direction, finding work as a dog walker and falling head over strappy sandals for the hot vet next door. Now she was spearheading the opening of Everland's rescue shelter as the new executive director.

"Hey, you!" Pepper glanced at her thin wristwatch, brows wrinkling beneath fashionably cut side-swept bangs. "Aren't you running late?"

"Yup." Tuesday restrained a grimace. The one drawback to living next door to such a capable, successful sister was frequently feeling like a hot mess. She cupped a hand to her mouth. "Lost my shoes."

"Again?" No surprise registered on Pepper's pretty face. They played their respective roles well, the responsible, dependable, reliable one versus the free-spirited, walking disaster. But when Tuesday's world in New York City had spun out of control, she'd headed straight here. Her big sister was true north even in the Deep South.

"Are we going to see you tonight?" Rhett called. They were hosting a potluck dinner around the theme of "Southern comfort." Pepper had entrusted her with the napkins. It wasn't meant as an intentionally insulting gesture, but unintentionally? That was a whole other story.

"Wouldn't miss it for the world!" Tuesday cracked a tight smile before driving away. Downtown Everland was more or less deserted this time of morning. The lovingly restored buildings dated back to the late nineteenth and early twentieth centuries, but the town was more than a hodgepodge of bright awnings, mom-and-pop-style storefronts, and cheerful planter boxes. The charm lay not just in the brick and mortar, but also the bighearted, warm, and welcoming (if eccentric) citizens.

A bay window etched with the words "What-a-Treat Candy Boutique" stenciled in calligraphy caught the morning light. She gasped as today's date hit home. It was What-a-Treat's owner Ginger Reed's thirtieth birthday. For a week Ginger had been informing customers that she was preparing to enter a mystical time warp whereupon she'd remain twenty-nine forever.

Kitty-corner to the shop sat city hall, the imposing brick

building framed by a profusion of late-summer flowers. "Perfect." She slammed on the brakes. If she hustled, she could pick a quick bouquet for her friend and leave it in front of the candy shop's door as a surprise.

She climbed from Pumpkin and raced over the damp lawn, crouching beneath an office window to grab Shasta daisies, goldenrod, and a few begonias. The blooms were vibrant, just like her new friend. In fact, they looked so pretty she picked a few more, and just a few more, and what the heck, now that she had this much, she might as well go the whole hog. After all, forever is a long time to stay twenty-nine.

A throat cleared behind her.

"Morning!" She squinted at a security guard, backlit by the bright morning sun. "Don't mind me. I'll be out of your hair in a sec."

"Well, Miss Knight, it's like this, see…" He shuffled from side to side. "There's been a report of vandalism."

"Really?" She glanced around, half expecting a lurker to be slinking from oak to oak, clutching a spray paint can. "Graffiti? Arson? Broken windows?"

The man removed his blue cap and studied the embroidered brim with particular attention before mumbling under his breath.

"Theft?" she repeated, unsure if she'd heard him correctly. "Who's dumb enough to steal in plain daylight?"

The security official grimaced. "The complaint was about you destroying city vegetation."

"Who gives a flying fig if I pick a few flowers?" The drape twitched in the window above, and her core temperature dropped. She pursed her lips. "Tell me, whose office is that?"

Dumb question.

"Mayor Marino requested that you be informed this space is Everland public property and not your own private garden."

"For Pete's sake." Her laugh was incredulous. The locals here were as charming as their town except in one respect. Their mayor had a stick shoved far up his (admittedly fine) ass.

"One more thing, ma'am." The security guard swallowed hard and adjusted his belt buckle over his straining belly. "I'm supposed to confiscate the flowers."

"Come on. They're picked." She waved the gorgeous bouquet under the security guard's nose. "The damage is done."

"Orders are orders, ma'am."

She glanced at the clock tower. "Crap. Is that the time?" Forget getting all "no justice, no peace." The foster kids would arrive in five minutes. "Fine. Here." She shoved the blooms into his arms. "Give these to the mayor with my regards."

"He's left the premises on official business."

"Well, inform him upon his return that he's *officially* a jerk." She fumed back to her car. Last week she'd taken J. K. Growling for a walk in the rain. They'd been minding their own beeswax, splashing in ankle-deep puddles on Love Street, when Beau Marino had driven by with a face like she was you-know-what stuck to the bottom of his shoe. He'd rolled down the window and told her she was jaywalking.

She'd told *him* where to stick it.

She also might have kicked a splash in his direction. She wasn't proud.

Balling her hands into two fists, she almost smashed a

lone Shasta daisy, the sole survivor of Operation: Bouquet Obliteration. Tossing the flower on the passenger seat, she cranked the volume to her beloved *Grease* sound track. Tuesday might look the part of a wide-eyed, angelic Sandra Dee, but she had Rizzo's soul.

She increased her grip on the steering wheel as she drove past the abandoned Roxy Theater, a crumbling eyesore off the otherwise neat and tidy Main Street. Even the for-sale sign plastered to the marquee had weathered to tatters. Once someone had built the place with grand hopes, but starry-eyed dreams had a bad habit of fizzling faster than a meteorite striking the Earth's atmosphere.

Tuesday knew all about that phenomenon thanks to two-time Tony Award–winning director Philip Chandler.

Pumpkin's wheels hit the road's rumble strip, the tactile vibration warning that she'd drifted too far right. She bit down on the inside of her bottom lip and corrected, taking shallow breaths to work around the asphyxiating knot in her chest. Despite the eight-hundred-mile distance stretching between here and Manhattan, the name Philip Chandler made her insides roil. Not every fairy tale had a happy ending, especially ones that started as "Once upon a time, a girl was duped by a narcissistic, cheating a-hole…"

A beep from the pink Cadillac in the oncoming lane interrupted her navel-gazing. Tuesday couldn't decipher Miss Ida May's face from beneath the straw hat garlanded with silk flowers but made sure to give her neighbor from Love Street a chipper wave. Miss Ida May administered the Everland gossip blog, the *Back Fence*, and was constantly trolling for a juicy scoop.

Drive along, ma'am. Nothing to see here.

No one in Everland knew the rumors, an ensemble actress trying to seduce her way into a breakout role. Or so the tall tale went. And whoever let truth get in the way of a good story?

Pepper could never find out about those last few terrible months in the city. Her sister didn't need another reason to think she was an idiot.

Tuesday had wanted to be a star so badly that she had allowed herself to be lured into her director's net of lies like a stupid fish, unable to escape. Tears prickled in her eyes, and she blinked hard, stamping them out. No pity parties were allowed in Scarlett O'Hara country. She'd take a page from the fierce heroine's playbook and not think about that now. Instead, she'd toss her head and sing.

The song ended as she passed Happily Ever After Land's main entrance on the town outskirts. A school bus turned beneath the sign that read Yo DREAMS START HERE. The "u" and "r" were missing. The only decent parking spot left in the staff lot was a tight squeeze beside a group of professional-looking people filing out of a deluxe minivan.

Terrific. Reverse parking with witnesses.

Tuesday lowered the volume to "Look at Me, I'm Sandra Dee" and swallowed a groan as her gaze locked on the tall, deeply tanned, dark-haired man in a gray blazer who towered over the group with intense "va-va-voom" eyes that would be completely sexy if not for the stony glare.

Her toes curled in her fake glass slippers as she fought the unwelcome pyrotechnics detonating in the pit of her abdomen.

Beau Marino, aka Hater of Random Acts of Joy.

When not calling security over war crimes against begonias, the man gave good face with his strong, dark features, aquiline nose, stern mouth, and an innately haughty air that earned him the town nickname of "the Prince of Everland."

She blinked first, and worse, her heart did that thing where it ran flailing into walls, or more accurately, her rib cage. This man's face had an irritating habit of setting off a chain reaction of unwanted physiological responses.

Stupid beautiful face.

It took three tries to park Pumpkin and she still ended up crooked. Whatever. Good enough. She set the hand brake and fished in the center console for bubble-gum-pink lipstick, taking her time with the application.

The stray daisy on the passenger seat gave her an idea. Tuesday might not know how to behave, but the princess would. "Showtime," she muttered before climbing out of the car, keeping her gaze wide-eyed and vacant. "Why, if it isn't the mayor! Oh me, oh my! Always a thrill to have local dignitaries visit our most humble kingdom," she trilled, inwardly smirking as a muscle twitched near his ear.

Stupid beautiful ear.

There wasn't a single good reason why such a mundane body part should look so freaking attractive. But it did. Then there were the three faint freckles dotting the center of the lobe, the second thing she'd ever noticed about him, after the pale eyes, blue irises cut by white rays and contrasting with his darker skin. Mesmerizing eyes that matched his tie. Unsmiling eyes that were…currently affixed to the wilting blossom clutched in her hand.

She broke the stem and stepped forward, shamelessly popping the daisy into his buttonhole. "A small token of my great esteem." She cloaked the needling tone inside her sweetest pitch. Her fingers grazed hard muscle beneath his suit. Dang, what was he packing in there? The muscles in her belly tightened before she blinked and straightened.

If he had any inkling of her agitation, he hid it well behind a narrow gaze, eyes riveted to her chest. "What *is* that?"

She glanced down with a grimace. A brown blob dangled from the satin bow in the center of her bodice. "Oh, shhhhhhhhhhh—ugar bowl." No hiding the fact that she'd inhaled a slice of peanut butter and banana toast for a rushed "over the kitchen counter" breakfast.

One of the group members, a middle-aged guy whose mustache gave him a walrus-like appearance, handed over a napkin stamped with the Mad Dawgs logo, Everland's popular bar and restaurant.

"Why, thank you, kind sir. Good to see chivalry is still alive and well among *some*." Tuesday dabbed her torso and gathered the remains of her dignity, lifting her chin like the Queen of England, not an underpaid actress in a stained dress and plastic shoes. "Now, to what do we owe the pleasure of your patronage?"

"We're from the Georgia Tourism Commission," a kind-faced, silver-haired woman with funky dangling earrings answered.

"Castles and Cauldrons! Haven't you come to the right place?" Tuesday plastered on a saccharine smile and wadded the napkin into a tight ball. Obviously Beau Marino had come to the park in a professional capacity. A man who called security over flower picking wouldn't have fun for fun's sake, not on a workday. "Why, Happily Ever After Land is the best time you can have around these parts with your clothes on."

The twitch in Beau's temple intensified to a thrumming

pulse. That vein could pop in three…two…What the mayor needed was a not-so-gentle reminder that life was an out-of-control roller coaster, so you might as well throw up your hands, laugh, and occasionally scream.

"The park just so happens to be hosting another very special group today," she chirped in her most singsongy voice. "A field trip of foster children awaits a royally good time."

"My oldest daughter fosters." The silver-haired woman clapped her hands. "Mind if we tag along? Observe the kids' reaction to the park?"

"I…" The mayor looked like he'd rather trim his nails with a chain saw, but he was trapped. "Of course, Donna." His lips curved at the edges, but Tuesday knew better. His flaring nostrils gave away his displeasure.

Her answering smile was 100 percent genuine. Time for Mr. Mayor to buckle up. He'd stepped onto her turf, and she intended to take him on one wild ride.

Chapter Two

~

Beau Marino plucked Tuesday's daisy from his jacket. But instead of tossing it on the pavement, he impulsively shoved it into his pants pocket, right next to his phone, the one his assistant, Karen, had lectured him to stay off of during today's tour.

"Keep your beak off that screen today, sir," she'd ordered as he'd left the office. "Remember to talk to actual people. You're getting good at it."

He'd mashed his brows. "Am I?"

"Well, better anyway," she'd demurred. "And smile... You have such a nice smile."

Introversion was a liability for someone in public office. He found it a hell of a lot easier to connect with constituents through social media platforms than to shake hands and kiss babies at town events. While not a natural "man of the people," he was committed to improving his community and making a difference, as corny as that might sound. His grave brand of cordiality was natural, and served him better than a politically phony persona.

After all, his constituents had elected him for a reason: to get things done. Improve the town's economy and make it more attractive to investment and growth. For the last six months, a large part of his strategy had been cultivating the Georgia Tourism Commission, lobbying them to grant Everland a "Coastal Jewel" designation, a coup that would yield a prime spot in their nationwide advertising campaign.

Today was a capstone event. Everything hinged on his town tour running smoothly, and here he was, right out of the gate, hitting a tiara-wearing speed bump.

"Right this way, ladies, gentlemen…and goblin." Tuesday Knight hiked the hem of her ridiculous dress and beelined toward the amusement park's side entrance, leaving him to bring up the rear like a sullen caboose. His forehead creased into a frown at the not-so-subtle jab.

The tourism board had to take him seriously if they were to take Everland seriously. The last thing he needed today was to get stuck playing court jester to her princess.

Sweat sheened the corded muscles in Beau's back, prickling against his dress shirt's cotton. The worst of the summer heat was over, but in another hour the relative humidity index would ratchet into the high eighties. His gaze latched on to Tuesday's pale arms, the delicate curve to her neck. How did she always look so relaxed and unaffected? She had an almost ethereal quality, as if floating through life.

Just last week he'd driven his best friend, Rhett Valentine, home after their usual Wednesday-night regatta. Rain bucketed down as he'd turned onto Love Street, and there in the middle of the road, Tuesday Knight had been kicking in puddles—barefoot—playing with her fat little dog, the one that looked like it had taken a running leap into a brick wall.

Such behavior wasn't normal. This was real life, not a musical number. Every time he set eyes on the woman, she bounced like Tigger, incessantly—relentlessly—cheerful. And who the hell had a name like Tuesday anyway?

No one with any sense.

"Care to elaborate on the park's history, Mr. Mayor?" Angie Robert, one of the junior commissioners, trailed an appreciative gaze down his frame. "Why, it looks as if this old place has been here an age."

"An astute observation, Ms. Robert." Beau tried not to stiffen at the woman's blatant scrutiny, sliding on his Ray-Bans to avoid her uncomfortable eye contact. "Happily Ever After Land is an Everland institution, built in the beginning of the twentieth century despite the fact that financing conditions proved challenging following the Panic of 1907, during that three-week crisis in the New York Stock Exchange, of course—"

"Once upon a time, a man had an ambitious vision," Tuesday broke in, spreading her arms in an expansively dramatic gesture. The group perked up as she breathlessly went on to spin the tale of Bartleby Hodgeworth, "a young, penniless dreamer who'd come to Everland with nothing but the clothes on his back and saw how this sleepy town a stone's throw from the Atlantic could be transformed into a place of magic and wonder, a place where children of all ages could forget their cares. To this day the park harkens back to the golden age of amusement—"

As much as Beau hated to admit it, Tuesday's bullshit had captivated the commission more than his formal spiel on the park's engineering and safety record followed by a monthly breakdown of visitor demographics. Instead she focused on tidbits such as how Hodgeworth insisted on painting buildings white for elegance and modeled the park's centrally situated palace after Balmoral Castle in Scotland.

Tuesday slipped to the end of the line as the VIPs filed ahead through the side-entrance turnstile. "You're welcome," she hissed.

It was disconcerting how she nearly met his gaze at eye level. Her height always caught him by surprise given she gave off such a dainty air, the kind that made a man instinctively slip into protection mode. Fucking stupid reaction, because here was a woman shot with steel. Her lips might be plump, pink perfection, but those caramel-colored eyes hinted at hidden mettle.

Who'd she be if she ever quit performing for two goddamn seconds and got real?

He curled one hand into a fist, rubbing his thumb over the base of his ring finger, the patch of skin now bare. Better to choke off the unwelcome curiosity and take that flashy "look at me" personality at face value. He needed to get mixed up with another drama queen like he needed a third nut.

Still, his stomach rolled over when the tip of her tongue put in an appearance, dabbing the center of her top lip. "I single-handedly saved your bacon back there. A riveting time line of financial collapses? Good Lord, you're like a human NyQuil."

"I have it under control. Or I did until you came along." Anger grated his voice. Any pretense of politeness frayed. She made a spectacle out of even the simplest interactions.

Her eyes glittered, and her jaw lowered, a chink in her serene princess mask. "If life were meant to be controlled, it would come with a frigging remote." And with that, she stormed off, taking the last word with her.

* * *

Tuesday bustled past the Skee-Ball booth while Lead Game Attendant Toots Landish wagged a finger. "Tick-tock, tick-tock, Princess, you're running la—Mayor! Well, now. Butter my buns and call me a biscuit. Ain't this a surprise?!" Her signature cat-eye glasses magnified her startled gaze as she snapped to attention, dusting the overhanging plush flamingos that served as prizes.

"The foster kids' school bus just pulled in. I'm going to head them off by taking the shortcut behind the carousel," Tuesday called.

"Going via the Magic Train Depot will get you there quicker." Beau folded his arms, his withering know-it-all attitude like nails on a chalkboard.

"Yeah. Thanks." She bared her teeth in a weak attempt at a smile. "Remember, good sir, I am a kingdom resident."

"And I grew up hanging around in the park." His brows furrowed in a death-ray glare. "Spent every summer on these rides."

"Apparently you rode the Tilt-A-Whirl a time too many and scrambled your brains." Ugh, she wanted to kick him right in his pompous, know-it-all attitude. "Trust me, going behind the carousel is much faster."

"Will you listen to sense? The train route will get you there in half the time."

"Carousel." It took Tuesday a few seconds to realize the sudden sharp pain in her palm was her nails stabbing into her flesh. Good Lord, forget about killing the mayor with kindness. She might just kill this mansplaining shit pickle outright.

Would it hurt him to admit that maybe—just maybe—she was right?

"Train." His tone was unflappable.

"Sakes alive, what a pair." Toots pointed a finger at Tuesday. "Listen here, Miss 'Once upon a time.'" She pivoted to Beau. "And you, too, Mr. 'Dark and Stormy Night.' You're both wrong with a capital dubya. Here's what you're going to want to do. Head straight toward the chair swings and make a right at the funnel cakes." She gave the nearest flamingo a satisfied pat on the head. "That'll see you there in half the time."

"Everyone, please take a moment to mark that woman," Tuesday announced to the group, fighting back her rising hackles as she smoothed her skirts. "She's been around this park longer than anyone else, even the current owner, Mr. Wilcox. A true local living legend."

The tourism board broke into obligatory applause, and Tuesday's heart warmed at the sight of Toots's flustered beam. Happily Ever After Land wasn't a dead-end job to her. She treated the other staff like family and had adopted Tuesday on day one. Her mothering style bordered on smothering, but there was no doubt she cared. A far cry from Tuesday's real mom, who was too busy playing perfect grandmother to her stepson's kids to mother her actual daughters.

"Mommy! Mommy! Look! Look!" A little pigtailed girl sprinted forward. "A princess, a real live princess!"

Tuesday snapped to the moment. No room for hurt or sadness here. She was in the happiness business, a professional smile maker. "By Merlin's beard, isn't that a gorgeous tutu?" She dropped to one knee and tugged the girl's coral-and-turquoise-colored tulle skirt.

"Your tiara is real pretty," the girl whispered.

"And you must try it on." Tuesday plunked it on her head and posed next to the child as her parents and grandparents snapped like paparazzi.

Thank you, the mother mouthed as the girl returned to them floating on air.

Tuesday stood, sparing a furtive glance to where Beau watched the whole scene with crossed arms. The disapproving gesture showed off his shoulders' latent strength and the gorgeously rich undertones of his skin.

She took a deep breath, inhaling the scents of kettle corn and saltwater taffy. His faint frown contrasted sharply with the amusement park's surroundings, the nostalgic feels of rainbow-swirled lollipops and classic rides. This place was a time machine to a sweeter, simpler period, but from the tortured expression on Beau's face you'd think they were at the Spanish Inquisition.

She readjusted her tiara and dusted her hands. And if she happened to be heating from her neck down to her good bits? Well, that could be explained away with three little words: this was Georgia. It didn't matter that Labor

Day had come and gone; the weather retained an August sultriness.

But as she walked, a shiver shot down her spine. She didn't need to turn to confirm whose cool blue gaze bored into her back. The only choice was to ignore him.

The foster kids clustered around the ticketing area. "Good morning, darlings," she cried, affecting her "royal" voice. She'd perfected the accent as a birthday-party princess back on the Upper West Side, where she'd made rent entertaining rich kids and smiling so hard her cheeks would ache on the subway rides home. Shove British, Scottish, and Irish accents into a blender and voilà—a vague fantasy lilt. That's what Grumpy McScowl seemed to misunderstand. Deep down, no one wanted reality. People craved feel-good; they wanted fun. Illusion.

In that vein, she gave the kids a quick run-through of the day's schedule, with less emphasis on rules and more on excitement. Most looked thrilled to be there, except for the eye-rolling tween in the back, the oldest in the group. Her lank hair had uneven black streaks, as if she'd colored it with a Sharpie. Raccoon eyeliner complemented the sullen "I'm here to have a terrible time" expression. Those oversized headphones blatantly advertised that she had no intention of listening to the orientation.

Tuesday shot the mayor a furtive glance. Had Grumpy McScowl ever gone through a rebellious emo phase? Nah. He was the quintessential speech and debate team type. A master debater. She froze midgiggle when his gaze flicked over and jolted her with a near-painful frisson of awareness. Warmth zinged through her inner thighs.

Did he ever do that? Touch himself?

God, of course he must. All guys did.

Stop. Regroup.

Note to self: Eat more than half a piece of toast in the morning. Low blood sugar caused deranged thinking.

"First stop, bumper cars!" she squeaked, her voice a little dry.

"Miss Knight." Beau stepped forward, halting her path.

Her wide-eyed gaze reflected in his aviators. She rearranged her features into scornful incredulity. "Can I help you?"

He prickled at her nettling tone and took another step closer. His cologne was vibrant, a mix of mint, green apples, and lemon. Warmth radiated up her thighs. Of course he went around smelling distractingly delicious.

"Am I a joke to you?" He ripped off his shades and stuffed them in his front shirt pocket. "Allow me to fill you in on the punch line. You don't understand what's at stake today."

"Let's see if I can guess." She dropped her fake accent to hiss back. Fighting was infinitely preferable to unsettling funny feelings. "An asteroid is hurtling to Earth? We're the only ones who can stop it?"

Two deep frown lines bracketed his full mouth.

"No? Huh. Okay, let me try again. This 'tourist board'"—she used air quotes—"is a group of day-walking vampires. Our mission is to ply them with rides so they forget to drain the town."

"Do you have to always be over-the-top? I'm trying to benefit the town here. That's it. End of story."

The tension around his eyes made her relent. This was a horse of a different color. "These guys could help Everland?"

"Yeah. And the park."

"Really?" Last week Toots had overheard Mr. Wilcox discussing the park's dismal financials with the Everland Community Credit Union CEO when she'd gone to his office to report that the Pirate Ship had been temporarily closed for repairs. Visitor numbers weren't booming, and Orlando was close enough that most people went there for their amusement park fix.

He inclined his head. "Really."

Happily Ever After Land needed a good sprucing up: modern rides, a fresh coat of paint, landscaping, and updated signage. The lackluster financial situation had set off a chain reaction. The more tired the place looked, the less people wanted to come. The old-world nostalgia factor went only so far.

She swallowed her pride, not her favorite flavor. "I'll do my best to ensure the commissioners have a good time." When she'd seen the Happily Ever After Land advertisement in the *Everland Examiner* classifieds a few weeks ago, it had felt like... 'I've played a princess before, so hey, why not?' She was adrift, and this place had ended up being one big cotton-candy smelling, whirligig life raft.

Beau stood close enough that she spied the tiny wound where he must have nicked himself shaving. "Hold up. Don't tell me that Tuesday Knight is being serious for once?" His eyes were the color of rain—not a wild cloudburst, but a persistent storm. The combination of his intense gaze and unexpected proximity toppled something inside her, like field grass in a torrent.

"I am perfectly capable of being perfectly serious." It was a trick to remain deadpan when her stomach played host to the butterfly Olympics.

"That's a surprise," he repeated, more to himself than to her, his gaze hooded.

She jutted her chin. "I'll have you know that you're looking at a Russian doll of surprises."

An indecipherable emotion flickered in his gaze. If she was the betting type, she'd wager contempt. "Guess it's good that I don't make a habit of getting curious."

She screwed up her features in an "ugh" face. This guy made her behave with all the grace of a six-year-old being denied a trip to Toys "R" Us.

"Hey! Princess? Princess? Can we go on that one?" A kid pointed at the Smash 'Em, Crash 'Em ride.

"Why, that's exactly our next destination, young squire!" She slipped back into the royal role, leading the charge as a dozen wiggly small bodies provided much-needed distance. "Saved by bumper cars," she muttered. Getting hot and bothered by Beau Marino was an exercise in reckless stupidity. She adjusted her bodice, wincing as her hardened nipples grazed the stiff lace. Much like pineapple pizza, chocolate-covered caramel, or cheesy French fries, she craved the wrong kind of guy. If she felt magnetism to a man, the sensation should come equipped with a red flashing light: *Stop! Warning! Emotionally unhealthy jerk ahead.*

She needed to be attracted to another jerk like she needed a third nipple. Face it. The mayor liked nothing about her. Nothing. Nada. No thing. Her romance report cards were solid F for failure, but no more. She wouldn't keep being the Rizzo, fascinated by the Kenickies of the world. If she couldn't control her attraction, she'd work hard on reeducating it.

She settled a hand to her throat, her pulse thrumming

against her damp palms. Time to knock it off and regroup. The rest of the day she'd double down on being a fabulous princess. Flip to "effervescent" in Merriam-Webster and there she'd be, blowing kisses and breaking into spontaneous song—a very nice, very wholesome, *very* G-rated princess.

Chapter Three

◡

Beau bided his time in the bumper car line while Angie Robert regaled her fellow commissioners with a convoluted story involving an angry woodchuck, a can of bug spray, and a fall into the Chattooga River. Up ahead, one of Tuesday's curls caught a light coastal breeze and skimmed back and forth over the place where her neck met her shoulder. With any other woman, the effect would have meant nothing, barely even registered; but with Tuesday...

He had a mad flash of that soft curtain of hair skimming his bare skin in a gentle caress. An invisible screw tightened in his jaw as his stomach tensed, as if punched, a strange, jarring sensation.

Tuesday Knight had a potent effect on men, an obvious fact, like fire is hot, ice is cold, nothing is free, and the Internet decreases productivity. Take the hapless bumper car attendant. She offered the teen a distracted smile and the poor bastard's Chuck Taylors became rooted to the cracked concrete, his mouth slack.

While the other commissioners chuckled at Angie's punch line, he pressed the heel of his hand against his temple. Fucking pointless gesture. The headache gained speed faster than Superman on Red Bull. Once upon a time he'd fallen for a member of Deep South royalty, a member of the old blood—blood who ruled the country clubs up and down the Gulf Coast.

There'd been no happy ending to that tale, and hell would freeze before he'd ever pursue another pretty princess. That way was closed to through traffic forever.

"Mayor?" The skinny young attendant wore a quizzical expression.

Shit. Beau was holding up the line. He adjusted his blazer and gave the kid a curt nod.

"Where'd you like me?"

"Pick a car, any car." The attendant closed the entrance door behind him. Only one left, and because God wanted to laugh at him today, it faced Tuesday, with her billowing dress bunched around her like a plume of cotton candy.

He climbed into the seat, struggling to arrange his long limbs in the cramped confines. Forget about the shorties; rides need to come with a height advisory for tall people. He made the fit, just, knees shoved to his chest like an asshole.

The foster group shrieked. They were all so young. Had it really been a quarter of a century since he'd run wild through this park with Rhett? A long time. Life moved faster as you got older. At thirty-five, days might be long, but years were short. As a kid, everything was about anticipation, the next summer-day adventure and a lazy bike ride to the river, fishing under the Kissing Bridge. Now his life felt more and more engulfed in retrospection.

Wham! Tuesday had put her glass slipper to the pedal and hurtled straight into him. His head snapped back, his back teeth knocking with an audible *clack*.

"Need a menu, Mr. Mayor?" she cooed. "'Cause you're about to get served." She hit him again. "No shame in losing when you're beaten by the best." Bang! Another slam. And another and another.

She'd wedged him against the wall like an angel—not of mercy but destruction, tiara askew and sweet evil in her laugh. This fresh-faced she-devil was nailing him, and from the fiery glint in her eyes, loving every second of it.

"Hold up," he called, unable to refrain from answering the challenge. "Don't cook me in your weak sauce."

"Weak?" Her brow furrowed. "What do you meaaaaaaaan!" He hit the accelerator, striking her head-on.

"Oh, it's on, is it?"

"Like Donkey Kong." He found himself returning her grin.

"On your left!"

"Right!"

Two foster kids T-boned him as Tuesday cheered, mischief in her eyes.

"Mayor, you've got a little something on your face." She playfully screwed one eye shut, as if to make a careful study. "That's not a smile, is it? Careful. Your mouth might get stuck that way."

Then she was off, cackling wildly, before sideswiping a commissioner.

After the ride, most of the commissioners lined up to go another round with the kids. Beau waited near the exit and made a note in his calendar for his assistant: "Book me into the chiropractor tomorrow." But he had to admit, it was the most fun he'd had in a long time.

"This is my first time at Everland." Donna Summer, the commission's executive director, appeared beside him. "I must say that I'm impressed. You folks offer a charming ambience and top-of-the-line Southern hospitality."

"Glad you think so." Beau allowed a shallow sigh, recalibrating back to the purpose at hand, presenting Everland in the best possible light. "Many merchants on Main Street have run their shops for decades, and we try to encourage the newer offerings to fit into the 'mom and pop' aesthetic. A Coastal Jewel designation will go a long way toward helping secure additional funding to finish off my revitalization plans—building a bandstand near the plaza's gazebo, getting the covered bridge painted, and restoring the Roxy Theater."

"It's rare to have a community retain such a quintessentially Americana character." Donna nodded. "You're no doubt aware, we'll be doing a site visit down the road to Hogg Jaw tomorrow."

No. He wasn't. His blood chilled. "Hogg Jaw?" Nothing doused a good mood like the mention of Everland's neighbor to the west and its biggest town rival. "They're positioned a little far off the coast?" Beau chose his words carefully.

Donna cocked a brow. "But they're nearer to the interstate and cater directly to tourists."

"True." He cleared his throat. It wouldn't do to disparage Hogg Jaw's kitschy offerings like twenty-four-hour laser tag, a pirate wax museum, a haunted house, and a horse track. "Here in Everland, we're developing a strategy that places a focus on history, combined with a vibrant Main Street. We have what it takes, but are farther off the beaten path and don't attract as many tourists as we'd like. Local businesses are forced to struggle year in and year out to make ends meet, and many residents drive elsewhere to make an honest wage. I mean to solve this problem."

Donna fiddled with one dangly silver earring and took his measure. "You grew up in the area, is that right? Local boy?"

"My father's ancestry is classic Caribbean hodgepodge, a little Afro-Bahamian, a dash of Dutch, and seasoned with some Venezuelan and Dominican Republic. Mama, on the other hand, now, she's from an original founding family, a dynasty that's all but gone. I'm the last of the line."

She smiled sympathetically. "No babies of your own yet?"

"Nope." He ignored the final word in Donna's question. Once he'd imagined them. But that door had been shut and bricked over for a long time.

"I heard about your poor wife." She rested a hand on the back of his. "Taken too young. My Mitchell passed on two years ago this October. Killed by a drunk driver on his way to pick me up from work. We were going to celebrate our thirty-ninth anniversary." Tears welled in her eyes. "Widowhood is the club no one wants to join."

He squeezed her hand back, his touch steady even as his stomach churned. "I'm sorry." This kindhearted woman mourned a long and happy marriage...unlike him. He swallowed forcefully, but the painful lump in his throat remained. It wasn't the time or place to say that his own relationship had smashed on the rocks, and from the wreckage his wife had left, only to drown in the company of another man.

Afterward, he couldn't grieve at being betrayed or rage over Jacqueline's affair—that she'd given up on them, their marriage. How could he be allowed those feelings when she was lost at sea? Lost forever. Her death denied him any self-righteousness or answers to the burning questions "Why hadn't he been enough? What could he have done differently?"

The only choice had been to numb the pain.

Kill the fury.

Kill the sadness.

The powerlessness.

The bone-crushing fucking waste of it all.

He pruned every feeling, cut every emotion until he was nothing but a trunk, solid, straight, and strong.

And that's how he survived.

Donna swiped her thumb under her eyes in a too-practiced gesture. "My friends say I should get back out there. But I can't. I just…I can't. How about you?"

But he could never quite cut off part of himself that felt like a fraud whenever he spoke to a real widow, someone who had known and lost true love. "I'm committed to my job." And that statement was God's honest truth. He'd found a way to stave off the helplessness, confusion, and pain, not at the bottom of a bottle or through mindless one-night stands, but through work. Punishing hours. Long meetings. Packed schedules. At his office, life made sense, had order. Decisions were made. Processes streamlined. Every ticked box felt like a foothold—a way to keep control.

Donna nodded sagely. "Staying busy helps."

And she was right. Just not in the way that she thought. He'd learned a hard truth. Staying single was better than being stuck in a shitty relationship.

The funny thing was that he and Jacqueline had seemed so good at first. It had been easy. Their opposite personalities fun. Until it wasn't. Then, no matter how hard he tried, how many hours he devoted, nothing improved. She was a drama queen and wanted him to heed every beck and call. There was no partnership, just her endless need for validation, for attention. He never knew what he'd find when he walked in the front door. Would she worship him today? Or despise him? The roller coaster was exhausting.

No one, not even his family or closest friends, knew how bad it was behind closed doors. How she broke dishes or would disappear for days at a time with no word, leaving him frantic until he checked the credit card balances and saw she was racking up the charges at malls around Atlanta. And after she died, everyone treated him with deferential sympathy when what he really wanted to do was scream that his life had been a sham, a nightmare.

Guilt and frustration isolated him. And so he worked, because at city hall he got results. And if people thought he didn't date or socialize much because of grief, he let them. The ruse was a hell of a lot easier than explaining how he'd rather remain single until the end of his days than enter into another toxic relationship.

If he ever decided to branch out again, he would grow old alongside a simple woman with no hint of drama. A woman where what you saw was what you got. No scenes. No production. No pain.

The bumper car ride came to an end and the two groups surged forward. "Okay, folks." He clapped his hands with forced enthusiasm as the commissioners filed out the exit. "What do you say we head on over to the Visitor Affairs office? I've asked the staff to run analytics and prepare a report on—"

"We can grab the dossier on the way out." Angie eyed Tuesday and the kids heading off to the next ride. "Let's keep up with their group. She's fun."

"A real live wire," another said. "I haven't laughed so hard in months."

"All in favor?"

"Aye," came the resounding answer.

"Well, then"—Beau forced a smile—"onward and upward to..." His heart sank as he noted the foster kids' direction. "The Lumberjack's Revenge."

A brown plastic log crammed with shrieking people dipped into view, eighty feet overhead. Dread sank through him like a brick as they plunged, screaming, down the steep chute. He took a step back and fished out his cell phone like a talisman. "I've got to make a quick call," he announced to no one in particular. He'd bow out and no one would be the wiser.

But fate threw a wrench in the form of a princess in pink. "Sorry to interrupt." Tuesday rushed over. "Those children over there are requesting that you go in their log. One of them says she won't even do the ride unless you're with her."

"Looks like you're rescuing a damsel in distress." The commissioner on his right slapped Beau's tense back. "Go on, son. Don't worry about us."

He wasn't.

Could anyone see the pounding pulse in his neck, his feet cemented in place?

"Mayor! Mayor! Mayor!" the children chanted, beating their fists in time with the words.

A fog of eerie calm descended. The line parted, and he took each step with the slow, measured cadence of a man approaching the gallows.

"Mayor! Mayor! Mayor!" The children piled into an open log, which gave a sickening lurch to the left. "Woo! Woo!"

"That's your seat there." A girl wearing a Braves ball cap pointed to the empty spot right in front.

His stomach churned. This town thought they knew everything about him, but they didn't know the half.

Not even his biggest fear.

Chapter Four

❧

"**Oh**. Em. Gee." Tuesday clapped a hand over her mouth. "I have no words." The English language was un-equipped to describe the image on the grainy screen in the Lumberjack's Revenge photo kiosk.

She might have failed to mention the teeny-tiny fact that the kids who had begged for him to go on the ride had saved him a special spot in "the Soak Seat," the nickname Happily Ever After Land staffers had for the first position in the log ride.

The souvenir snapshot captured Beau midplunge, his hands white-knuckling the sides, his mouth open wide enough to catch every mosquito in a five-mile radius. And there was the matter of his eyes.

Sheer terror.

Tuesday had to peek through her fingers. Oh God, oh God. Maybe this time she'd taken the fun too far.

"Is the mayor joking?" Robbie, one of the ride operators

filling in at the kiosk, rubbed a hand over his ginger peach fuzz. "He doesn't seem the type to play the clown."

It was impossible for her to tear her gaze from the image, his expression so unexpectedly out of character that she tittered, a guilty, nervous reaction. Why did she do this, get giggle attacks at times like these, the worst possible reaction? She was the queen of inappropriate laughter, cackling whenever scared, hurt, or stuck in an awkward situation. In the face of overwhelming anxiety, she couldn't hold back the floodgates.

"His face"—she gasped—"it's so—oops!" She'd given a very Sandra Bullock esque snort.

Robbie roared, actually slapping one knee. "Like a stray cat crossing the road while a Ferrari takes a bend at forty over." He cut off midgurgle and straightened as his cheeks blanched.

Ruh-roh. A sense of foreboding descended. "He's standing right behind me, isn't he?"

Robbie must have noticed his shoe was untied and dropped behind the counter.

Tuesday turned around slowly. Beau's crisp white shirt had been the epitome of businesslike good taste until its encounter with a few hundred gallons of heavily chlorinated water. The wet cotton plastering his chest left little to the imagination. She swallowed hard. Didn't he have a desk job? Nothing about those deliciously thick, hard slabs of pectoral muscle hinted at long sedentary hours in the cause of public service.

She'd never spared a second thought to the yacht he co-owned with Rhett Valentine berthed at Buccaneer's Marina. Swimming wasn't her strong suit, and Shark Week gave her hives. She'd just as soon shave her head as set foot on an oceangoing vessel. But her lack of water enthusiasm notwithstanding, Beau's impressive physique was suited to the open sea. Everything about him hinted at agility and capability.

Forcing her gaze to travel up over his corded neck muscles and to his furious expression, she pointed at the neon $9.99 sign. "Care to support the park with a memento of the ride?"

"I'll pass." He adjusted his gray knit blazer, his eyes the same color as chipped ice and his tone just as cool.

Her gaze swung south, stealing another gander at that strong chest. "Did you have fun?" she asked with exaggerated innocence. Provoking his bad humor would put an end to her oglefest.

"Think I travel with a spare change of clothes?" His Adam's apple rose and fell. "This. Is. The. Georgia. Tourism. Commission"—he bit off the words, practically spitting them out—"the statewide body for promotion. I need to win their respect so this town can be taken seriously, and look at me."

He was adept at masking his true thoughts and feelings, almost as good as her, but as his carefully guarded composure slipped, she found herself with a front-row seat to his hidden feelings. The anger. The embarrassment. The frustration.

Darn it. She must have been a Catholic in a past life because guilt gave her hives. She'd taken the prank too far, the same way she took everything in life. God, she hated being such a screwup. There had to be a way to make this right. She ground the heels of her hands into her eyes as the frustration built.

Think...

Think…

Inspiration struck right as he turned to leave. "Wait! Stop. I have an idea! I got you into this mess, and I can get you out!"

He didn't turn his face, merely glanced sideways through his thick lashes. "What?" He must be desperate if he was still speaking to her.

"Well…" She fiddled with a loose ribbon on the bodice. "I'm not saying you'll like it, but you'll be dry."

He managed a negligible nod even as his jaw muscles flexed. "Go on."

"I can't break off from the group, but Robbie can step away from the kiosk. Hardly anyone ever buys these overpriced photos." She turned to the boy gaping from the cash register. "Take Mayor Marino to the lost and found."

Beau gaped. "Lost and—"

"You'd be surprised what visitors leave," she countered matter-of-factly. "I suppose there's a little risk of lice, but a louse dies after seventy-two hours without a human host." She frowned, considering. "Louse. Is that right? Or is it lice? I never know which one is right."

"Oh no. No. No. No way in hell." He shoved a hand in his pants pocket. "Lice? Christ, Tuesday, I'm—"

"Going to trust me." She glanced down and blinked twice. Just what did her hand think it was doing on his wrist? From the way his powerful forearm muscles flexed beneath her palm, her unprompted touch surprised him as well.

There'd been a recent segment on a late-night news show about how attraction turned the brain into a hormonal jambalaya, hampering rational decision making. It wasn't a random cockeyed theory either. She was living the truth right here, right now.

Tingles radiated from her elbow as if she'd struck a funny bone. Jerking away, she balled her hand into a fist and backed out of his gravitational pull. She tugged the ribbon again, snapping it when he stalked away without another word, Robbie trailing sheepishly in his wake. It wasn't until his footsteps faded that her lungs resumed normal operations.

On a scale of one to trouble, this was a definite "uh-oh."

She'd fallen asleep before the end of the news show. Maybe she should look it up, see if there was an antidote. Hypnotherapy might provide another viable option, because she needed a cure once and for all to stop being attracted to jerky guys.

* * *

Ten minutes later Beau returned wearing a blue and orange Florida Gators T-shirt. Talk about adding insult to injury—he'd gone to Georgia, stayed there through his master's of public administration, a die-hard Bulldog who bled red and black. Hell, even a Tech shirt would have been better. But the only other choices in the lost and found box were a size small STRAIGHT OUTTA MY MAMA wifebeater and a dingy T-shirt that read I LOVE CUMMING (GEORGIA).

Trust me, Tuesday had said.

Yeah. Right. He'd trust Tuesday Knight as far as he could throw her. And given her scrawny frame could use a couple extra helpings of grits, he could probably throw her a good distance from Everland. Frowning, his gaze

lingered on her small hands, the butterfly-quick movements of her gestures. When she tossed back her head,
laughing at something one of the children asked, something about the delicate curve in her throat caught his
breath. She had an energy about her, an enthusiasm for
life that was contagious, drew people in with magnetic
force. He fisted the plastic shopping bag holding his sod-
den clothes, shoved down his head with effort, his jaw
clenched, and glared at a wad of chewing gum stuck to
the pavement.

Better. He blinked, the tightness in his chest easing a
fraction as he regained control. No more gawking. For the
rest of the morning, so long as Tuesday remained stuck in
his orbit, he'd remain detached and do his best to avoid any
further engagement. When that was unavoidable, he'd treat
her with a cool but civil politeness.

Yes. He gave an inward nod. Perfect. A solid game plan.

"Let's pop into Madam Magna's tent," she was saying
up ahead, pointing out a large red-and-white-striped tent.
"With any luck, she'll tell one or two of you your fortune
before lunch."

Beau arched a brow. Jesus, Madam Magna was alive?
That old woman had been pushing two hundred when he
was a kid. Stepping inside her tent, he glanced around. It
was like entering a time warp, the surrounds exactly as he
remembered: dim, shadowy, the outside world muffled. As
children, he and Rhett had dared each other to creep in and
spy, but Madam Magna had taken it in stride. Once she'd
busted him squatting behind a potted fern and said in a far-
off voice, "It will be all right in the end. If it's not, it's not
the end." After Jacqueline's unexpected death, the memory
had offered a measure of comfort.

A hush fell over the crowd. Madam Magna perched at a small circular table covered by an embroidered crimson brocade. A crystal ball was placed off to the side, while in front of her rose a stack of hand-painted tarot cards.

"Who seeks the unseeable?" Madam Magna drawled in a thick Eastern European burr. "Thirsts with a desire to know the unknowable? Craves answers to the ageless secrets? Whose loins quiver with the ache to understand?"

"Thank you, Madam Magna," Tuesday broke in. "So wonderful that you made yourself welcome to this group of children." Her tone was heavy on the *Cool it with the loin-quiver references in front of the under-eighteens, please.*

"Silence!" Madam Magna commanded. At the clap of her hands, the flames from the two gold-dipped candles on either side of the tarot cards sparked into the air. "There are those here with questions, and I have answers."

A freckled-nosed child looked around and sniffled. "I don't like this."

"Maybe we should get back to the rides." Tuesday took a step back. "We do have quite a lot more ground to cover before lunch and—"

Madam Magna clapped her hands again, twice this time, and the twin flames extinguished. A trio of girls screamed. Through the smoke the old woman intoned garbled words, rolling her head around and around, the sequins in her turban glinting in the half-light. She went rigid, gripped the table, and let out a guttural groan.

Freckle Face up front went from a bad case of the sniffles to full-blown hysterics. The girls on either side joined in.

"Should we call an ambulance?" Angie Robert shouted over the din.

"What's lost will be found," Madam Magna droned in a deep voice. "Dragons do not always win. Heroes come from the most unlikely places."

A crash boomed from the room's corner. The moody-looking girl who'd made a point not to join any of the group's fun dropped an unwieldy art portfolio. Paper spilled. Intricate ink sketches appeared to fill the pages.

"This is stupid." The girl squatted down, crushing the drawings to her chest. Her eyes were almost as black as the thick makeup surrounding them. "This is all f-fucking stupid."

"Ooooh, Flick said the 'f' word!" A kid in a purple sun hat tugged Tuesday's skirt with undisclosed glee as the tent erupted into a raucous mix of laughter and jeers.

The girl in black—Flick, presumably—fled. Tuesday's face tightened with worry, nothing like the ditzy princess from earlier, flouncing around the park seemingly without a care in the world.

"We need to go after her," she said, sweeping past him. "Come on, kids, hi-ho, hi-ho!"

In the chaotic span of twenty seconds the tent emptied, leaving Beau alone with five startled Tourism Commission officials and an ancient woman still gripped in some sort of a foggy-eyed trance.

"Do we leave her like that?" someone asked behind him. From the sound of their hopeful timbre that was the preferred choice.

"Go on ahead." Beau forced a tone of good cheer. "Meet me at Hush Puppy Heaven. I've arranged for us to stop there and grab a bite to eat."

"Hush puppies, you say?" The guy on his right perked. "Heard they make 'em good around here. That right, Marino?"

Beau's laugh came out less manufactured than he feared. "The recipe's a secret more secure than Fort Knox, but tell you what, I taste buttermilk in the batter."

"Mmm-mmm-mmm. Just the way Mama made 'em."

"See you in a minute, folks. Nothing to worry about here." He hoped his smile was reassuring. "I'll be along in a moment."

The group didn't appear to fully believe him, but they also didn't seem interested in challenging the point.

Once they left, he stepped forward and his foot slid. Under his shoe was one of Flick's drawings. A dragon seated on a throne holding a scepter. In fancy script she'd doodled, "Sometimes the dragon wins."

He frowned. Talk about an uncanny coincidence. No wonder the kid freaked. She'd looked barely thirteen, too. No one should be so cynical that young.

"Some see much but observe little." Madam Magna peered through the gloom with a stony-faced Yoda-like wisdom.

"Ma'am, do you have someone I can call to take you home and out of this heat?" As soon as he said the words he realized he didn't know where Madam Magna lived. Everland wasn't big, but she never pushed a buggy around the Piggly Wiggly or strolled Main Street. Where did she come from and where did she go?

"Life is a song," she said, regarding him steadily. "Music happens in the silence between the notes."

"Are you on medication or—"

She held up a silencing finger. "Listen. Hear that?"

Blood thrummed through his ears. "What?"

"You're a powerful man with many rules." She clicked her tongue. "Clever. Focused. Determined. And yet... blind. You do not see there is only one rule that ever matters."

"Which is?" What was he doing? Surely he wasn't taking this old woman's baffling mumbo jumbo seriously?

"The exception. But that's enough... It is time." Madam Magna stood in a creaky movement, her smile sphinxlike, and shuffled through a nearly undetectable slit in the back of the tent without further explanation.

Beau shook his head and folded the young girl's paper into his pocket. He'd woken today primed to sell Everland to the Tourism Commission, but all his best-laid plans had unraveled, and there was only one person to blame.

"I left Robbie in charge." The person in question burst through the tent's main entrance. "Did you call an ambul—" Tuesday's golden brows arched in confusion as she swiveled her head right and left. "Where is she? Where's Madam Magna?"

"She has an escape route," Beau said grimly. Tuesday was even prettier up close, her lips a pale champagne pink. If he were a different type of man, the sight might fizz away his common sense, leave him reeling a little, as if drunk.

"Wait, so she's not sick? Geez Louise, she really had me going. Let me catch my breath." She braced her hands on her hips and bent forward, shoulders heaving. "Do you have any idea how hard it is to sprint in heels? I'm about to pass out."

There were many places to look in the tent, all sorts of directions that weren't Tuesday's small, perfect breasts, the tops of which strained against the thick brocade. If he reached out, he could gather that cheap fabric in his fists and wrench it open like some plundering pirate.

"What?" She caught him out midstare, her laughter dissolving into a strained silence. Agitation charged his nerve endings, shot hot pulses down his spine. On and on the silence stretched until she sucked in her lower lip, then released it with a soft but audible *pop*, plump and glistening. His groin warmed at the unbearably fascinating sight. No more space remained in his head to strategize or assess consequences—a pure, primal want crowded out all reason.

He took a step, then another, and in doing so crossed whatever invisible line separated their personal space. Her lashes fluttered, her pupils dilating in the half-light, struggling to focus.

"What the hell is this?" he growled. "Why do you make me so damn crazy?"

"I...should go." She didn't so much as budge.

"Now." The helpless word emerged as a rasp. A plea.

The distance between their lips decreased. His vision blurred as her scent invaded his senses: sweet grass, grapefruit, and cucumber, fresh and light as a summer's day.

"Or what?" Challenge brightened her chestnut eyes.

"My God." His stomach constricted as if he were hungry—no, starving. The room's spicy incense smoke must be wreaking havoc on his senses. A lack of sufficient oxygen was the only explanation for this whole-body intoxication. The solid ground on which he'd built his entire self-control tilted off-kilter, sinking into invisible quicksand. Pure, unadulterated need tugged on his legs, threatened to suck him down to some kind of strangely wonderful hell.

"This." He fisted her thick blond hair, barely able to

register that it felt even silkier than it looked, before crushing his mouth to hers. When her lips parted in answer, her tongue sliding over his, tasting of pink cotton candy, all rational thought ceased.

Chapter Five

Tuesday enjoyed life's little unpredictabilities, how every day had the potential to be a grand adventure, although granted, of late, the hours tended to unfold with monotonous regularity. Gone were the excitement of auditions, the daydreaming walks past theaters like the Richard Rogers, the Gershwin, or the New Amsterdam, or opening a script on the subway like it might be her version of Charlie's golden ticket—a chance to be a star. A game-changing role.

Brushing her teeth this morning, the last thought on her mind had been that in a few measly hours she might be deep kissing the man who for all intents and purposes found her as annoying as a mosquito singing the song of its people.

And that wasn't the only surprise. That same man knew how to kiss.

Like...really knew.

Okay. Okay. She needed to stop—stop this, right now!—but it was like stepping into Willy Wonka's chocolate factory after a long diet of iceberg lettuce and rice cakes. Now she was getting her Augustus Gloop on. Her willpower was too busy saying things like "God," "yes," and "more" to be responsible.

Beau was a contradiction of strength and softness, his body hard even as he held her in gentle arms. His mouth moved with measured confidence, despite obvious hunger.

This wasn't black-and-white. Enemies. Lovers. This was a gray space, and who knew the murky middle could feel this damn good?

She wound her arms over his broad shoulders, lacing her fingers together at the base of his neck. His mouth stripped her of reason, of analyzing, of even trying to make a good impression. There wasn't style here. Or technique. This kiss was raw, real, and utterly ruthless.

His mouth devoured hers, and yeah, she'd been ravenous, too. The last time she'd been kissed—no, none of that; Philandering Phil had no place here. Whatever was happening, at least it was honest.

This kiss existed out of time. A parallel-world kiss. An alternate reality. A whole other dimension. As their tongues tangled, the known universe altered.

"I don't want you." His rock-hard bulge against her lower stomach begged to differ.

She nipped the indent in his top lip, her fingers digging into his borrowed T-shirt. It wasn't clear if she was pushing him off or pulling him closer. "I don't like you."

His frustrated exhalation heated her flushed chest. "Then what the fuck is happening?"

The naked confusion in his uncharacteristically helpless expression heated her blood. "I don't know," she whispered. "Wanna try again and see if we can find out?"

His mouth had an underlying tang like he'd recently eaten an orange. Imagine him feeding her one? Those big strong hands would split the peel, juice dribbling along his thick fingers as he pressed a segment to her parted lips. The thrill between her legs reached the intensity of a flyaway live wire. She writhed, burning in all her good places.

"Tuesday." He muttered her name like a prayer. "We've got to stop." Instead, he dipped to suck her neck, and her whole body tightened in a feline arch.

"I have a group," she gasped. *The children—think of the children.*

"Me too." His scruff worked in concert with his hot tongue to radiate tingles over her skin. "A VIP group."

Funny how "group" sort of sounded like "grope," and good Lord, she couldn't leave his biceps alone. She'd never seen him out of a well-fitting collared shirt. The sleeves always hugged his arms, but the professional buttoned-up look never invited touch. The ratty college T-shirt invited teasing finger explorations up his arm. Yum. No give anywhere, just ridge after ridge of hard, tantalizing muscles. He moved lower with a husky groan, his lips dragging over her clavicle, nipping and kissing until she dug her nails in and held fast as leg strength became nothing but a memory.

"This is crazy." His close-shaved head roughed the side of her cheek. God. His hands closed on the front of her dress. Was he going to rip it open like a plundering pirate? The idea of his wet, hot mouth getting anywhere close to her—

A throat cleared.

They both sprang back as if struck, breathing in harsh gasps.

Robbie shuffled in the doorway to Madam Magna's tent,

studying the back of his hands. He cracked a knuckle. "I, um, a few of the little girls needed to use the bathroom and I couldn't take them and—"

"On my way," Tuesday said breezily, slipping back into her princess character. It wasn't hard. Whatever just happened wasn't reality. What went down in a parallel world stayed in a parallel world. She stepped forward when a hand closed on her upper arm.

A hand she now knew had the ability to feel roughly calloused but also savagely tender.

"Your crown, Princess." Beau's voice was low in her ear. Her eyes half fluttered before she fought for composure. No! She wouldn't have an ear orgasm in front of Robbie.

"It's a tiara," she said in her snootiest faux accent, plucking it from his grasp.

No, she wouldn't meet his gaze.

No, she wouldn't linger.

And this would never happen again.

Never ever ever.

She replayed the words over and over in her mind, faster and faster, until the syllables grew strange and distorted, refusing to hold any meaning at all.

* * *

Tuesday Knight had kissed him to the brink of goddamn insanity and all she said afterward was *It's a tiara*?

Oh, hell no.

For the rest of the day, he led the Tourism Commission around Everland's other highlights, from the Kissing Bridge to his cousin's What-a-Treat Candy Boutique to the General's General Store. All the while he replayed her parting words on repeat, his smile and reserved good humor harder and harder to maintain.

As the group finally pulled away at the end of the day, the van disappearing down Main Street in the direction of Hogg Jaw, he answered his ringing phone with a bite. "Marino."

"Beau! Hey, my main man," Humph Miller boomed in his unmistakable baritone. "How's it hanging this fine day? To the left? Right?" He unleashed a phlegmy guffaw.

Humph had been the fraternity president back when Beau pledged in college. They'd kept in loose contact over the years. Rather, Humph kept in touch when it served him.

"Humph," Beau said, shoving a hand into his pocket. "Long time no talk. What can I do for you?"

"Hey, pal, you know what? I've been waiting for the wife to ask me that question since she popped out baby number four." Humph cracked up at his own joke. "My balls are the size of fucking watermelons."

Beau massaged his brow. Christ, what an asshole. "Congratulations on the new edition," he ground out. "I didn't even know Merris was pregnant again."

"Best part? Her breastfeeding titties are huge." More gravelly "good ol' boy" laughter.

Beau recoiled from the receiver, twisting his mouth in a grimace. Humph was a cashed-up, A-grade bastard. He'd married a society belle and in her company remained the epitome of a loving and chivalrous husband, but the second he stepped out of earshot he was the type to make crass remarks about women two decades younger.

"Hey, so is there a reason for the call? Because I'm up to my ears in—"

"Reason?" Humph belted out. "Depends on whether you

think Representative Marino having a nice ring to it is a reason."

Beau slammed his shoulders back. "Say what, now?"

"Did I stutter? And we're talking US Congress here."

"Not sure what planet you're on, but Everland isn't on any political map. I don't have the clout to bring in that sort of support in this district."

"Yet."

He paced. "Going to Washington takes money. I don't have much in the way of—"

"You know me. I know people. People with deep pockets. People who like to get things done. Are you a man who likes to get things done?"

"You know it."

"Judge Hogg had been in contention, but, well—after what happened..."

"An unfortunate episode." Everland disliked the judge, partly because he hailed from the rival town of Hogg Jaw and partly because he was a human garbage Dumpster fire, a grown man who took pleasure in bullying those he deemed weaker or less important. His bad behavior had finally caught up to him, and he'd been run out of town.

"Last I heard he was out on the Alabama border catching catfish in the Chattahoochee. Guess that's one way to handle a destroyed career. You replace him yet?"

"Not my jurisdiction, but there are people working on it."

"Interesting. Wonder who it'll be."

Hopefully not another whack job. He hooked a hand over the back of his neck and changed the subject. "And where exactly do I fit into this?"

"We're looking for someone with common sense, who can get things done."

"'We' being who?"

"Classic Marino." Humph unleashed a wheezy chortle. "Always lookin' a gift horse in the mouth."

"I like knowing who's buttering my bread."

What Humph offered was tempting. Lately a restless feeling had taken hold. The harder he worked, the more it grew. Maybe he was outgrowing the job and a new professional challenge was needed.

"What would you say if I represented business interests from all the way over in Atlanta?"

"I'd ask why they cared about Everland."

"Populations are climbing out your way. It's a good, wholesome place to raise a family, with low crime and affordable housing given the proximity to the coast."

"All points of local civic pride."

Humph scoffed. "Let's face it. Your shopping options suck balls."

Beau bristled. "Our Main Street won—"

"I know. I know. You came in second in that local business contest and no one is prouder of it than me, but I'm talking real shopping. Discount-Mart style."

"Discount-Mart?" Beau stopped in his tracks. Discount-Mart was one of America's biggest companies and headquartered in Atlanta.

"They've expressed interest in expanding into your market."

He looked up at the cloudless sky and rubbed his brow. "This town supports buying local."

Humph laughed. "Tell that to a soccer mom who can get her kids school shoes at seventy-five percent off, or the senior who needs one of those lights where you clap your hands and they pop on. What are those called again?"

"A clapper?"

"Yeah. Got four myself. Useful thing those, especially after a few beers. Anyhow, they've crunched the numbers and there's a prime piece of real estate ripe for the plucking. Could be expanded into an outlet mall. Maybe even a fancy water park. Already has parking lots paved."

"Don't tell me it's state parkland because—"

"That ratty-ass theme park."

"Happily Ever After Land?" Beau jerked.

"Old Joe Wilcox has been hemorrhaging money for years. Sharks smell blood in the water, and the hundred-year lease is up come winter. You broker this deal for Discount-Mart and you can good as count on a sizable contribution for grabbing that seat opening next year."

The United States Congress? Beau rocked his head back and rubbed his forehead. He was happy with his role as Everland's mayor, and more than content doing good work improving the community. But there was no doubt he could get more accomplished if he went all the way to Washington, got a seat on the Small Business committee or Appropriations. He'd been pouring his blood, sweat, and tears into getting the Georgia Tourism Board to designate Everland as a coastal Crown Jewel, but imagine if he could earmark funds on a national scale for the whole district?

"Folks are mighty leery of outsiders out your way," Humph pressed on. "But if a familiar, trusted community leader spearheads the deal, then this is as good as done. Think on it, Beau. Let's get that happy ever after for you."

Phaedra1953: I don't believe a word of it. Not one word. Robbie is a Brown, and you know what they say about the Brown family.

ScrabbleLuvR: Big-Mouth Browns. But what cause would that child have to lie? I think he saw what he said he saw. Mayor Marino and Tuesday Knight were playing tonsil hockey in Madam Magna's tent. It looks like the mayor is finally finding romance.

IdaMayI: No, no, no! Men don't know their brains from their bologna pony. Tuesday Knight isn't right for him. They are nothing alike. He'll only go and get himself hurt again. We can't stand by. It's time to investigate her.

Chapter Six

⌐

"Beau Marino kisses like a devil in disguise." Tuesday peeled back the lavender eye pillow and regarded her dog. "How is that possible? What planet slipped out of alignment during the last twenty-four hours?"

J. K. Growling settled her big head on her folded paws with a snort that made her feelings on the matter perfectly clear. *Not again.*

Too bad. Because Tuesday needed to process and this bed was her safe space, one place where she could drop all pretense and just be herself. "And he didn't do any of those alpha tongue jabs either. You know how I hate when a guy mows my face like a bacon cheeseburger. Talk about an instant deal breaker. But this was different. We...we...met in the middle. A give-and-take." She hugged a pillow. "But how can it feel so right when it's every kind of wrong? The mayor is nothing like me. He is so...I don't know, strait-laced, responsible, and pragmatic. I'd drive him nuts. He'd drive me nuts. Together we'd be a Costco-size container of mixed nuts."

J. K. Growing heaved a heavy sigh and closed her eyes.

"Come on. Aren't you supposed to be a woman's best friend? Pepper doesn't need to hear my drama, not when she's all wound up with her engagement and the shelter and those dogs and...Oh, no! What time is it?" Tuesday sat and checked the digital clock on her phone. Twenty past seven.

"Shoot. Pepper and Rhett's dinner started twenty minutes ago. Why didn't you remind me?"

The five text messages on the screen ranged from "Ready when you are!" to "Helllllloooooo????" to "That's it, we're sending Beau to drag you over."

She dropped the phone to her side. "Sending who?"

Someone knocked on the front door. Three strong raps.

Panic rose in her throat as she looked about wildly. Her cottage porch light was out. What if she didn't answer? That could work, right? Hunkering down under a throw blanket might not win any maturity awards, but this was about survival. Her pride was on the line.

J. K. Growling *woof*ed and barreled toward the door, scratching at the wood.

"Seriously? This is when you decide to show interest in anything other than dinner?" Tuesday hissed. "Traitor." No hiding now. She smoothed her hair and gave her reflection a critical once-over in the wall mirror. She'd treated herself to a lavender bubble bath after coming home and had slipped into dark-wash cutoffs and a coral-red cami.

No bra, but let's face it, her girls didn't require much heavy lifting in the support department. Gravity couldn't affect what wasn't there.

The knocking recommenced.

"Coming!" She ripped her fingers through the knotted tangle on the side of her head. Just because she didn't want to pursue some big, meaningful relationship with the mayor didn't mean that she wanted to look anything other than completely irresistible.

She flung open the door. He dropped his closed fist against his black-denim-encased thigh. *Geez Louise.* He'd traded his trademark blazer for a well-fitting gray T-shirt and an iconic leather biker jacket.

Now, that wasn't playing fair.

"Hi." It was a wonder she could manage a squeak when her mouth was drier than Death Valley.

"Hey." His mouth clamped as if he refused to allow a spare word to escape.

"Okay, well, cool, this was fun," she quipped at last. "Nice seeing you!" She pretended to shut the door.

"Wait!" He braced his hand, blocking her. "The dinner party."

"Oh, right." Her tone was mocking. "I'm sure you're all anticipating the napkins with bated breath."

"Napkins?"

"My vital contribution to the evening's success. What did you get roped into bringing?"

"Cake."

She cocked her head. "You grabbed something from Sweet Brew? I'm obsessed with their death-by-chocolate muffins."

"No bakery. My kitchen."

"Wait." She passed a hand over her mouth, but a giggle escaped, charmed to the tips of her toes by the idea of him in the kitchen, a dusting of flour on the tip of his nose. "You made a cake?"

He stared at her intently, as if searching for some secret mockery. "What's funny about that?"

"Nothing." She shook her head. "Nothing at all." The idea was adorable, and humanizing, and made her swoon more than a little. But it wouldn't do to tell him all that.

His gaze deepened, probing, studying every inch of her face. She refused to so much as blink or fidget. If this were an improvisation class, she was playing the role of "cool confidence." "I'm not sure." Better not to blurt out *the best kisser ever*.

"Look." He rocked on his heels. "About earlier—"

"Nope," she said lightly, raising a hand like a cop blocking traffic. "Not going there. I have no recollection of the morning. I appear to have been stricken with an incurable case of selective amnesia."

"Suit yourself." A thread of amusement laced his voice.

Did he see through her studied nonchalance? Or that her pebbled nipples contradicted her brave statement? "I need to change before dinner." She gestured at her cutoffs, swallowing thickly when his gaze skimmed her bare thighs. "Come inside a second?"

"Uh, sure. Yeah. Fine." He turned toward Pepper and Rhett's house like he'd rather walk back, but for some reason she wanted him in her space. Her territory. To get a better sense of her than the ditzy princess he had her pegged as.

"Can I grab you anything? A soda?" She offered a silent prayer of thanksgiving that no wayward bras were draped over the back of her sofa. "Wait. You guys call it Coke here, right? Even if it's Sprite? Or root beer? Luckily, I have Coke. Well, Diet Coke."

"I don't drink caffeine after noon."

"Why do you insist on acting like you're seventy?" she said with a laugh. "You're a grumpy old man before your time."

Bemused blue eyes met brown. "What would you have me do? Drink those coffee milk shakes that are so popular these days?"

"Did I say seventy? Never mind. Your inner child must look like Benjamin Button. I'll have you know, my drink of choice is a double espresso, hold the cream and sugar."

Philip had always made the same order for her, a "double shot espresso," explaining no one with any taste would spoil the coffee by adding milk or sugar, or God forbid, artificial flavors.

He gave her a skeptical once-over. "Really?"

"What can I say." She met his questioning tone with an air of mock superiority. "I'm a coffee snob." But was she really? Because before Philip imposed his drink of choice on her, there'd been Zepher, the Brooklyn DJ with a thing for chai lattes, which she drank dutifully even though cardamom hurt her stomach. And before that was Bruce, the Staten Island firefighter who considered five-dollar coffees "horseshit," trusting only the burnt jet fuel that came served in Styrofoam from his corner deli.

No guy ever seemed to care to know what she actually wanted, content for her to play a role, be who *they* wanted at the time, what made *them* feel good.

Beau gave a disinterested one-shoulder shrug. "I mostly stick with water."

"Yes, water is good. Love water." Her nod was emphatic, even as internally she was reeling. She loved pleasing people, even if it meant compromising her own happiness. "Probably because I'm an Aquarius."

He gave her a strange look because what was she even talking about? First, water was fine, but half the time she forgot to drink enough, and second, did she have to agree with every beverage choice of every guy whose tongue had ever entered her mouth?

No. Maybe it was time to quit being such a people pleaser and try just being herself...Tuesday, the one role that never felt quite right.

J. K. Growling lumbered up with a soggy, well-chewed tennis ball and dropped it at his feet, snub tail wagging.

"Feel free to ignore her; she's such an attention seeker." She inched toward the hall, desperate for a moment of distance, a chance to take a deep breath and regroup.

"I don't mind." He shoved his hands deep in his pockets. The gesture didn't do much to hide the broad swathe to his shoulders.

"Suit yourself," she said thickly, feeling a prickle creep up her cheekbones—a blush heating her face. "But fair warning, because once you start, she'll never let you go." As she walked into her bedroom she realized with a start that the same could go for her.

Chapter Seven

Tuesday's house had the same sweetly exotic fragrance she carried in her hair—jasmine or lilies. He liked it. He liked it too much.

Beau rolled the wet ball across the cramped living room for a second time, trying to concentrate on taking shallow sips of breath. Poor dog had one of those "only a mother could love" faces.

The ball rolled into the hallway, and J. K. Growling disappeared around the corner, returning a few moments later with something white wadded in her mouth.

"What do you have there, girl?" A tissue? Tuesday wouldn't want that getting shredded all over the floor. "Give it here." He dropped into a crouch and froze as she deposited a flimsy lace thong into his outstretched palm.

He gaped at his hand, mortified and not a little turned on. What the...? Tuesday ran around Everland wearing these?

He hardened in an instant, hit by wave after wave of sexy mental images.

"All set?" She flew back into the room in a strapless emerald sundress that offset her sun-kissed skin and platinum hair to perfection.

"Yeah. Sure. Good to go." He bolted upright, stuffing the scrap of lace into his pocket, grinding his teeth so hard he risked cracking a molar. Shit. His pocket? But it was either that or confess and look like a pantie pervert.

No thank you.

J. K. Growling huffed a satisfied grunt and ambled away, stubby tail wagging, and leaving him in one hell of a predicament. He'd felt a certain sympathy for the dog up until that point.

That compassion ended tonight. This very moment.

"What's wrong?" A furrow creased between Tuesday's brows.

"Nothing." He racked his brain, trying to remember the exact amount of last month's power bill, the capital city of Oklahoma, anything to ward off his impending erection. "Except that we're keeping everyone waiting."

"That's on me. Sorry. Oh, wait. I almost forgot the all-important napkins." She dashed into the kitchen and returned with a paper bag. "Mission accomplished. Let's roll."

Outside, they walked down her driveway. "Yours?" she asked, opening the picket fence gate and making a vague gesture toward his black Ducati Scrambler.

"Yeah." He cast her a sideways glance. Everyone in town knew his bike. It wasn't like her to stumble over small talk.

Unless she was unsettled, too?

Which was somehow even more unsettling.

"I've never ridden on a motorcycle." The statement

didn't sound like a flirtatious suggestion for an invite. Just a statement of fact.

Well, shit. He didn't know what to think, not about any of this. The tiny panties in his pocket were fucking with his brain function.

"Want to?"

He felt her own sideways glance. Shit. Did *that* sound like a flirtatious suggestion?

Sort of.

Was it?

Kinda.

His upper lip twitched as frustration tugged at his belly. He didn't know how to do this. Be witty. Banter. Life was a hell of a lot less complicated when he didn't kiss women.

She unleashed a nervous giggle. "This is weird, huh?"

"Most definitely. Listen, here's the situation. It's a full house next door. We're going to need to act natural," he said.

She flashed a thumbs-up. "No artificial weirdness. Acting is what I do best."

He slowed his pace, frowning at the uncharacteristic bite in her voice as a female laugh poured out Rhett's window. "I mean it. Lou Ellen's here." His friend's big sister. "That woman roots out gossip like a truffle-hunting pig."

"What happens in Madam Magna's tent stays in Madam Magna's tent." She paused, wrinkling her brow. "Well, except that I spilled the beans to J. K. Growling."

An unhealthy level of curiosity spiked. How'd she described their kiss?

"Yoo-hoo, Mayor Butter! I declare if it isn't the man of the hour!" Miss Ida May bustled around the side of her house brandishing a pair of pruning shears. "Are your ears

burning, sugar? Did you know that I had my annual physical this morning and sang your praises to the new nurse?
A pretty thing, too, fresh in from Jacksonville. She's home-
sick, bless her heart, and could use a few more friendly
faces in town. And your face is..." The older woman trailed
off, taking in his frustrated scowl, the one he'd worn ever
since slipping the world's tiniest panties into his pocket.
"Well...seeing as how you're a real kind man and all."

"Your garden looks stunning," Tuesday chimed in to
change the subject. "I'd love to stop by and pick your brain
on landscape design."

Beau chewed the inside of his cheek. She didn't seem to
want to hear about this nurse. *Interesting.*

"My, doesn't that sound nice." Miss Ida May gave Tuesday a noncommittal smile before turning her attention back
to Beau and shaking her shears. "Her name is June." Her
wink was the definition of suggestive. "Like a June bug.
Ain't that the cutest thing?"

"Indeed." Beau gave her a nod. "You go on and have
yourself a nice evening."

"You too, sugar."

"'Night, Miss Ida May!" Tuesday said, and the woman
looked her up and down, *tutt*ing her tongue three times before returning to her rose garden.

"What crawled up her petticoat and died?" Tuesday muttered after they had moved out of earshot. "She acted like I
was a Roundup-resistant weed or something."

Beau remained silent, not about to share the most likely
theory. The *Back Fence* appeared to be breaking their long-
standing embargo against meddling in his personal life.
Looked like they wanted to set him up with a suitable
woman and had determined that Tuesday wasn't a candi-

date. Which meant the busybodies had discussed him and Tuesday. His mind seethed with the thoughts.

Goddammit. The last thing he wanted was his love life put under Everland's microscope. He wasn't in the mood for his love life to be henpecked over, or for these panties to be burning a hole in his pocket—the barely there whisper of lace, the string holding the two impossibly small triangles together.

Was she wearing a pair like this now?

"Who ran over your cat?" Tuesday gently elbowed him in the ribs.

Her touch, even in jest, put him on edge. "Don't have any pets," he shot back. "I work too late most nights to be responsible for one."

She rolled her eyes. "Um, have you ever heard about this thing called a figure of speech? Don't go biting my head off just because Miss Ida May got under your collar."

"She didn't." He hadn't raised his voice, so why did it feel like he was yelling? "I'm fine."

Her eyes hardened as she flicked her hair back over her shoulder. "Suit yourself."

He sucked in a deep breath as they walked back across the street. There were two options. This woman would either drive him crazy or give him a heart attack. He'd been raised to believe he could achieve whatever he put his mind to conquering. No challenge was too far out of reach. No obstacle insurmountable. And in many arenas of his life that had proven true. Except one.

Love.

He'd failed in his marriage. Jacqueline had left him on New Year's Eve while they were visiting his family in Bermuda. He'd let her go that night, assuming she'd be back the next day and they'd try again, even as it was becoming obvious their relationship was ending. But she hadn't come. Instead, she'd been sailing off with a man she'd met at the marina's bar, showing as much disregard for the storm warnings as she had their vows.

Now if a woman ever gave him a shy smile, or brought him a peach cobbler, or let her hand linger on his arm a little too long, he couldn't reciprocate. The wall he'd built around himself was too damn high. Instead he worked. Worked out. Sailed. Lifted. He got the occasional pitcher of beer and watched a game at Mad Dawgs. Worked more. Won an election.

He wasn't sure if he'd ever get a second shot at forever, or if the risk would be worth the reward.

But if not, there was always his never-ending inbox.

For now it would be best to chalk the Tuesday kiss up to an uncharacteristic lapse in judgment. Except it wasn't just a kiss. It didn't happen in a vacuum. His nostrils flared as heat flushed through his body. His dumb ass had been the one to kiss her.

But she kissed your dumb ass back, a voice whispered.

Tuesday paused outside Rhett and Pepper's front door and wiped one eye, glancing down. "I got an eyelash," she said to herself, blowing it off her fingertip. "Time to make a wish."

He let out a breath of frustration, and fine, yearning. What was it about this woman that simultaneously pulled and repelled him like a mad-spinning magnet? Made him ogle as she unselfconsciously licked hot fudge from her fingers at a church ice cream social, or ventured into a rain shower to play in ankle-deep puddles, or donned a tacky princess dress to make a bunch of foster kids smile?

The maddening truth was that he wanted her. He was drawn to whatever offbeat rhythm throbbed inside her heart, the one that made her look at the world in a way so different from himself.

But he'd never win a woman like that. How could a serious, stiff, workaholic ever make a happy-go-lucky, free-spirited drama queen happy?

He couldn't. It would be the opposite of easy.

More laughter poured through Rhett's cottage windows. Beau's stomach soured with irrational jealousy at the sounds of carefree happiness, his hand frozen on the door-knob. His best friend was the local vet, and Pepper had assumed responsibility as the executive director for the soon-to-be Virginia Valentine Memorial Everland Animal Rescue Shelter. He didn't begrudge his friend, but maybe, hell, he wanted some happy himself.

As he and Tuesday entered the house, a cheer went up.

"Hey, hey, the gang's all here." The General draped a burly ginger-haired arm over the back of his husband's chair. The gold hoop winking from his ear was a perfect match for his gold incisor. "And not a second too soon. I'm hungry enough to eat the southbound side out of a north-bound cow."

Beau took in the crowded table. For better or worse, these were his people. The General and his husband, who went by the Colonel, co-owned the General's General Store, an upmarket take on an old-fashioned small-goods store. Beside them sat Lou Ellen, Rhett's bossy big sister, and her husband, Snapper, who hadn't spoken in public since uttering "I do" at his wedding. Next came his bubbly second cousin Ginger, owner of What-a-Treat Candy Boutique and, since his parents moved to Bermuda, the closest thing he had left in town to family. The bookish man in the tweed jacket opposite was Cedric Swift, an Oxford history professor rumored to be writing a book about Redbeard's missing treasure, although more than a few credible rumors circulated about how he was often spied early mornings transecting the river bottoms in the hopes of actually making the grand discovery.

"Take a seat, Princey Baby," Lou Ellen sang. She loved to needle people, and it took concentrated effort not to give her the rise she sought. He'd endured the tongue-in-cheek nickname of Prince ever since he could remember. That's what happens when you're the heir to a dying dynasty and resident of the largest home in the county.

He slid into the empty chair, and Tuesday took the only other one available. A six-inch gap separated their legs under the table, a six-inch gap filled by a nearly palpable tension. Never had he been so physically aware of another presence. Something nudged his foot. The pointed toe of an utterly silly shoe.

His fork hit the corner of his plate with a loud clatter.

"Christ on a cracker!" Ginger spun her head so fast that her thick black curls bounced against her cheeks. "What's gone and gotten you all hot and bothered?"

"Lost my grip." On that point he told the truth. He just didn't elaborate that what he was really losing his grasp on was his mind. At this point, all he could do was remain outwardly calm and pray to survive the next few hours in Tuesday's proximity, not getting distracted by her mouth, or the ache he felt when staring at her lips. "Got a cold one in the fridge?" he muttered to Rhett.

Escape was the answer.

"Sure do. Anyone else?" Rhett glanced around the table.

"I'm all set, thanks." Pepper gestured to her half-full glass of white wine.

"We'll go another round," the Colonel said, indicating him and his partner.

Tuesday leaned back with a grin. "Got any tequila in the house?"

"Maybe?" Pepper frowned in Rhett's direction. "But no margarita mixer."

"Even better," Tuesday shot back. "I'll take mine straight with no chaser. Hold the salt and lime." She broke the ensuing stunned silence with a wink. "Kidding. Geez, you guys need to lighten up or I will need that shot."

Pepper shook her head with a half-amused eye roll. "Hey, did you hear from Dad today? I got a postcard of a saguaro cactus. He's traveling the country with his girl-friend in a refurbished Airstream," she informed the group.

Tuesday shook her head. "I haven't checked my mailbox since Friday."

"They're en route to the Grand Canyon."

"Everything sound okay?"

"You know how Dad is with communication." Pepper shrugged. "He didn't say much about anything but the food. Apparently he and Susan have formed a wicked addiction to chile rellenos."

"Mmmm. Add that to a future potluck." Tuesday took a deep breath. "Everything tonight really does smell deli-cious."

Ginger nodded in agreement. "Great idea to build a menu around the theme of Southern comfort."

"Mr. Smarty Pants here gets the credit for the brilliant suggestion." Pepper beamed at Rhett. "We've got oven-baked ribs, creamed spinach, buttermilk mashed potatoes, roasted squash with brown sugar, and Beau's famous flour-less chocolate cake."

Ginger heaved a happy sigh. "Mama Marino always was the best baker in town. How are your folks these days?"

"Folks, as in parents?" Tuesday showed him a sly, mischievous wink. "You mean you weren't constructed in some uptight cyborg factory?"

The table gasped, and it took Beau a moment to realize they were frozen, waiting for his reaction. He wasn't a guy anyone ever dared tease.

"Tuesday!" Pepper's hand flew to the side of her neck.

But Tuesday was too busy checking out his chest to pay much heed to her sister's startled admonishment. Her gaze traveled the span of his shoulders as she idly plucked apart one of her napkins. The shredded pile grew in front of her like a tiny snowdrift.

They locked eyes. The tiny gold flecks in her irises were like a crowd of stars, and her kissable mouth, tugging in one corner, was restless with unasked questions.

She wasn't afraid of him.

No. That wasn't it. No one at the table feared him, or the town at large.

But he never invited familiarity. Rhett gave him shit, but he'd been his best friend since kindergarten. No one else besides his parents ever bothered to build a bridge around his natural tendency to keep the world at arm's length, to look deeper and see the guy who existed beneath the reserve.

"Why, his mama was born in Belle Mont Manor and raised right here in Everland." Ginger snapped him back to reality. It surprised him a little to hear her jump to his defense. "A Southern belle debutante."

"But one who cared more about adventure than her china

pattern," he said, clearing his throat, showing he hadn't taken offense. Tuesday liked to poke, but he was begging to tell she didn't mean it meanly. In fact, he sort of liked it. "My granddaddy owned a yacht and insisted his only child learn to sail. She took to the challenge like a duck to water. Got me and Rhett into the sport."

Rhett nodded. "I haven't seen her equal."

"She marched to her own drummer. No way was she ever going to be content as a sorority president. Back then girls weren't allowed on the sail team. There was no co-ed. During a summer in college, she met my dad on her first solo sail to Bermuda. He tended bar at a dive near the marina. They should've had nothing in common, but something clicked while he fixed her a Rum Swizzle. And the rest, as they say, is history."

Beau settled his elbows on the table. All eyes were on him. Lou Ellen's mouth was practically on the table. That's the most he'd said all at once at one of these dinners, ever.

He continued, his gaze trained on Tuesday. "Mama wanted me to grow up in her hometown, put down roots. Dad got along with most folks in town, but Bermuda was in his blood. After I went off to college, they signed the deed to Belle Mont over to me and downsized to a condo back on the island, not far from all his people. They spend six months a year bouncing around the Caribbean, two of the happiest people I know." He smiled around the table. "Present company excluded."

"A toast." Cedric raised his glass. "To love. To those who found it and those of us poor souls who are still searching."

"Hey, us singles aren't that bad off." Ginger shrugged. "We still get to look forward to our first kisses." She gave a dreamy sigh. "There's nothing like a first kiss, is there?"

At the mention of the word "kiss," Tuesday sneezed three times so loudly that Pepper and Rhett's four dogs, Faulkner, Steinbeck, Fitzgerald, and Kitty, broke into uneasy howls.

"Oh, my nerves," Lou Ellen gasped. "Do they have to be so loud?"

"It was a very nice toast," Ginger reassured Cedric over the din.

"Certainly was." Rhett slid back his chair. "And aren't I supposed to be topping a few of you off?"

"Hold that thought." Tuesday jumped up so fast she knocked the table edge; the floral arrangement in the middle tilted precariously before Cedric got it righted. "Oops. But you sit down, Dr. Valentine, and keep making more of those googly eyes with your gorgeous fiancée. I'll get the drinks." She poked Beau in the shoulder and announced, "And the mayor will continue his commitment to community service by helping me."

The rational part of Beau's brain registered that everyone around the table blinked in unison. Tuesday might be an actress, but at the present moment she wasn't a study in subtlety. And even still, his senses were heightened, her casual touch sending acute waves of sensation through his core, flooding his groin in heat.

"Be right there," he said, clearing his throat, keeping a cloth napkin casually positioned over his hardening cock as he rose and followed her into the kitchen with horrified amusement, two contradictory emotions that he was beginning to realize were commonplace near Tuesday, and not altogether enjoyable.

But this situation was new, and confusing, and he didn't want it to be on grand display. Especially with Lou Ellen, who'd be telling half of Everland what transpired tonight on the drive home and the other half at the coffee shop in the morning.

Once around the corner, safely out of sight in the kitchen, he paused, bracing his hands on the counter, letting the cool granite seep into his hot palms. "They're onto us."

"I'm sorry. I am so rattled," she whispered back with a grimace, collapsing against the fridge. "What do we do?"

"We?" Beau hadn't been a "we" in years, and even then he and Jacqueline had never felt all that much like a "we." "We get the drinks like you said. You have one. Two maybe. Then we eat."

"Good, yes." She nodded. "I can do that." She took a deep breath. "Get the drinks. Drink a drink. Eat. And that comment I made about cyborgs. I hope you know I was kidding. I mean, of course you had parents—"

"Two very nice ones."

"They're still together?" Tuesday's voice took on a wistful tone.

He pulled out a few beers with a nod. "Yeah. For over thirty-five years."

"Impressive."

"They make it look easy." His parents had that way about them, a kind of hand-holding, easy back-and-forth relationship that made other people want it, too. He'd thought their marriage was normal, what everybody had, and when he'd first met Jacqueline it had felt easy, too. Sexy. Fun. Addictive.

Until it didn't.

No fairy tale ever said that you could fall in love and get it wrong, that it could be a battle that became a protracted war with no clear winners and losers. That something that seemed for a fleeting moment so right could go horribly wrong.

"My parents married for bad reasons," she said. "They couldn't keep their hands off each other." She grimaced. "I can remember as a little kid they were always kissing and hugging. I thought it was so gross. But they were too different. They might have had the attraction, but nothing went deeper. No roots, so it was easy to pluck out."

"I'm sorry to hear that."

"That's life, right? Not enough happy endings to go around."

He frowned, despite her flippant tone, there was a flash of hurt in her eyes, a pain quickly hidden behind a blithe smile. The ringing of his phone cut the silence. He glanced at his hands, each clutching a beer. "Mind reaching into my pocket and getting that?"

She glanced at his waist, cheeks flushing. "It seems intimate."

"It's after hours. If someone's calling, it's probably important."

"What could possibly be happening? The high school quarterback climbed the water tower and got stuck? An armadillo wandered onto Main Street and held up traffic? This is Everland and we're at a dinner party." She crossed her arms. "Relax. Take the night off."

"I don't have that kind of job where you punch in and punch out." He had three more rings until it went to voice mail. "Please."

Her face softened at the "please." "Ugh. Fine." She reached for the pocket that held her panties. Shit. His mind whirled as his heart stopped, and a sense of dizziness overtook him, ready to tumble him into a rabbit hole of panic.

"Never mind," he growled, stopping her in her tracks.

She arched a brow. "What's that supposed to mean?"

He stepped back. "It means never mind."

"What? You ticklish?" she asked, amused and alarmingly inquisitive.

"Yeah, something like that." He wasn't, but if she pulled out her white thong, she'd forever peg him as a pervert. "Forget about it."

"Stop being a big ol' baby man." Her hand dipped into his phone pocket. All that separated her fingers from his thigh muscles was cotton. "Although...baby? Man? Guess that's redundant."

Blood whooshed into his groin. Fuck. Disaster wasn't quite averted.

She glanced at the screen and smirked. "Humph Miller? Is that an actual name someone gave their child? Oh, darling," she mimicked in a high-pitched Mary Poppins voice. "Why, I do declare, he looks just like a Humph."

The phone stopped ringing. Shit. Humph was a pain in the ass, but he only ever called with a purpose.

"Humphrey," he bit out. "His name is Humphrey."

1 new message lit up on his screen.

"Looks like Humphrey can wait until after we eat."

He met her brow arch with one of his own. "You're more annoying than Janice in the Water Department, and she replies all to every e-mail."

She slipped his phone back into his pocket and the edge grazed his growing erection. He swallowed a groan, his breath uneven.

She leaned in close, lips grazing his neck. "What do you want to bet that you're notorious for marking every e-mail as 'high importance'?"

"Hey-o! Those drinks coming sometime this century or what?" The General's baritone boomed from the dining room. "I'm thirstier than a camel in a turtleneck sweater."

Her low chuckle hit his skin in a soft puff.

Something growled. Shit. It was him. His body tensed, his heart thundering in his chest as she walked out of the kitchen murmuring, "Six points for Gryffindor."

Whatever that meant.

For the next hour and a half he tried to think about everything from sports scores to the agenda for tomorrow night's city council meeting, anything that wasn't the feel of Tuesday's lips grazing his neck. Over dessert she offered breathless, husky moans while devouring his chocolate cake slow bite by slow bite.

He snuck her a sideways glance only to find her staring back.

"So good," she murmured.

God help him he wanted to knock everything off the table, rip off her top, peel off that tiny sundress, nudge apart her sweet thighs, and see what other sounds she was capable producing. She thought his cake was good? Wait until his imagination got cooking.

His knees twitched, sweat prickling the back of his neck as agitation set in. He needed to get a grip. His body might be ready to rut Tuesday into tomorrow, but his mind sought to cut and run, jump on his bike, and hightail it to safety. He'd just begun to string together an urgent excuse to leave when Pepper suggested everyone move into the living room to play old-fashioned parlor games. Cedric suggested charades, and everyone agreed, getting up from the table.

Five minutes later, they were all resituated with fresh drinks in hand.

"What fun! Why, I haven't played charades since Girl Scout camp way back when." Lou Ellen rested her head on Snapper's shoulder, snuggling into the love seat.

"I've never played," Beau said flatly, kneeling by the television. He was trapped in a hell of the sweetest kind, but it was hell nevertheless.

The source of his torment gave a disbelieving gasp, plopping next to him. "What do you do during the winter?" Tuesday asked.

"It rains for a few days, and sometimes we have to put on a sweater. Otherwise it's probably the same as a New England summer,"

She had a small smudge of chocolate on the corner of her bottom lip, so small no one would notice, unless they made a careful study of her mouth.

Pepper explained the rules in her no-nonsense lawyer tone while passing out thin slips of precut paper. "You write down ideas, like famous quotations"—she pantomimed quotes signs in the air—"movies"—pretended to look through a lens and crank an old-fashioned camera—"books"—pretended to read—"plays"—she made a flamboyant gesture—"songs"—she feigned bursting into song—"and finally...television shows." She made a box with her fingers.

Rhett burst into spontaneous applause, and she leaned down to plant a kiss on his forehead with a giggle, "Aw, thanks, baby."

Beau's gut worked itself into a knot. Look how Pepper and Rhett made being happy look easy. So did Lou Ellen and Snapper, snuggled on the love seat, and the General and the Colonel, sprawled on the green striped couch. Even Ginger and Cedric appeared comfortable sitting cross-legged on the ground.

He and Tuesday sat cross-legged, their knees a hair-breadth apart.

They weren't easy. They were…He didn't know.

But, God help him, he wanted to find out.

Chapter Eight

What made Beau's hands intriguing? Tuesday couldn't tear her gaze from the broad knuckles and visible veins. If he gestured just so, palms out, rough calluses appeared, lining the pads. No doubt hard-won through sailing and fodder for dirty fantasies as he stood in the center of the living room rug and pressed his middle and pointer fingers together to make a box.

"Okay, what do we got here? A television show," the Colonel muttered under his breath, kneading his temples. "Our Netflix addiction might finally come in handy."

Beau held up three fingers.

"Three words?" the General mused, crossing a leg and leaning forward. "*I Love Lucy! Will & Grace! Beverly Hills, 90210?*"

Beau shook his head.

"Don't stand there staring like a blind bat. Do something," Lou Ellen ordered, scooting to the edge of her seat.

Beau curled his lips back, baring his straight white teeth.

"Vampire!" Tuesday shouted before she had time to think.

Beau nodded and waved his three fingers.

"Oh!" She clapped her hands. "*The Vampire Diaries*! Too easy."

"Got it." Beau flashed a thumbs-up, and she threw her arms into a victory V.

"What? How?" Pepper swiveled her disbelieving gaze between them. "Did you peek? That was impossible."

"What can I say?" Tuesday shimmied in her seat. "I've got the gift." Easier to gloat than be startled at her strange telepathy with the mayor.

"A gift, huh?" Beau took his seat and glanced over, the rare twinkle in his eye replacing his usual penetrating stare. "What's it called. Humbleness?"

"Did you just make a joke, Mayor Marino? Quick, someone check out the window and tell me if there's a flying pig." Hearing Beau speak fluent sarcasm was unsettling. Her sanity found it much easier to keep him in a sexy-but-too-stiff-and-bossy box. Watching him willing to look silly while playing a parlor game was a whole other receptacle. Her abdominal muscles tightened as if bracing for a sudden impact. She'd been so certain that she had this man pegged—more evidence that she didn't know how to read someone.

But he didn't have a slick veneer of charm like Philip. No, he wore his faults on his overstarched sleeve. Not a bad boy but also not laid-back or funny.

Charades carried on and everyone took another turn. When it circled back to Beau, he got up and placed his hands on either side of his mouth.

"A song? A song. A song. Okay, Snapper, you love music. You got this, sugar." Lou Ellen executed a quick but complicated cheerleading-routine clap.

"Here we go." Beau held up eight fingers with a grin.

"Eight words? This is going to be a mouthful." Ginger flopped back against the couch, her riotous black curls bouncing around her chin.

Beau slapped his chest, then stared around the room.

Everyone returned the stare with confused expressions.

"Tarzan?" Cedric ventured.

"You might need to work on your math skills, History Boy," Ginger said with a good-natured chuckle.

Beau slapped his chest again.

Tuesday mashed her lips together and shifted in her seat. Bless his heart, as they said down here. Beau Marino might be as sexy as heck. He might even be an amazing elected official. But there was one thing he was not.

A good actor.

He pulled his brows together and glowered, jabbing a finger to his forehead, face screwed in concentration.

The answer struck faster than a midsummer lightning storm. "When I Think About You I Touch Myself!" she blurted, jumping to her feet and throwing up her arm in a high-five.

"Bingo!" Beau slapped her back, his fingers interlacing with hers for a fraction of a second before he readjusted his jacket and turned his attentions to the map of Georgia pinned to the far wall. "How'd you guess?"

She didn't have a pat answer. It was like she'd read his mind.

"I say, that was uncanny." Cedric swigged his dark beer, stating the obvious.

"Downright spooky if you ask me," Lou Ellen added. "Technically it's "I Touch Myself" but I'll let it slide given the circumstances."

Steinbeck, Rhett's golden retriever, *woof*ed in assent. The other two, Fitzgerald and Faulkner, wagged their tails. Kitty, Pepper's dog, kept right on snoring.

"Well, now." The General glanced at his watch. "This has been a hoot, y'all, but we better mosey home and check in on Fido." Fido was the General's pet alligator. The Colonel tolerated the animal but made it clear it was his husband's quirky responsibility.

Kitty, Pepper's puppy, whined by the back door.

"Yep, it's getting to be about that time." Pepper yawned behind her hand. "Hey, Beau, are we still on for lunch tomorrow? I want to get your insight on the shelter's final building plans before they go to the planning review committee."

He conferred with her as Tuesday watched from a discreet distance. Imagine being in charge of so much. She barely managed responsibility for J. K. Growling. As much as she hated to admit it, his understated authoritativeness was superlatively sexy.

"Thanks for coming," Rhett said, handing over her purse and distracting her.

"It was fun." She meant it. Especially charades. "We should do it again soon."

"Maybe go French," Rhett said. "And after dinner we'll watch *Amélie*. Pepper's choice."

"Ooh la la! *Oui*, we love that movie!" Tuesday pirouetted. "Maybe this time I'll get upgraded into bringing something that people can actually consume?" She waggled her eyebrows, trying to stamp out a flicker of annoyance, because guess what? It sucked not to be taken seriously. Sure she was a hot mess, but sometimes it would be nice if the more responsible folk weren't quite so patronizing. Just because she misplaced her shoes and car keys a few (dozen) times a week didn't mean she was incompetent in all things.

Her sister didn't mean to hurt her—even if her words stung—and so she gave her sister a quick squeeze before turning for the door.

"Hey, hold up. I'll walk you out." Beau's comment had a too-studied note of nonchalance.

Pepper and Rhett exchanged a glance. Ginger nudged Cedric.

Yes, Beau Marino was a terrible actor.

But in the grand scheme of things, maybe his transparency went in his favor. It made him the polar opposite of a lying, cheating, Tony-award-winning director who said they were finalizing their divorce when really his wife was on an extended work assignment to Europe. If she asked to go out in public he berated her until she felt like she was the problem. Then said wife came back to surprise said director for his fortieth birthday and claimed Tuesday was a conniving home wrecker rather than dishing a helping of blame on her husband.

Beau wasn't Philip, but could she trust him?

Her dating track record had been woefully devoid of good guys with the exception of Ryan Shelby in fifth grade, who'd always slipped her his chocolate milk at lunch. Wait, scratch that. Didn't Ryan Shelby also serve time for mail theft after high school?

Being attracted to bad boys seemed exciting, except for the part where they were, well…bad. Dating one or two assholes was an unhappy part of a girl's life, but her jerk record was unbroken.

She waited until they cleared the front porch steps before speaking. "They're definitely suspicious."

Beau deliberated a moment. "Yeah. But they'll be too polite to ask questions."

"Maybe to you." Tuesday grimaced. A furtive movement caught the corner of her eye. Rhett and Pepper jumped back from the window, both pretending to be busy drawing the curtain, but holding the same string.

They crossed the street. Beau stopped at his bike and drummed his fingers on the curving metal frame. "Mind if I come in? I meant what I said about clearing the air."

She considered his request. A frank adult talk *would* put the whole matter to bed.

No, wait. Scratch that. Not bed.

She ducked her chin, grateful for her long veil of hair, and let her gaze land across the street. In the big old house, Miss Ida May was visible through her front window, holding court in her dining room in front of an open laptop. Behind her leaned in the illuminated faces of Phaedra Fairweather and Lucille Munro. The three not-so-secret editors of the *Back Fence* were intent on whatever they were studying online. At least they were distracted from the events unfolding in the middle of Love Street. After the way Miss Ida May had eyed her earlier, Tuesday sensed they wouldn't approve of her bringing Beau indoors after hours.

"Sure," she said firmly, leading the way to her cottage. Her pace was brisk, a Manhattan stride, one that meant business. "It would be great to get on the same page."

She opened her front gate with gusto. Yep, this chat would be easy-peasy. He'd come in. They'd agree this morning had been nothing more than a big mistake, and then she'd tell a joke that would make everything okay. After that they'd return to being nemeses.

Because they hadn't had their first kiss. They'd had their *only* kiss.

Chapter Nine

⁓

Tuesday pushed open her unlocked front door and they stepped inside, staring at each other in the dark room. It was a look that went too long and felt as intimate as a caress. Of course she'd heard the old expression about being undressed with eyes. Well, Beau was doing a mighty fine job of stripping her bare.

"I'll get the light." She bent to flick on the side table lamp. Had he really come to talk? What if he was here because he saw the same things Philip had—the blond hair, the happy-go-lucky smile, her up-for-anything attitude—and assumed she'd be great for a romp but nothing serious?

She kept her chin tucked to her chest, arranging a stack of celebrity gossip magazines, keeping her face shielded behind a veil of hair.

What an idiot. Beau was probably after one thing. She didn't need to play Twenty Questions.

He cleared his throat. "So here is what I'm thinking—"

"Let me guess." She drew herself to her full height. "Because I kissed you, you think that I'm going to sleep with you?"

"Sleep with *you*?" Two bemused lines creased his forehead as his eyes flew wide open. "What are you talking about?"

Her cheeks scorched with embarrassment—talk about misreading the situation. Philip was eight hundred miles away and still his poison circulated in her veins. Beau wasn't marking her as an easy lay. He wasn't considering her, period. God, could she be more of an idiot?

She endured his inquisitive gaze, chin held high as he scanned her beet-red face as if it were tattooed with a map of the missing Redbeard treasure. "That's not how I want you to think of me," he said. "We don't have much in common, but I respect you."

She huffed a mocking laugh; it was that or climb the walls. Because like it or not, Beau Marino wasn't a jerk. He wasn't Mr. Happy-Go-Lucky, but he wasn't here to take advantage. Rather, he stood there like the portrait of a perfect Southern gentlemen despite those rather wicked low-slung jeans and the weathered leather jacket. She was the one with her mind in the gutter.

"Forget it," she muttered. "You say north, I say south. You say left, I say right. I swear we could probably argue whether the Earth was round."

His jaw clenched. "It's an oblate spheroid."

She blinked. "Excuse me?"

"The Earth. It appears round from space, but it is squished at the poles and swollen at the equator."

She stared, openmouthed, as he took a step toward her. He was tall, but so was she. They stood nearly eye to eye, but he was broader. Hard-bodied. Male. Not the type to talk her ear off or go on and on with hours of mushy pillow talk. It took him a while to warm up, but he wasn't shy. His quiet confidence settled something loose inside her. He'd never manipulate her to take advantage. But that didn't mean he was safe. His serious gaze felt dangerous in another way, especially when it fixed on her mouth just so.

"Tuesday." He stepped closer.

She slanted her mouth in a smile. "The Earth is squished and swollen, huh? That would have been a fun physical science class." Humor was her only defense against this overwhelming confusion.

He shook his head but didn't come closer. "We're off point. Listen. I'm not in the habit of acting like I did in Madam Magna's tent. Fuck it all…" He skimmed a hand over the top of his head, his features open, vulnerable even. "I haven't kissed a woman since my wife."

She hadn't known about Beau's Bermuda-living parents, but it was impossible to live in Everland for more than three days and not overhear offhand comments about his deceased wife, always accompanied by a headshake and a vague sympathetic comment.

In this moment he wasn't the no-nonsense, confident leader, but a fellow lost soul. "I'm sorry," she whispered, taking a deep breath. "So very sorry."

"Everyone is *sorry*." He spit out the word like it was a vulgar phrase. "I don't want pity. And I don't deserve pity, trust me."

"Then I won't give it to you." She dropped her shoulders. Not everyone had believed she was a conniving home wrecker in New York. Some friends had been sympathetic, and that had almost felt worse. She wouldn't put him in the same position.

His phone rang again.

"Saved by the bell one more time," she said with forced brightness. "Go ahead and take the call. I need to let my dog out. We can reconvene after and make a game plan for going forward." That sounded very businesslike and take-charge.

Relief washed over his features. "Good."

Now they'd talk over the afternoon's mistake like two grown-ups, sweep the memory under the rug, and return to regularly scheduled mutual dislike. All would be right in the world. "Great. Feel free to take a seat."

He gave her pink-striped couch and peacock-patterned throw pillows an impassive glance. "I'll be out front," he said, opening the door and disappearing onto the porch.

She helped her old Boston terrier hobble down the back steps and into the yard. J. K. Growling sniffed around a magnolia while Tuesday sank onto the stoop. A warm, buttery light shone over the side fence, separating her yard from Pepper and Rhett's cottage. Jazz poured through their kitchen window, muffling conversation but not their laughter and the occasional dish clink.

Tuesday swallowed the unexpected upwelling of jealousy with a grimace. Her sister deserved every single bit of goodness that crossed her path. She didn't begrudge Pepper anything, and yet sometimes it hurt. Because Tuesday had tried to play the game, and had gone all in on the idea of love, but unlike Indiana Jones in front of those hundred goblets, she'd chosen unwisely. Now she had a past more checkered than most checkerboards. Why were all the men she dated jerks? How could her asshole detector be so broken?

The what-ifs could stretch to the moon. What if she hadn't been so desperate to be liked?

It wouldn't have been so easy to be manipulated for starters.

What if she had questioned the unsettled feeling she'd gotten whenever Philip had made a glancing reference to his supposedly ex-wife?

What if she'd walked out after he'd put her down, rather than ignoring his sob stories about a troubled childhood?

God, she'd let him play her emotions like a fiddle. Saying how his wife had broken his heart. That he was alone. Wounded. That Tuesday was the only person who'd ever made him feel whole. She was special. A talent. No, they couldn't go out together. He didn't want to share her. What they had wasn't for the world. It was just for each other. If she could be smarter. Prettier. Skinnier.

Different.

First he'd invited her to read for him at his apartment after they met in the elevator when she was on her way to work at a birthday party on the floor above him. He'd held the door and asked for her number. When she'd gotten in the elevator she'd squealed. Of course she'd heard of casting-couch auditions, but it wasn't like that. He actually had her read. Praised her performance. Called her his budding star.

It took two to have a dysfunctional relationship. Her, the victim.

And him, the asshole.

He'd groomed her, flattered her, dazzled her until she couldn't see that she was being led down a dark path by a guy who got off on abuse and humiliation. A spider who spun his web around her so delicately, so lightly, that she never knew she was trapped until he'd sucked her almost dry. She'd been with her share of jerks, but Philip was special, a class all his own. He drained her of self-worth, of confidence, of love.

And afterward, when she was nothing but a husk, all she could do was stare in the mirror at herself, as if maybe if she looked hard enough she'd see the answer to the biggest why of all…

Why had she chosen to fall for a man like that?

She stood and tilted her head back. No breeze from the coast tonight. What she wouldn't give for a bit of autumn coolness to temper the overwarm dark. Or air-conditioning.

A deep voice drifted over the roof. Beau. On the phone. Working as always.

But the lost feeling on his face, how to reconcile it with the clipped, masculine take-charge tone.

"Tomorrow's no good. I'm booked solid," he said in his usual curt voice. "I have time Friday, a half hour at noon."

Friday? It was only Monday. His days were that packed?

He made a disgusted sound. "I don't give two shits what Discount-Mart says. I'm not in a hurry. Happily Ever After Land means something to this town. Any potential closure needs to be considered from all angles."

Closure? She froze, her heart forgetting a beat. Discount-Mart, the chain store? What was going on?

"The Tourism Commission paid us a visit today. If they support Everland for their Coastal Jewel campaign, then I'd be hard-pressed to advocate for the park's closure. It's a little tired, but it provides historic value to the town."

He went quiet a moment. Something wet rubbed over the back of her knee, and she squeaked. J. K. Growling's nose. She'd been eavesdropping so hard that she hadn't heard the old girl lumber up the stairs.

The tenor of Beau's voice changed, increasing in speed. "Listen, man. I can't talk. We can meet Friday. All right. 'Night, Humph."

It was wrong to eavesdrop, and now the evidence was inadmissible. She couldn't say anything without sharing it had been overheard.

And first she had to figure out what was going on. Because no one would close Happily Ever After Land. She set her shoulders. The real world was a hard place. Good guys—and gals—could lose. Undeserving villains could win the day and never pay for any of their vile deeds.

That's not the way this story would end. The park existed as a place of hope, of simple joy and happiness. Once upon a time, she hadn't been able to save herself. But no longer.

This princess would kick some dragon tail and take names.

Chapter Ten

B eau hung up and went back inside Tuesday's dollhouse cottage. Humph Miller had been relentlessly self-serving as usual—no surprises there—but the million-dollar question was which option would be best for Everland? Keeping Happily Ever After Land and continuing to pursue a long-game tourism and revitalization strategy, or pursuing immediate results with the Discount-Mart deal but risk losing the unique small-town ambience?

Humph's big fat carrot about supporting a bid for higher office didn't factor into his decision. The reason people were disenchanted with politics was because of corruption, the idea that values could be bought and sold. When he first ran for mayor he promised himself that if the role ever clashed with his ethics or beliefs, he'd find another occupation. That was the biggest problem with career politicians, those who began to see it less as a calling and more as a paycheck. He might be able to do more good in Washington, DC. But he'd lose being grounded in his community. Being anchored to the real work of government, its power to improve individual lives.

He sank onto the pink-and-white-striped couch, taking in the overwhelmingly feminine room, from the peacock-patterned throw pillows, to the tiny curios, to the vase of yellow roses, lilies, and sunflowers, to the rhinestone tiara hanging from the coat hook. The whole atmosphere was light and delicate, contrasting with the black leather furniture and dark, muted color scheme of Belle Mont Manor.

A floorboard creaked. Tuesday hovered in the doorway, and he swallowed thickly. In addition to deciding on the best outcome for Everland, he needed to figure out one here, too, between them.

"What happened this morning," she said crisply. "It was a mistake." She spoke nothing but the truth, but that didn't erase the sting.

"You're a great kisser," he blurted, addressing her pink-painted toes. Shit. Where did that come from?

Her cheeks flamed. "Um, thanks?" He liked her little blushes. That was the problem with Tuesday; she was addictively adorable. Her guileless gaze might conjure strong protective instincts, but it took only a good long glance at her clear eyes to spy the strong-willed spirit that dwelled inside.

This was a woman who could kick ass and take names if the situation required.

Both versions were appealing—the innocence and the strength. Too damn appealing.

"You're my best friend's fiancé's sister. This is Everland. We're going to see each other like it or not." Did he like that idea?

Her face softened a fraction. "I don't want to fight."

"Can we call a truce?"

An emotion crossed her face that he couldn't begin to decipher. "I'm not sure."

"What can I do to make you sure?" He squinted, regarding her more carefully. Tension rolled off her in waves.

She opened her mouth, but ran her hand over her lips as if to shove the words back inside. "Let me get back to you on that."

He wrinkled his brow. Something was up. Her gaze shuttered like windows before a hurricane. But it was hard to think rationally while she daintily chewed the corner of her lip.

"How about we call it a night, okay?" She avoided his glance.

No. It wasn't okay, but it would have to be. He liked this about Tuesday, seeing her set boundaries and take charge of a situation, steering it to how it could better suit her. She had such a strong sense of self, personality poured out of her, a raw, vital energy that was heady to be around.

What if she wasn't all show? What if she was just that great?

He swallowed hard, trying to dislodge his heart from his throat.

Those were questions that were safer to ponder from afar.

"I'll see myself out." He rose and turned for the door, but she was at the end of the coffee table, blocking that route. He stepped right only for her to follow suit, not anticipating his move. They ended chest to chest.

"Sorry. Let me go the other way," she said, but he'd already done it.

They stood closer still. He pressed the tip of his tongue against the back of his teeth.

Her head tilted back and she regarded him through hooded, hazy eyes. Before he could finish thinking "fuck it," the choke hold loosened on his self-control. Their lips tangled, a slow, tender, mutual assault, and there it was again, the ignited chemistry, white-hot and right.

Whatever they couldn't manage to speak they shared now, tasting each other's frustration, fear, hope, loneliness, and desire. A small, wounded part of himself brushed against hers, and the pain was sweet. He couldn't get enough of her mouth; he'd never get his fill of her lips.

"This is a bad idea." She pushed him down on the couch and landed in his lap, legs straddling his hips, her dress hiked high, baring her satin-smooth thighs. When she leaned in to resume their kiss, she rocked against the thick heat in his pants and didn't pull away. If anything, she leaned in harder with a breathless, "Oh God."

They froze, sharing breaths, pressed hard, close and aching. He skimmed her shoulders, let her hair tickle his fingers.

"I've seen these kinds of situations before," she murmured, pressing her forehead to his. "In movies."

"Glean any valuable insight?"

"The couple always decides to sleep with each other."

"That a fact?" he rasped. Maybe he should give movies more credit.

"It's always this shtick about how sex will help them get out of each other's system." Her laugh held a mocking note. "As if that's ever going be the case. It's the worst trope ever."

"Why?"

"Attraction doesn't always lead to good places. Been there, done that. Nope. Nu-Uh."

"Spoken like a princess from Happily Ever After Land?" he teased.

Her gaze flew up to meet his. "Attraction blinds people to reality."

She had him there.

Her expression grew more bashful. "And it just so happens that I'm attracted to you."

He winced as she shifted her weight. He was so hard it hurt. "I seem to be in a similar conundrum," he ground out.

She licked her top lip in a quick, self-conscious nervous gesture. His gaze riveted. This wasn't a mere crush on her mouth but a full-scale obsession.

"First step is admitting there's a problem."

Her smart mouth made him grin. "It appears we can't keep our hands off each other."

"Right. So the key is physical distance. At all times." She pushed back and stood, took a step back, then two more. "Five feet. That seems reasonable. Three in a push."

He rose and moved in the opposite direction. "Ground rules."

"And we don't speak about this to anyone. That way it never happened, like a tree falling in the woods or however the old saying goes."

"My lips are sealed." He headed toward the door and made himself place his hand on the doorknob. "Good night, Tuesday."

"Have a safe drive home, Mayor," she returned.

He closed the door, and the wind chime hanging from a nail on the porch rafter tinkled in the wind, spinning around and around and around. It took him a full minute to muster the strength to walk down the front steps, get on his bike, and drive home.

Close call, narrowly avoided, but the fact held no relief. Just a lonely, weary sadness.

Chapter Eleven

~

The next morning Tuesday doubled down at Happily Ever After Land, posed for photographs, hammed it up with guests, and studied the surrounds. She could still close one eye and imagine elegant men in bowler hats and women in bustled skirts and parasols promenading the leafy paths, but the last hundred years hadn't been kind to the park. The grand old dame looked tired, the surroundings battered by sea air and faded by time.

The souvenir shops needed fresh paint. The Fun Slide and Drop Tower had CLOSED FOR REPAIRS signs hanging from their entrances. Algae coated the water surface of the kiddie boat ride. And yet, even still, the place retained a vintage charm, from the clickety-clack of the wooden roller coaster to the soaring one-hundred-and-twenty-foot Ferris wheel.

But condemning the park in favor of a Discount-Mart and an outlet mall? Talk about committing small-town sacrilege. Everland was special because it wasn't like any-where else and retained an indefinable lost-in-time appeal. The workers here relied on the park, not just because of a paycheck, but also because it was a home. A place of be-longing, family, and friendship.

She entered the staff break room stomach rumbling from watching visitors devour toffee apples, funnel cake, and saltwater taffy. She'd forgotten to eat breakfast and on-the-job snacking was strictly forbidden for a princess. Other rules were no sitting, no using a public restroom, no playing with a phone, and no breaking character.

Unless in here. The break room was the safe space for the talent.

A clown snored in the corner of the room under a poster that read YOUR MAMA'S NOT HERE. CLEAN YOU OWN MESS. Z-Man, fast asleep as usual. There were conflicting reports on whether his real name was Zack, Zane, or Zebidiah, but there was unanimous agreement on how he'd earned his nickname. Sneaking on-the-job naps wherever possible. He played the park mascot, Merry Perry, and not only endured the swelter-ing months in the red wig and thick makeup but also had the ten-years-service ribbon taped to the front of his staff locker.

She opened her locker and removed the Sweet Brew car-rot cake cupcake she'd been dreaming about all morning. She'd be more likely to forget putting on underwear than to miss a meal. And let's face it, baked goods fantasies were less dangerous than those relating to certain men, specifi-cally of the mayor variety.

"Hello, lover," she murmured, cradling it in her hands. "Yup. I'm fitting this whole baby in my mouth." She got as far as peeling off the foil when there came the thunder of footsteps.

"Greetings, my beautiful true love!" Gil burst into the room, crossing to her in four exaggerated hops before posing with a smooch-lipped face and fluttering lids.

"In your dreams, Kermit." She patted the top of his head. "It's not me; it's your class. I'm a mammal. You're an amphibian. We're from opposite sides of the magical kingdom."

"Love knows no sides."

"Maybe not." She giggled. "But alas, we couldn't provide the kingdom the required heirs."

Gil feigned deep thinking. "I think a hybrid frog-human could make our kingdom great again." He snatched a bite from her cupcake.

"I hate you!" she cried.

"You love me," he countered, wiping his lips in satisfaction. He attended night school at the local community college and was in that twenty-year-old "the world is my oyster" stage. Who wanted to rain on that parade?

She'd never had a little brother, but if she did, she imagined he'd have been like him. He loved chasing her around the park, cajoling her for a wayward kiss to the delight of the guests, but in the break room they kicked back and traded gossip over the day's cute boys.

Gil might be a frog, but he hoped to meet his Prince Charming someday. Toots strolled in next, right on schedule, along with Caroline from Janitorial Services, who never spoke above a whisper. Lettie Sue was preceded by a loud sneeze. She was a single mom and the park hypochondriac. She continuously quizzed Caroline about the cleaning product ingredients and followed the outbreak of every rare disease in the national news. She'd recently been convinced she'd contracted the bubonic plague from the park's chipmunk population. It turned out to be dehydration after working the Visitor Information in hundred-degree heat.

Hot on her heels was Eugene, aka "Mean Gene," the quintessential grumpy old man, who was the only person who ever put an idea in the employee suggestion box.

Toots said it was always the same thing: "Remove the suggestion box."

Tuesday had been welcomed into this ragtag gang of misfits, no questions asked. At lunch politics and religion were strictly off-limits, while discussions of celebrity scandals and teasing were not only allowed but encouraged.

Except today she was the bearer of serious news. How could she share Beau's conversation from last night without putting them in fear of losing their social network and livelihoods?

"What's the latest in the world?" Toots asked, picking up the *Everland Examiner*.

"The park's under attack," Tuesday blurted. "We're in danger of being torn down to make way for an outlet mall and a Discount-Mart."

All conversation ceased. The vending machine hummed in the corner.

Oops. She'd meant to ease into the dialogue gently; instead her lead-in was "the house is on fire and we're alllllllll gonna diiiiiiiie."

The room fell silent. Z-Man had jolted awake during the hubbub. "Say what?" He plucked off his rubber nose.

"Happily Ever After Land has been losing money for years, and outside interests want to stop the bleeding by tearing us down and building a Discount-Mart and an adjacent outlet mall."

"Says who?" Toots demanded.

Tuesday chewed her inner lip. She couldn't out the mayor. This group might gather battering rams or pitchforks and storm city hall.

"I'm not at liberty to reveal my source."

"Pshaw." Toots scoffed. "Sounds like a tempest in a teapot to me. Why, this park has stood for one hundred years. It's listed on the National Register of Historic Places."

"Is not," Eugene grumbled.

"It should be," Toots shot back.

"Could there be another reason?" Lettie Sue dabbed her nose. "What if we're positioned too close to the swamp across the road? I had wondered about all them mosquitoes. Or worse, what if nuclear waste is leaching into the ground-water?"

"Has your tinfoil hat fallen off again?" Mean Gene barked as Tuesday said, "No. No. None of that. My, um...inside source made it sound like we are in dire fiscal straits."

"We're in the happiness business," Gil piped up. "You can't put a price tag on joy."

"I love the sound of delusional people." Mean Gene folded his arms and rolled his eyes. "Everything is for sale for the right price. That's the world we live in."

Caroline mumbled something, but hard to say if it was in agreement or dissent. Normally she went along with Toots and Lettie Sue.

"Listen." Tuesday banged her fist on the table, right into the cupcake. "Darn it!" She licked the frosting off the side of her hand. That wasn't going to waste. "I'm telling you, my source is real."

"I'm sure you believe what you say," Toots said kindly. "But we've struggled for years. Somehow the place always gets along on a song and a few extra prayers."

The others muttered their assent.

"The princess speaks the truth."

The room went silent as a tomb at the sight of the turbaned old woman in the doorway. It appeared the fates had seen fit to grant her an unlikely ally. In Everland they don't hide crazy; they drape it in gauzy fortune-teller robes and give it a job.

"Madam Magna," Tuesday said deferentially. "I didn't see you lurking back there." The woman had a disconcerting habit of appearing and disappearing at will.

The tenor of the group shifted. Madam Magna commanded a sense of shock and awe. Even Toots wasn't immune to her presence. If Magna said she spoke the truth, they were going to listen.

"Has anyone spoken to Mr. Wilcox?" Lettie Sue dabbed her upturned nose with the ever-present red hankie she stored in her shirtsleeve.

"You will soon have your chance." Magna vanished back through the doorway. Tuesday was half surprised that thunder didn't follow her proclamation.

"The old broad is inhaling too much incense smoke." Mean Gene feigned taking a hit off a joint, brave to grump now that she was gone.

"Afternoon, my favorite people!" Mr. Wilcox ambled into the break room, a broad smile creasing his plump face. "Y'all look as upset as a T. rex trying to make his bed."

"The man of the hour," Gil said.

"Who?" Mr. Wilcox made a show of looking around. "Me?"

"Cop a squat, Boss Man," Toots said, pulling out a chair.

"I'm more nervous than a turkey on Christmas." He finished with his trademark machine-gun *heh-heh-heh*. The more unsure Mr. Wilcox became, the more folksy he got. He took the offered spot, brushing imaginary lint off his suit jacket.

"Go on. Tell him, Princess," Toots ordered.

Tuesday pointed at her chest and mouthed *me?* Guess that's the first rule of gossip. If the urge to gossip strikes, don't partake in front of the entire break room. She folded her hands and placed them on the table. "We understand that the park is facing serious financial trouble."

Sweat sheened Mr. Wilcox's bald head. "We've had better times."

"And there are suggestions that Everland is being pressured not to renew our hundred-year-lease that's up next year."

"An oversight. The town offered the land as a gesture of goodwill. To see if it might attract more visitors. We were founded on a dream. A dream of the town."

"Or a nightmare," Eugene muttered.

"So it's true? The park might go out of business? Make way for a Discount-Mart and an outlet mall?" Gil sounded disbelieving.

"But it doesn't make sense," Lettie Sue said. "All this infrastructure? Where will that go?"

"They'll tear it all down." Mr. Wilcox's voice cracked, his rheumy eyes bright with alarm. "Haul it off for scrap. Sell a few rides to traveling carnivals. There's talk of donating one ride to the Smithsonian for a museum exhibit."

"The conversation's as far gone as all that." Toots pursed

her lips, and deep lines bracketed her mouth. "And you never said a word!"

"It ain't over until it's over," Mr. Wilcox said. "The lease could be renewed. I am trying to figure out a way to convince the mayor to see reason. With his support—"

Toots shook her head. "You couldn't convince a man out of a wet paper bag. You're a good man, boss, but you ain't got any sense. You'd start on those nervous jokes and annoy everyone into shutting us down."

"You can do it," Caroline whispered to Toots. "Speak with Mayor Marino. Get the city behind us."

"But it's always my way or the highway. Politics don't work like that. They require more finesse."

"That's it," Eugene announced. "We're doomed."

"But this place brings so much joy," Gil said. "It just ain't right. We help make Everland special."

Z-Man squeaked his red nose, looking thoughtful. "Princess here wins people over."

Everyone turned to face Tuesday.

She gulped. "I do?"

"You keep the kid trips in line better than anyone we've ever had."

"You're likable." Lettie Sue nodded slowly. "Everyone likes you."

She arched a brow. "Except Mayor Marino."

Toots whipped off her glasses and narrowed her eyes. "Especially Mayor Marino."

She snorted. "You might need to up your prescription, see the situation clearly. He despises me."

Gil coughed. Robbie was his little brother. No doubt he had blabbed about catching her kissing the mayor.

She shot him a warning glare and he clammed up. The

kiss was an aberration. Hatred was as strong an emotion as love or desire. That's all that happened there. Nothing more.

"Wilcox, that's it, that's your lobbyist," Toots said, wagging a finger at Tuesday.

Tuesday stared at her cupcake with longing. "But I just said—"

"Quit your malarkey. The mayor is interested in you. You've got his attention. When you're around, he doesn't look anywhere else. You connect to folks. You're genuine. It's why all visitors gravitate to you." Toots didn't sound like she'd be swayed.

"He's arrogant. I don't like *him*," Tuesday protested weakly.

"Sure, he might be a little stiff, but he grows on you."

"So does ringworm," she muttered.

"And your smile lights up the room," Gil said. "Why even ol' Mean Gene here can't help but smile back."

Eugene gave a rueful smirk. "Kid's got a point. You got a way of making people feel good inside."

"A natural leader." Z-Man nodded.

"Our savior." Caroline pressed a hand to her chest.

Tuesday never suffered from stage fright and could ad-lib through most any situation. But it seemed her improvisational powers had run out. She surveyed the room. Who was this persuasive, strong, charismatic leader that they spoke of? "Are you guys sure you're talking about the right person?"

"Deal me in." Mr. Wilcox threw up his hands. "I thought this was a job for a knight in shining armor. Maybe what we really need is a strong princess in heels."

Eugene rapped the table with his knuckles. "Let's put it to a vote."

"All in favor of making Tuesday Knight the official Happily Ever After lobbyist say aye."

"Aye."

It was unanimous. Getting the park their fairy-tale ending was up to her. But she wasn't a heroic leader. A dragon had defeated her, chopped up her self-confidence and spit her out.

The group stared with trusting eyes.

Her next breath was shakier than one of James Bond's martinis. What could she do?

Play the part. If they wanted a leader to save the park, she could pretend.

At least she still knew how to do that.

Chapter Twelve

~

Beau frowned at his in-box, idly clicking his favorite retractable pen. His e-mails bred like rabbits. The latest was from Janice in the Planning Department, the woman notorious for hitting "reply all" to every single damn query. This one simply said, "Got it! Thanks!!!!!!!"

Sixteen people had been forced to read that exclamation-laden response.

His frown deepened. Maybe the solution rested in a municipal resolution banning frivolous e-mails. Each time he got cc'd on a group e-mail, which he did all day, every day, he hoped maybe this one time no one would hit "reply all."

Ping!

Another e-mail. This one from Councilman Jerry Merryfox. His personal specialty was waiting until a group e-mail thread was finally poised to expire, then resurrecting it with a long-winded non sequitur that served no purpose other than to demonstrate the basic ability to connect his fingers to the keyboard.

But because people loved to weigh in on anything that required an opinion—even if that opinion was "Should we purchase a new coffeepot for the council chamber room?"—the whole conversation would rear back to life like a Hydra that refused to die.

A notification popped up from his calendar: Listen and Lead 3pm

He rolled his shoulders and cracked his neck. That was more like it. The purpose of being mayor wasn't to broker staff infighting over the merits of vanilla versus hazelnut coffee creamer; it was to improve his community. Listen and Lead was an initiative he had implemented his first month in office. Twice weekly he'd open the doors and clear his calendar between three and five o'clock to hear from any Everland resident who wanted to stop by.

"Mayor?" His assistant's voice came over the intercom. "Your first L&L is here."

"Very good. Thank you, Karen." He gathered the report he'd been skimming and neatly stacked the pages. Even the worst fifteen minutes spent engaged in a constituent chat was better than listening to Councilman Merryfox drone on during a conference call about how life was better before the advent of the Internet, all the while munching on something crunchy out of a foil bag.

"Good afternoon, Mayor."

That voice. Only two people in Everland spoke with a New England cadence. One was engaged to his best friend. The other?

His hands slipped from the report he was stacking and his left index finger got one hell of a paper cut. He plucked a tissue from the box on the corner of his desk and pressed it to the wound before looking up.

He glanced up without raising his chin. This vantage point afforded a direct line of sight to a navy-blue ruffled bow skirt and two long gorgeous legs in a confident stance. He raised his gaze higher, to the narrow waist and torso, the arms tightly folded over the chest, partially obscured by white-blond hair, narrowed brown eyes framed by a heavy fringe of lashes.

"What brings you in today, Miss Knight?" Her bright gaze wasn't a punch to the gut; it carved his bones with all the ruthless efficiency of a diamond cutter, remaking him into something new, strange, and multifaceted.

He nipped the inside of his lower lip. Or just made himself a stupid, poetic mess.

"Aren't you going to offer me a seat?" Her eyebrows shot up as she pointed her chin to the two empty visitor chairs before his desk. "Here I've been thinking Southern gentlemen were famous for impeccable manners."

"Yes. Of course." He half rose, sweeping his hand in a take-a-seat gesture, knocking over his pencil holder in the process. Christ. Look up "agitation" in the dictionary and there his dumb ass would be whenever this woman was in his sphere. "What can I do to you? I mean, for you. Do for you."

Tuesday let him marinate in his faux pas, taking her time sitting and crossing those long legs. "You listen and I'll lead. I'm here in an official capacity."

He blinked as he sank back down. "I see." He didn't. But what else was there to say?

She leaned forward. "You'll be interested to know that Happily Ever After Land has appointed me lobbyist. I'm here to promote the park's importance to the Everland community and put forward a case as to why we should retain our lease and remain in business for another hundred years."

He was silent, absorbing her words, their implication.

"I'm a passionate person, Mr. Marino." She tapped a finger to her lower lip.

He scowled at the unwanted memory of the honey-sweet taste of those lips. This was a distraction. *She* was a distraction, one that he could ill afford. "Look, let me be clear, Miss Knight. I have a great deal of, um, passion for the park. In fact, pirates aside, you could consider it Everland's true treasure."

"Indeed," she answered drily.

A warning *clang*ed deep in his brain. The timing of her appointment was too deliberate to be a coincidence. An ache spread beneath his shoulder blades, a tight knot of twisting muscle. The call with Humph outside her cottage; she hadn't overheard—

"I believe it's *my* turn to be clear, Mr. Marino. You cannot allow developers to build a Discount-Mart and outlet mall on the property." Tuesday slipped from coy to businesslike brisk so fast he got whiplash. "Don't bother denying the plan. I heard you last night. Every. Single. Word." She opened her hand and pantomimed a mic drop.

He cursed the unsettled color burnishing his cheeks. *Shit.* She had him against a corner. No way out. No move. Unless...he threw her off her game.

"I'm not surprised you were nominated," he drawled, leaning back in his leather chair and drumming his fingers on the desk. The action steadied him, a reminder that this was his office. She was on his turf. And he'd be damned if she'd put him on the back foot. "No." He gave his chin a musing rub. "You strike me as a woman able to hold the most...interesting positions."

She blinked, a nearly imperceptible hesitation, before her chin rose a fraction. "When I find a position worth holding, I maintain it." Challenge radiated from her gaze. Her thoughts were almost audible. *You want to play innuendo games? All right, let's dance.*

"Fine." His nostrils flared. This could be fun. "I look forward to working with someone so...skillful." He rocked his seat, crossing a leg over his knee.

Her fingers balled into a fist, her knuckles white, even against her pale skin. "We are a job creator for local residents, not to mention it's a visitor draw card."

"Wilcox starts his park staff at minimum wage," he rebutted. "They might get a job, but it's not going to do much to support a family. As for a draw card, I'll give you that. It was, sixty years ago." He held up an open hand, silencing her protest. "The Tourism Commission seemed enamored with its potential, and I suppose that I have you to thank for contributing to the good impression. If we secure nomination for the Coastal Jewels Campaign, the town gets a cross-the-board boost, and that includes the park. But if we don't? Then what? We need economic progress, Miss Knight. Events like the Village Pillage or Harvest Festival are popular for locals, but they aren't drawing in outsiders who spend money at restaurants or patronize Main Street.

"We won second place in America's best small-town contest, and all it got us was a plaque on the plaza gazebo. Sure there were bragging rights. The bonus to pissing off Hogg Jaw. All good things—don't get me wrong—but you know Snapper, Lou Ellen's husband."

"Of course." She inclined her head warily. "At least, a little."

"He's a good guy, an honest family man. Did you know that he commutes an hour to Statesboro every day? One hour. One way. And he's typical of many others in town. We need good jobs closer to home and to build our reputation in the tourism sector. The General and my cousin Ginger are only just hanging on. Gunner over at Mad Dawgs does a decent trade on beer and pizza, but Michelle, who works here in this office, and her husband just went off to France to visit his family for two months. She said it was to improve their twins' language skills, but I can't help wondering if it's really because Chez Louis is struggling and they are seeking other opportunities. It's hard for folks to afford fine dining here."

He reached for his water glass and took a sip before continuing. "I intend to develop telework relationships with larger companies, but that's further down the track, after we finish putting the final touches on the high-speed rural broadband initiative that I spearheaded my first year in office. You should have seen how we operated out here before that." He shook his head ruefully. "Sending paper airplanes would have been faster."

She'd remained uncharacteristically quiet. Maybe he'd put her to sleep.

"Sorry if this line of talk bores you," he said tightly, setting his glass back down on the coaster. Never would he admit the fact that hurt him, how what he'd just shared wasn't a matter of pride, but what mattered to him on a bone-deep level.

He shouldn't expect the woman across the desk from him to give two shits. Jacqueline hated when he talked shop. If it wasn't a gossipy conversation about the reality-television couple that tried to join her parents' exclusive country club, planning their next Caribbean trip, or inquiring how their financial investments were doing that quarter, she lost interest fast.

"I'd never have believed this in a million years, but..." Tuesday's mouth drew in at the corner. "Your job is actually...sort of...fascinating."

He hid his shock behind a bland expression, trolling her features for signs of suppressed sarcasm.

"Knock that off," she snapped.

"What?"

"Trying to tell if I'm messing with you." She pushed a wave of hair behind her ear. "I say what I mean, and I mean what I say. You love being mayor."

Love. He turned the word over in his mind, a term that didn't rest easy in him. "This community has given me a lot, a great childhood and support during rough personal times. Guess I want to give back."

"I think we can work together." She inched to the edge of her seat. This time a genuine smile creased her face. "We haven't seen eye to eye on much, but hear me out. This town means a lot to you, and Happily Ever After Land means a lot to me. The people who work there, they treat me like family. They believe in me." Her voice softened, taking on a wistful note.

Kinship. The last thing he'd ever expected to feel toward Tuesday Knight. Just as he started getting used to his unwelcome physical attraction, this strange connection came along to kick him in the ass.

"Alone none of us can do diddly-squat," she continued. "But if we band together we can do so much. Think about the park's promise. 'Happily Ever After.' We have to believe that's possible, right?"

He glanced at the bookshelf behind her, at the empty space where a brass-framed wedding photo used to be, one he had taken down a long time ago, when he wasn't much more than a boy. A chill slithered up his spine. Tuesday's impassioned words were persuasive, but he governed in the real world. Fairy tales were nice. But happy endings weren't the norm in the real world.

"What you say sounds like a nice story." His lips flattened. Her very presence in his office was a danger, lulling him. He had a job to do here, and that meant thinking with his brain, not his dick. "But as mayor, it's my duty to deal in reality, not make-believe. I concede that might be hard for a drama queen to understand."

He hated himself for the flash of hurt in her gaze, but he couldn't do this. Their out-of-control physical chemistry was bad enough. Imagine actually liking Tuesday? More than liking. That would venture from dangerous territory to an outright calamity.

"Correct me if I'm wrong, but you have your own nickname. Prince of Everland. Ring any bells in that thick head of yours?"

The intercom buzzed, and Karen chirped, "Mayor, your next appointment is waiting!"

How did Karen always manage to sound so relentlessly chipper? She attached an exclamation mark to every sentence. Maybe it had something to do with the two dozen long-stemmed red roses delivered to her desk every Friday before noon. "My husband," she would say with a shy laugh. "What can I say? Wally loves spoiling me!"

Once upon a time he'd had a woman he'd wanted to

spoil. Except nothing was ever good enough. Jacqueline had looked like a perfectly normal Southern belle: pretty, perky, and cheerful. But inside was a gaping hole, one he'd tried and tried to fill. Their marriage had been a bitter lesson.

No matter how hard a person tried or struggled, no matter how just the cause, not every challenge could be overcome. When his wife informed him of her intent to file for divorce on Christmas morning in a sunny boat slip in Bermuda, any illusions of being a white knight shattered.

He wasn't a hero, and here was Tuesday Knight acting like somehow all he had to do was raise a sword, lead the charge, and all wrongs would be righted. It wasn't fair to be angry at her innocence, but when did fair ever matter?

"Mayor?" Karen's voice came through the intercom again, this time more quizzical.

"One more moment. Thank you." He scrubbed a hand over his jaw, suddenly exhausted.

"You know I'm right," Tuesday said mulishly. "About working together." And the shitty truth was that she was correct.

"The situation isn't black-and-white," he snapped.

"It is to me. But you go on to your next meeting." She stood and subtly wiped her palms on her skirt. Was she as nervous as he was? The memory of their kisses filled the corner of the room like a smirking elephant. "Today was about touching base," Tuesday said. "I'll be seeing you soon."

"Next Tuesday." He cracked a knuckle.

"Excuse me?" She froze midway to the door, turning with a raised brow.

"Next L&L happens in a week. On Tuesday." He dragged his gaze to her face, debating whether or not to ask the question that had been nagging at him for a month. "Why are you named that anyway?"

An emotion skimmed her face, one he couldn't readily decipher, like everything about this frustrating woman.

"Long story." Her impish smile returned. "Who knows? Maybe the mystery will give you something to anticipate." And with that she strutted out the door.

Don't look at her ass.

Yeah. Right.

At least he managed to save his groan until after the door *snick*ed shut. The story about her curious name ranked significantly lower on the things he anticipated about their next meeting.

Chapter Thirteen

⌀

Tuesday stumbled out of city hall, reining in her runaway breath. She reeled half a block before bracing against the weathered side of the abandoned Roxy Theater. Her trembling thighs ached as if she'd done an advanced-level spin class, probably because she'd been hard clenching them for the last fifteen minutes. The delicious sight of Beau looking all dominant behind that polished oak desk in his starched white shirt and perfectly knotted cobalt-blue tie had sizzled her senses.

Weird. She'd lived in Manhattan for how long?

Long enough.

If there was one thing that city had in spades besides rats, rude cabbies, tourists posing with grungy-looking cartoon characters in Times Square, and fabulous pizza, it was suits. Donald Draper–looking types waited at every crosswalk and she never so much as eyed one sideways. The buttoned-down and uptight look was so not her type. She'd have nothing in common with a man like that. In her world, the newspaper's financial section existed to clean windows along with a spritz of vinegar.

Only one cure existed for a crisis of this caliber. Ice cream.

She pushed off the side of the building and turned onto Main Street. No doubt clarity waited at the bottom of a root beer float. The brass bell over the What-a-Treat Candy Boutique door chimed as she walked into the welcoming old-timey emporium, greeted by crooning forties big-band style music and mouthwatering sugary smells.

"After the usual?" the owner, Ginger Reed, called from behind the counter, where she busily arranged Jordan almonds and bright licorice allsorts on a brass cake stand display.

"With an extra scoop, pretty please, and three maraschino cherries on top." Tuesday grinned. She hadn't lived in Everland long, but she already had "a usual." Normally two scoops of Ginger's homemade vanilla bean ice cream followed by a generous pour of local sarsaparilla cured any ailment, but after that meeting three were in order.

"Am I ever glad to see a friendly face." Ginger adjusted a bobby pin in her vintage pin-curl ringlets. Her shamrock-green dress was covered in tiny strawberries and set off her vivid emerald-green eyes. "Although at this point, even old Mean Gene would have been a sight for sore eyes."

"Been a quiet day?" Tuesday asked, perching on a high stool.

"Slower than molasses." Ginger slid open the ice cream display's glass panel and dipped the metal scoop into the bucket.

What-a-Treat had a black-and-white checkered floor, copper tin ceiling tiles, and shabby chic shelves crammed with shiny glass jars full of colorful hard-boiled sweets, everything from butter mints to horehound candy sticks, jawbreakers to humbugs. There was even a corner devoted to classic lollipops in rainbow corkscrew twists or round swirls. The very air was infused with the sugary scents of childhood nostalgia.

Ginger's impish smile didn't reach her eyes. "Summer's over. That means the big 'tourist rush' is finished, too." She crooked her fingers in sarcastic quote marks. "This was the slowest July and August on the books."

"Hmmm." Tuesday tapped her lower lip. "Well, if you need the support, that means there's no choice but for me to go ahead and order an extra-thick slice of your sea-salt caramel fudge, too." She hated the worry lines creasing the space between her new friend's brows.

Ginger wagged a finger, and her dark curls bounced against her round cheeks. They were around the same age and shared a love for all things made from cream and sugar, key ingredients for any firm friendship. "You don't have to—"

"Stop. This isn't some sympathy-order upgrade," Tuesday said, beating her to the punch. Her bank account didn't have many zeroes, but she was a firm believer in the power of an occasional "treat yourself" moment. "In fact, you're the one doing me a favor. I just got out of a meeting with the mayor. Sugar therapy is much needed."

"My cousin?" Ginger popped the lid on a glass bottle of old-fashioned sarsaparilla. "What day is it? Were you at one of Beau's Listen and Leads? They're getting quite popular. My guess is half of it has to do with his big baby blues. I'm jealous of how pretty they are. He seriously lucked out in the gene department."

Tuesday ignored the question even as her brain frantically nodded in agreement. "You're looking at the newly appointed lobbyist for Happily Ever After Land."

"Why does an amusement park need a lobbyist?" Ginger asked curiously.

"I don't have the strength to explain without the assistance of a thousand extra calories." Tuesday giggled.

"Coming right up." As Ginger set the mug on the counter, a drip of melted vanilla ice cream slid down the frosted glass. Behind her hung a framed photo of a kind-looking older man bouncing a much younger Ginger on his knee.

Ginger's grandfather on her non-Marino side had opened the shop in the postwar forties and had passed away two years ago. He'd raised his granddaughter, and she wasn't willing to close the store. Perhaps What-a-Treat struggled, but Tuesday had the sense that no matter what, Ginger would fight to preserve her beloved granddaddy's sweet legacy.

Beau wore responsibility day in and out like an invisible mantle. So many people counted on him to make decisions that would directly impact their lives. Toots, Mean Gene, Z-Man, Gil, Letty Sue, Caroline, Mr. Wilcox, Ginger, the General and Colonel, Delfi at Sweet Brew, and Ginger here, and all the other local businesses and residents.

The only one who had ever counted on Tuesday was J. K. Growling.

"You two made quite a pair at Pepper's house. During the charades game you were completely in sync."

"In sync? Hardly." Tuesday scoffed. "Trust me, Beau and I have nothing in common." Except for a shared weakness for impromptu make-out sessions.

Ginger chewed the bottom of her lip. "He smiled at least four times that night."

"Uh, that's what people do when they play a game."

"He doesn't. Or at least hasn't. Not easily, and not like he meant it. He was happy. I haven't seen him that happy since…I don't even know."

"He lost his wife."

"He lost Jacqueline long before she died." Ginger's gaze shuttered as she removed a brick of fudge, placing it on a cutting board. "Tell you the truth," she murmured, frowning, "I'm not sure he ever had her at all."

Tuesday tried wrapping her brain around that startling piece of information, but the idea was too big, too jagged, too oddly painful to grasp.

Beau's marriage hadn't been happy? So what? There were many troubled marriages? It wasn't her business, and yet…and yet the fact made her throat tighten, made her next breath ragged and shallow.

"Oh shit!"

"Good Lord!" Ginger started, chopping off an extra-big square from the sea-salt caramel fudge. "What's wrong, honey?"

Tuesday shrugged, looking around in confusion while trying to recalibrate. "That wasn't me." Outside the open window a small birdlike girl with raven-streaked hair squatted to collect loose-leaf drawing paper.

"Hey! I know her." Tuesday leaped to her feet. "That's Flick."

"Isn't she one of kids staying out on the Boyle farm?"

Ginger asked. "They've been fostering since their youngest, Tommy, moved to Valdosta last year."

"She was in my Foster Friends group at the park yesterday." Tuesday strode toward the door. Flick was the angry one who colored her hair with black marker and knew no restraint when it came to mascara and eyeliner application.

Tuesday opened the door and raised a hand to cut the sunny glare from her eyes. "Hey, you! You keep dropping things."

"Well, if it isn't Captain Obvious." The girl sneered. "Sit tight. I'm sure you'll get your own crappy superhero movie soon."

Whoa. Tuesday had always vaguely assumed she'd have kids until two years ago, when a friend from high school had called to cry in desperation about her sleepless, sexless life. After that Tuesday had moved that particular life goal from her "Must do" list to "Maybe." Might be time to downgrade it to "Nope."

Tuesday bent to grab the closest paper and pasted on her most sparkly birthday-party princess smile. "What you need to do is get yourself a new backpack."

"No kidding. A backpack?" She slapped a hand to her forehead. "A *new* backpack! Hell's bells, aren't you a genius!" She proceeded to roll her eyes so hard there was an honest-to-God risk they might get stuck that way.

So much for the power of the sparkly smile. "I only meant to say—"

"I also need a real nice mommy and daddy." The girl's lip curled so hard that the small gap between her front teeth was visible. "But being a princess and all, it must be hard for you to know what life is like outside your perfect castle.

Let me clue you in. It's not all balls, fairy godmothers, and pixie fucking stardust."

Her voice sliced with paper-cut intensity, but didn't hide the pain in her eyes. Still, it took one actress to know another. Flick wasn't this hard-ass routine. It was the mask she wore to keep herself safe.

And Tuesday knew all about those.

She straightened. Flick didn't need fake cheerfulness, but straight talk. "We got off on the wrong foot. Why don't you come inside and you can choose whatever you want?"

"Two things," the girl shot back, hugging her art pad to her black T-shirt, one that read I HATE YOU in an angry green neon scrawl. "First, there's no you and me. You are you. I am me. End of story. Second, everyone knows kids aren't supposed to take candy from strangers."

Tuesday offered up a prayer. *Serenity now*. Mask or not, Flick's anger was real and looking for a punching bag. "You're absolutely right. Okay. Let's back up even further. My name is Tuesday, Tuesday Knight. There." She clapped her hands. "Now I'm not a stranger, and trust you me, I know what it's like to have a bad day."

For a moment the girl appeared to soften. Her shoulders slumped a fraction before she shook her head, steel back in her spine. "Try a bad life."

Tuesday's throat thickened, but pity wouldn't help this kid. "Follow me," she ordered in a don't-mess-with-me tone she'd often heard Pepper employ to great effect.

To her considerable relief, the girl huffed a sigh but complied.

"Hey, Ginger?" Tuesday walked back up to the counter. "Can I get a sundae for my new friend Flick here. I'm talking the works."

"Got a favorite ice cream flavor?" Ginger asked.

The girl mashed her lips into a thin white line.

"Found yourself a regular chatterbox, didn't ya?" Ginger said finally.

"I keep telling her to pipe down," Tuesday quipped, making a "talk, talk, talk" gesture.

"Whatever," came the mutter.

"Good choice, Miss Flick," Tuesday said, moving her handbag so the kid could have a place at the counter. "I like your name. Sounds like what you'd name a fairy."

"Whatever, *Tuesday*." The girl paused as if she'd gone too far. "It's short for Felicity." She ducked her head, scraping at the ragged edge of her hard-bitten thumbnail. "But that's my mama's name, and I don't want nothing to do with her or any of her twelve boyfriends. You know, give or take, depending on the week."

Ginger pulled a banana split dish down from a shelf, loading it with scoops of vanilla, strawberry, chocolate. She expertly halved bananas, and covered the whole thing with homemade whipped cream, a sprinkle of peanuts, and a smattering of shiny red maraschino cherries.

"Um, so that looks amazing," Tuesday said as Flick's eyes bugged out.

"It really does, doesn't it?" Ginger cheerfully agreed. "But we're not quite done." She poured a generous dollop of hot fudge over it and ladled fresh marshmallow fluff, which she browned to mouthwatering perfection with a tiny blowtorch. "There. I do believe this here is the finest banana split you'll find in all of Dixie."

Flick's lower lip gave an almost imperceptible tremble as a shaft of happiness broke through her stormy features.

Tuesday allowed a small inward sigh. How many wars

could be prevented if world leaders negotiated over banana splits?

"So you live on the Boyle farm?" Tuesday asked.

Flick gave her a suspicious look, but couldn't readily answer with her cheeks stuffed to the gills with strawberry ice cream. She settled for a curt nod.

Tuesday poked at her ratty art pad. "Why haven't they bought you a backpack?"

"They did," Flick answered after a swallow.

"What happened to it?" Tuesday asked.

She scooped more marshmallow fluff. "Got stolen."

"At school?" This was like playing the most frustrating game of Twenty Questions in existence.

"Greyhound." She swirled a cherry through the hot fudge and popped it in her mouth before answering. "Last week."

Tuesday sized the girl up, careful not to let a frown creep onto her face. This kid seemed like the type to bolt at the first sign of pity. She was elfin, small for her age. Her eyes might be ancient, but that didn't mean she wasn't vulnerable. "What were you doing on a bus?"

"Running away." Flick added a silent "duh" to the end of the statement.

"Where to?" Tuesday pushed her float away, her stomach churning at the idea of a little girl alone on a Greyhound, where anything could happen. No one should have to face that much pain, bitterness, and hardship, especially not a child.

"New York."

"I see." Tuesday met Flick's gaze without flinching, knowing it was important, a test of sorts. But there was no answer key. "So you—"

"That's it. Too many questions." Flick jumped off her stool, skittish as a rabbit in a foxhole.

It took all of Tuesday's self-control not to grab the girl's arm, figure out a solution right then and there. But if she forced it, she would blow everything. "Don't get too excited." Her nonplussed tone belied her racing thoughts. "I ask everyone questions. I'm nosy. It's what I do." She jumped off her own stool. "And I also do that in this." Time to bust out distraction. She executed a complicated tap-dancing routine. When in doubt, she always turned up the drama. It usually drew people out of their comfort zones and made them feel less alone.

When she at last came to a stop, Ginger broke into spontaneous applause. Even Flick looked unwillingly impressed.

"You really want me to like you, huh?" she asked, cutting straight to the chase. She didn't seem upset about the fact though. Her gaze narrowed curiously.

"Sue me. I like a challenge," Tuesday shot back, slinging her arm around the girl's fragile shoulders.

"Oh, thank heavens, there you are." A middle-aged woman paused in front of the window before bustling inside. "Hey, sugar," she said to Ginger. "I'm sorry if this one was any bother. Come on, you," she ordered Flick. "We've been searching high and low. The van is loaded and we've got to get back to the farm and water the chickens."

"Afternoon, Mrs. Boyle!" Ginger called.

Hmm. Flick's foster mom. Tuesday sized her up. The matronly woman seemed friendly enough if a little harried, and a lot annoyed.

Mrs. Boyle plucked a lace handkerchief from her purse and dabbed her upper lip. "I've been busier than a moth in a mitten hunting around for you. What did I say about running off without a word? I've talked myself near blue in the face. One minute you were right there in the library checking out the comics and the next...poof! Nowhere to be seen."

"There was a cool-looking tree outside the window, and I wanted to sketch the way the sun hit the branches and...never mind." The soft look fled from the girl's face. "Forget it," she said abruptly, her brows dropping like a thunderhead as her expression went stormy. "It was stupid. I was stupid. This was stupid. Sorry that you're stuck with such a stupid kid."

Mrs. Boyle shook her head, clicking her tongue like a worried hen. "What am I going to do with you?"

"Let me run away," Flick muttered to her combat boots, face reddening as if she was painfully aware every eye in the room rested on her.

"Again with the back talk. We've been over this." Mrs. Boyle's tone suggested this wasn't the first conversation of the sort she had conducted with her foster child.

"I just took over the lease on my sister's cottage." Tuesday broke into the conversation. "It needs decoration. I left most of my things behind in New York."

"You lived in the city?" Flick stared with a faint glimmer of interest, taking the bait.

Tuesday nodded. "Near Hell's Kitchen." She turned to address Mrs. Boyle. "I must say that I admire Flick's style. She's got natural talent."

"Her style?" Mrs. Boyle asked as though Tuesday might have suffered a recent brain trauma.

Tuesday gave her an encouraging smile. "Her artwork."

Flick didn't lift her gaze, even while a natural pink hue spread beneath the caked-on blush.

"Tell you what," Tuesday persisted. "If it's okay with you, and it's okay with Flick, then I'd like to invite her to my house later this week. I want to commission some art."

"Art." Mrs. Boyle looked surprised, but not as surprised as Flick.

"What's the catch?" The kid sounded more suspicious than pleased.

"What can I say?" Tuesday answered. When she was a girl she'd bring home any stray animal that needed to feel loved. Not that she could explain the impulse to the girl. "I like to support the arts."

And as she smiled, Flick's face lost some of its hardness.

She wanted to help take care of the girl, but she didn't know the first thing about taking care of anyone. Even herself.

Was she up to the job?

Chapter Fourteen

Ma Hogg hunched over her yellow Formica counter stirring ice cubes into a pitcher of mint-sprigged sun tea as the wheels of Humph Miller's Cadillac crunched over the driveway gravel. She swung her still-sharp gaze to her cat-shaped wall clock. The wide eyes and plastic black tail moved in time to the second hand.

"Three minutes late." Her lips pursed as she tapped the wooden spoon on the glass rim. That fool was getting entirely too big for his britches.

The car door slammed. "Hello!"

She gripped the spoon handle at the boomed greeting. Was that boy born in a barn, hollering like a stuck pig? If she were fifty years younger, she'd take this here wooden spoon straight to his heinie. Humphrey was an imbecile, cocky and brash.

She'd use him like a tissue before disposing of him.

Plastering on a feeble smile, she picked up the plastic tray and shuffled toward the door.

Ever since her fool of a son, Aloysius, had allowed himself to be run out of the county, she'd been forced to give
up her bedridden ruse. It had been a risky gambit to blow
the useful frail invalid cover. When the world looked at her,
they saw someone so *old*, an elderly woman with humming-
bird bones and a back stooped by osteoporosis. Easy to
disregard. To underestimate. Every last wrinkle and strand
of her blue-rinsed hair invited dismissal.

She coughed a wet chuckle. Aging might be for the
birds, but it had a few uses. Especially when it came to the
business of revenge. All the better to be misjudged by your
enemies.

Everland had laughed at her boy. Bumbling Aloysius deserved their scorn, but when someone laughed at a Hogg,
they laughed at Hogg Jaw. And Ma Hogg *was* Hogg Jaw.
Born and raised, went back generations, all the way to Captain Redbeard's second mate, Ezra Hogg, who'd founded
the town.

She halted at the screen. Humph was already rocking
on the porch swing like he owned the place. Her blood
simmered and bubbled. This man needed his silver spoon
shoved where the sun don't shine. "Hey! Highness! How
about helping with the dagnabbit door?"

Humph rose with a muffled grunt of annoyance. He considered her a bother. What he hadn't considered was that if
he failed, she would make his life worse than the fifth ring
of hell. He was unfaithful in his marriage. She knew all the
skeletons in her foot soldiers' cupboards. Secrets were useful things. She made a hobby out of collecting them like
other women did spoons or vintage Pyrex or ceramic fig-
urines.

He opened the door. "There we go." She handed over the

tray and reached for the carved cane propped by the door. All part of the act.

She'd walked three miles before sunup.

He set the tray on the small table and poured them each a glass. "Mighty nice day," he said stiffly.

She managed a convincing enough smile. "What progress have you made with Mayor Marino? Close to wrapping up that park deal?"

A test. She knew full well the answer was no. In fact, he hadn't come close.

A trio of hens scratched around the front yard. The noise Hump made deep in his throat was a near-perfect match to their nervous clucks.

She fought back her own mounting urge to peck him. She needed this man because he had a connection, however tenuous, to Beau Marino. Now, there was a man without a single skeleton in his closet. He associated with no unsavory characters. Good Lord, he had been an Eagle Scout and had never looked back. There'd been that nasty bit of business with his wife, but even there she couldn't dig up dirt, just fact after fact about a man who tried hard to save a failing marriage.

How revoltingly boring.

"The park conversations are moving ahead. We're getting there," Humph blustered. "In fact, the deal's as good as done." He was a soft-boiled egg, hard on the outside but was easy to crack and liable to make a mess of things. There was nothing worse than a man who overestimated his abilities while underestimating those around him. Her husband, bless his heart, had been the same way.

Millard. The weak fool, bless his soul.

Turned out her son was forged from the same weak stuff.

If only the dear Lord in his infinite mercy had seen fit to grant her a daughter made of her own mettle.

Everland had gotten the better of Aloysius. Now they'd rue the day they ever turned up their snobby noses at Hogg Jaw. She'd make sure Happily Ever After Land closed in favor of a cheap job infusion. The county would get their coveted "Coastal Jewel" designation, but it would be Hogg Jaw wearing the crown.

If a woman wanted to get something done in this world, she'd have to do it herself.

"As good as done?" She clicked her tongue. "My, my, my, and here I have it on good authority that Mayor Marino hasn't committed to anything. In fact, he has been meeting with the Georgia Tourism Commission. And you know who else is talking to the commission to get that status? Me." She slammed the jug of sweet tea on the coffee table so hard that the glass cracked down one side. Tea leaked through, pooling around Humph's shiny black shoes.

"And just how is that sweet intern of yours? What's her name again? Tina?" She smiled as Humph's hand shook hard enough to spill his tea. "A little bird told me that she's quite the multitasker." Ma Hogg removed her eyeglasses from the end of her nose, dropped them on their chain against her bosom. "Does your wife know how good she is at multitasking? Merris just gave birth to... what is it now?" She pretended to count on her fingers. "A fourth child?"

Humph made a strangled sound.

"Listen good, Bucko." She dropped the pretense, her voice steel. "You don't have a red cent to your name. Those alligator-skin shoes and fancy car are bankrolled by your wife's high-flying daddy. Your wife, whom you've been cheating on with a good-for-nothing gold digger who thinks you're a big shooter. But all you've got is a checkbook of blanks."

She picked up her cane and brought it down hard, smacking his kneecaps. Not enough to break anything, but he'd sport a lasting pair of nasty bruises. "There are things at work here that you can't begin to understand.

"Your job is to know your place in the pecking order." She picked up a piece of toast off the tray and threw it for the chickens. "Me? I am the bird. You? You're the worm. And you know what worms do."

"No." He choked.

She thwacked her cane across his shins. "No, ma'am," she barked.

This time he yelped. "No, ma'am."

"Worms make their home in the dirt." She jabbed her cane in the direction of his car. "Now start digging until you unearth something useful. Go on, git."

Phaedra1953: I've gone and done a bad thing. I'd baked my famous chewy peanut butter cookies for Pepper's animal shelter's bake sale. But *The Bachelor* was on the DVR, and you know that last rose ceremony was a nail-biter. By the time it had finished, I'd devoured the entire plate. Every last crumb. I'm a stress eater, what can I say? But now I have no donation and my dress for the Fall Ball doesn't zip.

ScrabbleLuvR: I'm boycotting *The Bachelor* after last week. I don't think any of the hussies left have class. And I had to drive Earl to the podiatrist this morning so I couldn't bake. Instead, I passed on my favorite cookie cutters to Ida May to see if they got a rise out of her. Speaking of bachelors, has anyone heard if Beau Marino is bringing a date to the ball? Will it be Tuesday Knight?

IdaMayI: Those were dirty cookie cutters. Lucille Vernon, I'd say you need Jesus except it is too funny. You should have seen the look on Pepper's face when I dropped off our *Back Fence* contribution. Also, about that Tuesday Knight business. Well, well, well. There are some chat boards in New York City that are making *very* interesting allegations about little Miss Princess. Turns out she has quite the skeleton in her castle.

Chapter Fifteen

The ocean was as calm as a lake. Beau gestured at the *Calypso*'s limp sails and slumped his shoulders. Sometimes Mother Nature was a real bitch. "Ready to head back, or keep racing along at two fucking knots?" There wasn't so much as a breath of wind. Any hopes for a decent sail were bust.

"I vote to stay out unless you're itching to get back to something at city hall." Rhett stretched his long legs on the foredeck and nodded to the five gallons of fuel lashed to the deck. "We've got a full tank and a freshly topped jerry jug. Why not putz to the closest anchorage and have a cold one from that new Hogg Jaw brewery?"

"Ten four." Beau stuck on his shades to cut the sun glare on the water. "I'll motor to the northwest side of Hope Island. Shouldn't be too crowded if we put in by the creek."

It took a half hour to let down the sails, fiddle with the choke on the finicky engine, and get to the pine-lined cove framing a sliver of golden sand devoid of people.

"All right, you're right. Even a no-wind day is better than most spent on land." Beau lowered the anchor, not budging until he felt it set on the bottom.

"That's the spirit." Rhett dug in the ice-packed cooler for two beers. "Now, what's on your mind?" He popped the cap before passing over a bottle.

"Not much." Beau picked at the label.

Rhett shrugged before taking a long swig. "Shit, that's good, hoppy as hell. And fine. Suit yourself. But just so you know, I'll be right over here, in case words start coming out."

Beau studied his buddy's relaxed profile as he enjoyed his beer. Rhett had stumbled on the real deal after being jilted at the altar. His ex-fiancée, Michelle, was a good person, even if she'd royally screwed up by panicking the morning of the wedding rather than ending their relationship face-to-face. But Beau had always half understood why she'd pulled the stunt.

Rhett had a hell of a big heart. A good guy who never wanted to let someone down, even when his long-term relationship had devolved into nothing more than friendship. He'd stuck by his original youthful commitment, for better or worse, despite any private misgivings. It had forced Michelle to go with her gut, needing more from life than a sense of stubborn obligation. But the two had eventually worked it out, and now both lived in Everland on good terms.

"Got big plans for tonight?" Beau resisted the urge to cringe. Small talk came as natural to him as a drunk cow on roller skates.

Rhett made a noncommittal gesture. "Pepper has her hands full organizing a bake sale fund-raiser for the shelter and Lou Ellen asked to borrow our wolf pack." His big sister took their dogs from time to time to entertain her five hyperactive children.

"Must be a change going from Everland's most confirmed bachelor to happily engaged?" *Drunk cow. Fucking roller skates.*

"The funny thing is that Pepper makes me more of who I am, not less." Rhett caught his gaze. "Thinking about getting back out there?"

"Me and Jacqueline got together first semester in the dorms at UGA. I've never *been* out there," he snapped. He'd thought by marrying young they were getting a jump-start on forever, but if love was blind, marriage was one hell of an eye-opener. All they'd done was jump into the fast lane of making each other miserable.

"Couldn't help noticing that you and Tuesday hit it off at our dinner party."

"So?" Beau scrubbed all feeling from his tone. "We've got nothing in common."

"So...don't know if that's the whole truth." Rhett shoved his hat back and swiped a hand over his forehead. "From where I sat, it looked like you shared a deep love for driving each other bat-shit crazy."

Beau managed a casual chuckle. But Tuesday had made him admit one thing. He *was* crazy lonely. He might not be the right guy for her, but his failure with Jacqueline didn't mean he could never get behind the wheel again. A woman could be out there, one he could make happy.

He swallowed more beer. Hard to get out the next words, even to an old friend who wanted nothing but the best for him. "Suppose I have been thinking about dating. Last night I drew up an itemized list of positive attributes for a potential partner ranked from 'must have' to 'nice to have' to 'lesser importance.'"

"Say what, now?" Rhett winced. "Jesus. Is this list also in alphabetical order? Color coded?"

He ignored the jibe. "I thought I should start by trying to find someone more like the female version of me."

"You?" Rhett coughed into his fist. It seemed to be masking laughter.

He flexed his jaw. Maybe talking was a bad idea. "It wasn't anything fancy. I'd like someone who enjoys being out on the water and who's career minded. See, I have big plans for Everland's future development, plans that require commitment and elbow grease. I need someone who'll appreciate that work can be life and that's okay."

"And a fellow workhorse will make you happy?" Rhett didn't bother hiding his skepticism.

"Yeah." Beau shoved away the mental image of Tuesday kicking in that damn rain puddle or straddling his lap and kissing him stupid. "I don't know. Maybe."

Rhett pulled an unconvinced face. "Got to say, I doubt it, man. I doubt it very much. But you know what, I'm going to do you a solid. There's a new Realtor in town. Meredith Green. Have you heard of her? Total overachiever. I met her in line at Sweet Brew and she had her business card in my hand in under twenty seconds."

"Sounds promising." Beau's gut clenched. This was exactly what he'd asked for, so why did his body reject the idea like a bad virus?

"I'm going to shoot straight though, man." Rhett gave him an indecipherable look. "Love doesn't follow rules, and it sure as hell doesn't always make sense."

"My parents came from two different worlds, but look how easy they had it. My marriage . . . wasn't."

Rhett frowned. "All relationships take work. Even the good ones. The trick is finding someone worth the effort. But know what? I'm going to swim and cool off before we head back." Rhett seemed to realize he'd hit the end of his endurance and stood, ripping off his shirt. "And now we can scratch 'sharing deep thoughts about love' off our friendship bucket list."

"It's been real," Beau shot back.

Rhett chortled like a smug bastard before diving into the crystal-clear water.

They spent the rest of the trip back to the marina trading good-natured insults and engaging in general shit talk. If Rhett happened to insert Tuesday into more than a few stories, Beau pretended not to notice, even though he ended up chewing his cheek half bloody to avoid asking follow-up questions.

He shouldn't be curious.

He shouldn't wonder.

Tuesday shouldn't be a topic that interested him on any level other than that of an engaged constituent.

Ignoring her shouldn't be this hard, should it?

"I'm going to get you Meredith's number," Rhett said as they pulled into the slip in the late afternoon. "Because you think it's what you want. But remember." All joking erased from his tone. "Careful getting what you ask for."

* * *

Tuesday bolted upright. "What the heck?"

The peacock pillow that had just bounced off her nose tumbled to the floral-patterned rug next to the couch.

"Rise and shine, sunshine," Pepper chirped in an annoyingly perky voice.

"Ugh. What time is it?" Tuesday rubbed her sand-filled eyes, disoriented.

Pepper waved her ever-present wristwatch. "It's 1:37 on a Saturday afternoon."

"And your point is?" Tuesday ignored her sister's disapproving tongue snick in favor of rolling over and burrowing her face into the back of the couch.

"My point?" Pepper grabbed her by the shoulder and rolled her back over. "That unless you're sick, nap privileges get revoked the same time as diapers."

"How are we related? Naps are the best thing to do on a lazy afternoon. Wait, correction." Tuesday flashed a wicked smile. "The second-best thing."

Her sister held up three fingers. "One, naps make me feel like crap. Two, they aren't productive. Three, I have perfected a sleep schedule and refuse to throw it off."

"Have you been binge-watching YouTube makeup tutorials or something?"

Pepper knit her brows.

"All I'm saying is that you do an exceptional job masquerading as a human." Tuesday plucked the fallen pillow and hurled it back at Pepper. "I want to know what foundation lets you cover up your green skin and scales, you no-nap monster."

"Why, you little..." Pepper jumped on top of Tuesday and pinned her arms.

"Get off, you goose. I can't breathe."

"Don't let your mouth write a check that your body can't cash." Pepper proceeded to tickle her relentlessly.

"Oh my God. Oh my God, stop. Oh my God, please."
Wetting herself became an actual concern. "Please, I beg
you," she pleaded between peals of laughter.

Pepper finally relented and retreated to adjust her perfect
A-line bob with a smug expression. "Glad to see I still got
it in me."

"But for real." Tuesday sat up and tugged down her T-
shirt. "You don't nap during the day?"

"Never," Pepper answered.

Tuesday mulled the disturbing admission for a moment.
She definitely took after their free-spirited father, who believed siestas were the key to a long life.

"But what about last week? Remember how I came
over in the middle of the day and you and Rhett were in
the bedroom and..." She clapped a hand over her mouth.
"Rhett. You. Bedroom." She made a gagging sound
through muffled fingers. "Oh, good gravy, I totally busted
you, didn't I?"

"Yup. In flagrante delicto." Pepper burst out laughing.
"Rhett was mortified."

"Gross. Gross. Gross." Tuesday shuddered from the horror. "You hornballs need to start hanging a sock in your
front door."

"That would go over well with Miss Ida May. She'd
probably invest in a periscope."

"Do you know the *Back Fence* started a poll predicting
when you're going to get knocked up?"

"No they haven't!" Pepper went four shades of red.
"There isn't even a wedding date yet."

"It was the poll right beneath picking the best time of
year for your impending nuptials. Wait, no, it was beneath
the one trying to give you guys a nickname. Choices were

Alett and Rpepper. Terrible mergers to be honest. 'Rpepper' sounds like a nasty itch, doesn't it?"

Pepper stared toward the ceiling and took a deep breath. "I've been practicing meditation every morning. It's the only way I'm going to survive small-town life. In Moose Bottom most people lived in the woods. We weren't ever in each other's business like this."

"The *Back Fence* tagline is true though; they truly do share 'all the news you care about.'" She glanced at the tablet on her coffee table and bit her lower lip. Better to focus on small-town gossip than scroll through Broadway tattle on the *New York Theatre Guide*.

She shouldn't have looked. Looking was dangerous, stupid, and pointless because she was never going back to that world. After reading about all the latest castings, she'd forced herself to sleep in order not to go cry in the shower.

"As much as I'd love to hear what the specials are at Mad Dawgs, who is rumored to be carrying on with a handyman, or drama about the upcoming Fall Ball or Harvest Festival, I have my own share of small-town melodrama," Pepper said. "That's why I'm here. Do you have the goods for the bake sale?"

"Goods?" Tuesday stretched until her lower back gave a satisfying pop.

"'Good' is maybe a little ambitious, but I mean your baked good donation."

Tuesday clasped a hand over her mouth.

Pepper narrowed her eyes. "Oh, come on. You didn't forget."

"I'm so sorry," Tuesday said. "I spaced it. I've had so much going on."

"Yeah." Pepper eyed her disheveled living room. "I can

see you've been busy. Never mind. It's just a bake sale to raise money for the Everland animal shelter. You know, the one I'm the new executive director of and in charge of getting the last fifteen thousand for the capital campaign. I thought I could count on my one and only sister to help support the cause. And she promised, so you know…"

"I do know!" Tuesday swung her feet off the couch and stood. "Gah. I'm sorry. I'm such a mess."

"I didn't think it could get worse than when the *Back Fence* biddies dropped off their donation, a plate of gingerbread cookies with the men and women all having conjugal relations."

"Not going to lie—that's sort of funny," Tuesday said with a giggle.

"Some things can never be unseen," Pepper replied grimly. "I might never recover."

"Okay, I can salvage this. I have a pack of chocolate chip cookies in the pantry. How about I whack them on a pretty plate and call it good. They are chewy and extra chocolate chip."

Pepper thought it over. "Nothing X-rated."

Tuesday flashed her old Girl Scout sign. "Scout's honor."

"What the heck, that would be great. Thank you. Every dollar counts."

"I am sorry for letting you down. I know how much the shelter means to you."

"Get a planner. Write a few things down."

"Yes." Tuesday nodded. "Yes, that is exactly what I should do. Planner. Calendar. Maybe some cute pens. Stickers for the planner. Ooh, washi tape. I could start wearing pencil skirts and smart-looking updos."

"Come back to real life." Pepper touched her shoulder.

"You don't need to get carried away and throw yourself overboard by assuming a new role. I love you just the way you are."

"Hot mess and all?" She studied the black-and-white photograph of the tightrope walker balancing between two New York City skyscrapers that hung on her wall.

Pepper nodded. "Hot mess and all. How about start with a weekly calendar and check it each day?"

Tuesday sighed. Pretending to be organized and actually being so were two vastly different things. "Do you want help for the bake sale?"

"There are five volunteers meeting me at the community center to do pricing. I'm more than covered."

Tuesday stood and walked to the kitchen to get the cookies. "Text if you need me to stop by and pitch in. I'm going to the Everland Library," she called.

"That wasn't my first guess," Pepper called.

Tuesday popped her head back out the kitchen door. "I want to read up on the art of persuasion. Happily Ever After Land is trusting me to be their lobbyist. Imagine *me,* Pepper. Mr. Wilcox, Toots, Lettie Sue, Gil...all of them need their jobs and not just for the money." The odd collection of misfits were a real family.

Pepper's features softened. "Everland's gotten to you."

"I don't know what's happening." Tuesday ducked back in the kitchen and opened the cupboard with too much force. "The park isn't my dream job any more than being a birthday-party princess. But the place is special. It's what I need right now, and more importantly, it's bigger than me. I can't afford to mess up Happily Ever After Land. Not like I messed up New York or even your bake sale. I have to research, get it right."

"Forget the bake sale a sec," Pepper said, walking in behind her. "You know that you've never given a straight answer as to why you left New York. All you said was you weren't involved in anything illegal. I'm sure you meant those words to be comforting, but I've been worried. Performing on Broadway was your dream."

"Emphasis on the *was*."

Pepper cast a pleading look. "Don't shut me out."

"I'm not trying to." Tuesday opened the pantry, grabbed the cookies, and tore open the package. "I'm not trying to be mysterious. Look. It's just...I...got hurt and am embarrassed about it." She dumped the cookies on the plate and arranged them in a circle. "For the first time in forever I've started feeling like I'm moving forward and don't want to go backward right now. I want...I need to keep looking ahead. Please."

Pepper chewed the corner of her lip. "You know evasiveness drives me crazy."

Tuesday exhaled in relief. "It's one of my superpowers." Her straightforward sister was going to give her space. Pepper was the best.

"Do you need my help knocking sense into Beau? Should I barricade myself to the park gate opening until he agrees to your demands?"

Tuesday swallowed back tears as she handed over her half-assed bake sale donation. Despite it being new to her, Everland felt familiar with Pepper here. Home was more about the people than the place.

"I don't need you to go the full civil disobedience hog just yet. But do you have any insights on how to sweet-talk the mayor? All I know about lobbying I've learned from binge-watching the first season of *House of Cards* this week. I'm grasping at straws here."

Pepper leveled one of her intense, MRI machine–style stares, scanning her from head to toe. "I'm going to take the liberty of administering a hefty dose of straight talk."

"Oy," Tuesday quipped, trying to ignore the unnerved sensation in her stomach. "This sounds serious, Doctor."

"Here's the truth, honey." Pepper rested her hands on Tuesday's shoulders. "I've never seen Beau Marino look happier than when you happen to be occupying the same airspace."

Chapter Sixteen

"**Y**ou're in luck, pretty lady!" Tuesday plucked J. K. Growling's leash off the coat hook. "I've got just enough time to squeeze in a quick stop at the dog park en route to the library!"

The Boston terrier scrambled for the bedroom at breakneck speed.

"Hey, hey, hey! Wait just a second." Tuesday chased after her, addressing the wiggly lump under the unmade pile of blankets. "Nap time's over. Up and at 'em. We both need the exercise." Plus she had to clear her head. Pepper's parting words about Beau had fogged her common sense.

She made Beau happy? She passed a hand over her mouth as if to wipe off her stupid grin. No way. Impossible. But her sister was one of the smartest people she knew.

What did it all mean?

J. K. Growling whined and wheezed as she was unceremoniously uncovered and clipped to the leash. They walked the few blocks through the bright, breezy autumn weather, past the workman cementing the bronze Davy Jones bust back onto its post in Everland Plaza, the dog statue Judge Hogg had attempted to steal before being run out of town during the summer.

Through the wrought-iron fence, Doc Valentine, Rhett's father, held court at his usual picnic table, playing Scrabble with other regulars as their dogs ran amok in a happy pack.

"Want to play?" he called, adjusting his ever-present red bow tie. "We're starting a new game." He was a stern sort of fellow, but he had gradually warmed to Pepper and now treated her with a courtly politeness.

"Thanks, but I'm not a big Scrabble player."

"We take all sizes," the General added, patting his hefty belly with a guffaw.

Tuesday smiled but backed away slowly. "I'm not a big Scrabble player" was code for "if I never play that horrible game again it will be too soon."

On some level she understood the appeal and had spent many winters playing it against her sister back in Moose Bottom, but therein lay the problem. Because the reality was that she'd spent many winters *losing* at Scrabble. Her spatial sense was nonexistent and her spelling skills atrocious. She was one of the few people who thanked the Sweet Baby Jesus for autocorrect. Otherwise she'd never even bother using the words "definitely" or "privilege."

Plus, it was a universally accepted fact that die-hard Scrabble players liked little more than gloating after a big win.

A prickly sensation spread across the center of her back as she wandered over beneath the expansive shade of a hundred-year-old oak. She rolled her shoulders and turned.

Nothing there. Not even the General's pet alligator, Fido, was in sight.

Huh.

She picked up a twig and threw it for J. K. Growling, who sat and watched it fly overhead.

"You're meant to get that," she said.

J. K. rolled onto her back with a wet sigh.

The prickly feeling returned. This time she counted to three before whirling. A shrub shook past the dog park fence, one low branch bouncing in a direction opposite to the wind.

Someone was watching her.

"Come on, lazy bones." She popped the leash on J. K. and gave the Scrabble Squad a hurried wave before heading out the gates and around to investigate. She'd lived in New York long enough not to take bullshit behavior. Assertiveness had its uses. Time to root out the lurker.

"Hello?" She bent down. "Anybody home?" It was a little silly to address foliage. Sillier still when the green vegetation yielded no answers. What did she expect? It wasn't like Beau Marino would be crouching in there with a rose.

Her stomach turned. Of course not. What a stupid idea.

Better to get moving to the library before it closed. *Aha.* She sighed in relief. There was a logical explanation for why that disturbing mayor thought had wormed into her mind. She was off to check out books on influencing others, interpersonal communication without conflict, all with him in mind. As she turned to walk, a white flicker caught the corner of her eye.

An illustration rested on the grass. A doodle of a dragon. No, not a doodle. The attention to detail was painstaking. That took real talent and didn't deserve being abandoned on the ground. She swiveled her head right and left, gaze scanning for any signs of Flick. Not only did the girl appear to have an affinity for dragons, but this image bore her unmistakable style—so much raw talent. Tuesday brushed her hand over the inked scales, the menace in the creature's glare. Sketching such powerful animals must give Flick a way to snatch back a semblance of control in her otherwise powerless situation. So why abandon it as if it meant nothing? Impulsively, Tuesday rolled the illustration into a tube and tucked it in her bag before walking up the front stairs. She'd have a few more questions for that kid the next time they ran into each other.

The Everland Library was an old repurposed mansion, three stories tall and with enough detailing to resemble a layered wedding cake. Tuesday tied J. K. Growling to a lamppost and went in.

"We're closing in twenty minutes," the librarian said to Tuesday as she entered.

"No problem. I know exactly what I need." She beelined to the nonfiction area having already researched the titles she needed.

After she gathered her selections, a glass case at the far end of the aisle caught her gaze. She walked closer—a display about the old Roxy Theater. The old playbills caught her attention, plus a few masks, two scripts, and a diorama of the interior.

"Sorry, that installment went up last week. Wonderful, isn't it?" Cedric Swift stepped beside her, removing his glasses to give them a quick swipe on his 221B BAKER STREET T-shirt.

Some whispered Cedric had a screw loose, but she never found him to be anything other than perfectly British, always apologizing unnecessarily when not making self-deprecating comments or huge understatements like "it appears a bit wet" when there's a "torrential downpour."

"I'm devastated it closed." She leaned close enough that her breath fogged the glass. "Look at the stage. That chandelier. So many wonderful details."

"Yes. It doesn't seem right it's going to be condemned."

Her jaw dropped. "What?"

"The fire department is requesting that it be torn down."

"No!"

Cedric sighed. "There's not enough people in town to justify restoring such an icon, more's the pity."

Tuesday studied his face as if seeing him for the first time. Sure the accent was appreciated, but he'd also struck her as a little forgettable, lanky, ginger, and studious with his wire-rimmed glasses and bookish demeanor.

How wrong she'd been. While his face was a little on the studious side, his jaw was square and his eyes straddled an intriguing no-man's-land color between blue and green. His hair, cut in a traditionally conservative crew cut, erred on the thick side and was the shade of burnished copper. Good Lord. He was a male version of a dirty library fantasy.

And her surprise at his looks was met with a surprise of even greater magnitude...She wasn't attracted to him. In fact, as she studied his earnest, thoughtful features, another face rose in her mind. One more serious and prone to scowling. A mouth not given to easy smiles. And eyes that weren't warmed by any suggestion of green but remained firmly rooted on the cooler end of the color spectrum.

"Are you trying to decide whether or not to laugh?" he asked. "Because I assure you it would be quite all right. Everyone around here seems to have that reaction to me."

She blinked, struggling to regroup. "No, no, nothing of the sort. But I do have to ask, why are you here, in Everland? It's not exactly on the academic beaten path."

"Depends on the field. I happen to specialize in the Age of Sail, from the Battle of Lepanto straight through to the Battle of Hampton Roads, and want to write the definitive account of Redbeard's legacy."

She cut to the chase. "Is the treasure real?"

He shrugged. "It's been long dismissed as rumor. A fool's errand."

"So is that a yes or a no?"

He gave a rueful grin. "I rather consider myself something of a great fool."

She rubbed her hands. "Any theories where X marks the spot?"

His smile increased in size. "If I knew that, I wouldn't be standing here."

"Too busy leapfrogging through piles of wealth?"

"Not bloody likely." He made a scandalized noise. "It belongs in a museum to be appreciated by future generations."

She dropped her hands to her sides. "Let me get this straight. If you found a buried treasure, you'd stick it in some dusty museum?" She'd more likely than not fill a bathtub with gold and roll around it in before throwing a huge party for everyone she had ever met.

"Absolutely." He opened his arms wide. "Preferably right here in Everland."

She giggled, charmed by his earnest expression. "Okay, Indiana Jones."

"Go on, poke all the fun you want." He reset his glasses. "But history is more than a bunch of boring names and dates. It's stories. Who doesn't like stories?"

"Huh. You're right. I never thought of it that way." She adjusted the colorful bohemian scarf around her neck. "And buried treasure is a story that would draw people in, huh?"

"Certainly would. Maybe enough to open the Roxy again, too."

Their thoughtful faces reflected back from the glass display case.

"Closing time," the librarian called.

After Tuesday checked out her books, she went outside, and there, crouched next to J. K. Growling, was Flick.

The girl stopped petting the dog and scrambled to her feet.

"Hey, you!" Tuesday called, reaching for the art in her bag. "I've got one of your drawings." The penny dropped. Flick must have been the one following her today.

But rather than coming forward, the girl turned heel on her combat boots and sprinted up the cobblestone street.

Chapter Seventeen

∽

For the next week, Beau doubled down at work. He put in punishing hours, paid careful attention in subcommittee meetings, made personal visits to each city council member, and read every last one of Janice's reply alls. Anything to occupy his brain from instant replays where Tuesday straddled his lap and kissed him until his lungs were near bursting.

Finally came the night when his desk was clear and no unread messages remained in his in-box. "Now what?" He flicked into the spam folder and scrolled. Want a one-night stand and carcinoma? "Maybe? And no," he muttered, his eyes glazing over the strange subject lines:

Make four mill dollarz in the next twenty-three hourz!!!

Enlarge your c*#k.

Open me or miss out on the best opportunity of this lifetime.

Only the most best qualitative drugs for your unhappy erectile situation.

Is the president a secret hippopotamus?

No use. He highlighted and clicked "delete all" before taking out his wallet and removing the Realtor's card that Rhett had given him. Meredith Green's small smiling headshot suggested tenacity. He'd asked around and heard tell she'd done well in a big Atlanta firm before deciding to cut loose and set up a brokerage of her own. He twirled the card through his fingers.

He kept meaning to ask her out for lunch. And kept forgetting.

He tossed the card on the desk and glared at the stack of clippings Karen had cut from the *Examiner.* She made it a habit to share anything that pertained to his office. This week the Letters to the Editor section had been blown up by a barrage of letters from happy visitors to Happily Ever After Land extolling the virtues of the park. All appeared genuine, if a trifle coerced, but he sensed Tuesday's unseen hand behind every double exclamation mark.

"Enough." He rose from his desk and stalked to the window. The town was deserted at this hour, except for the lights farther up Main Street, the local crowd closing down Mad Dawgs. A burger and a beer sounded welcome, but that meant conversation.

His running shoes were propped against his office coat closet. A better option than sitting on a bar stool or heading home to the empty Belle Mont mansion, the one his parents had signed over to him as a wedding gift in the hopes that he'd fill the many rooms with children's laughter.

Instead, he'd managed to fill it with yelling, the sound of broken glass, recrimination, and disappointment.

He yanked the curtains shut and stalked to the closet, changing into his jogging sweats. His reflection stared from the full-length mirror hanging on the back of the door, and he curled his lip before yanking the hoodie strings tight.

Better to stay far away from Tuesday. She was everything bright, and he didn't dare besmirch her with darkness.

He locked up the office, left the empty building, and ran until the breath tore from his lungs. As his feet pounded the sidewalk, the lights from the windows showcased the lives inside like movie vignettes. Along Forever Lane people were watching late-night television programming, reading a book on the couch, or chatting on the phone, each one a world unto themselves. Their own happiness. Their own sadness. Their own struggles. Their own individual daily triumphs. Some he knew about. Some he'd never know.

He passed Always Court. Ahead was Love Street. He hadn't intended to go this way. He ran faster, turning right. Jesus, of course he did. Love Street had pulled him in with magnet-like force ever since he'd left city hall.

Inside Miss Ida May's Victorian home, the *Back Fence* ladies huddled around a table, their faces glowing from the screen as they pursed their mouths in collective concentration. He had to laugh. What were those troublemakers up to now? On the other side of the road, Rhett and Pepper sat cross-legged on the living room floor playing Scrabble on their coffee table. Rhett must've cracked a joke because Pepper burst out laughing before planting a kiss on his lips.

He glanced away, stomach churning, a fucking happiness voyeur. The next house was the smallest cottage on the street, like a doll's house and blue as a robin's egg and surrounded by a white picket fence. The lights were all off inside. Disappointment skimmed across his chest like a hard-flung stone.

Tuesday was already asleep, and here he stood like a dumb ass, hoping without fully admitting to himself that she'd be a fellow night owl and that whatever drove him out to these evening streets kept her awake as well. He set his hand on the front gate latch and the night-chilled metal seeped into his skin. What if he opened the gate, walked up, and knocked at the door?

Would she let him in?

Would she be happy to see him?

Would she be the woman who straddled his lap and kissed him to insanity or the cool, collected version who primly crossed her legs in his office?

Both versions had their appeal.

No. Dammit. He waved off a mosquito. This madness had to stop.

He sprinted all the way out to the Kissing Bridge, pausing to suck air and listen to the bullfrog chorus before circling back to Main Street. Instead of Tuesday's breathless moans, he tried imagining what the town might look like to fresh eyes, say a tourist out for a pleasant weekend vacation. The brick-front stores, the brass streetlights, the attractive window displays held nothing but potential. This town had what it took. If Everland could be chosen as part of the Coastal Jewel campaign, it might be the leg up they needed.

He slowed for his cooldown, and up ahead squatted

downtown's biggest eyesore, the old Roxy Theater, boarded up these past twenty years. The fire department recently requested to have it torn down, and he understood their reasoning. It was a fire hazard, and every so often Everland or Hogg Jaw High School students broke in to host impromptu parties or get up to trouble. He'd had his first kiss at the Roxy at fourteen.

He'd been putting off the fire chief's teardown request in the hopes of returning the old theater to its former glory. As he paused to drag his forearm over his sweaty brow, he froze at the low *thump* behind the wall. He dropped his hand to his side and cocked his head. The *thump* happened again. His heart gave an extra thud. Someone was inside. There came the subtle creak of careful footsteps, too big to be a stray cat or rat. He checked his hoodie pocket.

Shit.

His cell phone was back at his desk. Calling the sheriff was out of the question. Adrenaline coursed through him. Why not go in? He was fit and could take down a trespasser if it came to that. Most likely it was a kid being stupid…Understandable, because he'd been a stupid kid once, too. But stupid kids shouldn't risk endangering their lives by accidentally starting a fire, or falling through a termite-ridden floor.

The front door was boarded over with yellow WARNING: NO TRESPASSING signs. The intruder must have jimmied opened a side window.

Hunching, he prowled the perimeter. Sure enough, on the west-facing wall, a plywood board had been pried off a window and propped against the foundation. He hoisted himself up and swung a leg over, easing inside. As his feet hit the ground, there was a crash.

"Dammit," he muttered. An old popcorn maker lay on its side. For a second silence reigned. Footsteps pounded up behind him, and as he spun, white-hot pain exploded behind his eyes and his knees slammed the floorboards.

Whack!

Intense pain shot between his shoulder blades.

Whack! One more explosion on the back of the head, and nothing.

* * *

Tuesday knew she was unlucky in love, but killing the first guy she'd been attracted to in months was going too far, even by her track record.

"Come on, come on, come on!" She slapped the side of Beau's face. "Wake up."

He groaned, his thick lashes fluttering.

"Come on, Beau. Yell or something." Was he breathing? His chest rose and fell—a strong, fine chest, too. She yanked her hand away like she'd touched a hot oven plate and tugged the hoodie down off his head. Her palm stayed dry. No blood.

"I'm so sorry." She took his hand and held it between her own. She hadn't been able to stop looking at the dragon Flick had drawn and finally had called Mrs. Boyle and asked if the girl would want to spend some time with her, go on an adventure, do something fun.

Flick was at counseling, but Mrs. Boyle said she'd ask her and phone back tomorrow. Her tone had been "don't count on it." After that Tuesday hadn't been able to sleep, so she'd gotten up and gone for a walk. When she passed the Roxy tonight, she'd gotten a wild hair to explore the interior.

Chalk it up to missing the theater. Even an old one

that hadn't been in use since Reagan was president. Maybe Nixon even. She'd wandered the moth-eaten red velvet chairs and climbed onstage for an impromptu Rockettes routine just like she'd done as an understudy for the group at Radio City Music Hall.

First, though, she'd wheeled the dusty old kettle popcorn cart beneath the window. The abandoned theater definitely registered on the creep factor. A simple "bad guy trap" would at least notify her if anyone else tried to enter.

It seemed like a funny, paranoid impulse until the cart toppled over. Her heart had paid a visit to her throat before she'd reacted on instinct and self-preservation, grabbing a two-by-four from against the stage and bashing the giant in the hoodie creeping through the window.

Unfortunately, the guy happened to be Beau, whom she'd struck three times.

She lightly slapped his cheeks. "Wake up, please. Wake up." What to do next? Give him mouth-to-mouth. No. Stupid idea. He was breathing. He was breathing, right? She leaned down closer to inspect just as his eyelids slammed open and he lurched forward, wrenching his nose on her chin.

She flew backward and landed hard on her butt, legs splayed.

"Fuck." Beau clutched his face, his face twisted with pain. "What the hell were you thinking?"

"I couldn't fall asleep, so I took a walk and got curious about the theater. What possessed you to come creeping in here?"

"I felt restless after work, so I went for a run. And *I* heard someone creeping inside the theater." He massaged his brows and groaned. "Jesus. You have a hell of a swing, you know that?"

"It's true," she admitted. "I was the star hitter for the Moose Bottom Mavericks back in high school. We were undefeated senior year."

"Moose Bottom?"

"My hometown. Moose Bottom, Maine. Granted, it took almost half the girls in my grade to make up the softball team and—no! No, no. Please don't get up."

He looked at her. "Not lying here all night."

"Let me call nine one one. Shoot. That's what I should've done right away. Get you an ambulance."

"No!" He tried to rise and collapsed back on his knees.

"Don't try to be a tough guy," she said curtly. "I remember this one time my dad was working on the side of his barn and the ladder tipped and he fell and walked two miles on a broken—"

"If you call emergency services, the entire town will know we were here together tonight. The dispatcher is Miss Ida May's niece." He hooked a hand around the back of his neck with a groan. "Also, Lucille has taken it upon herself in the name of civic duty and general nosiness to resurrect the *Everland Examiner* police blotter. The minute any of those women catch wind of this, it will go straight on the *Back Fence* blog, and no one will talk of anything else for three weeks."

"And it would compromise me as lobbyist." Tuesday hugged herself close. "We're alone. It'd look like I was trying to take advantage to advance my interests." Like what happened in New York. She swallowed before her throat could close up and she'd choke. "How many fingers am I holding up?" She shoved a hand in his face.

"I'm fine. Let me sit a second and breathe."

"Why is this place boarded up?" Tuesday shone her flashlight around the space. The red velvet seats were damaged with age, but there was no denying the grandeur of the space. The acoustics were flawless. She sang a few bars from *Grease*'s "Summer Nights" and had been pleasantly surprised with how it sounded.

"It was built by the original owner of Happily Ever After Land," Beau said.

"No kidding?" Tuesday beamed the light to the ceiling. An old brass chandelier twinkled in the light. "Holy cow, that's cut crystal."

"Yeah, during the park's heyday." Beau rolled his shoulders with a muffled groan. "Everland must have seemed poised to become a real destination before Hogg Jaw pressured the highway commission to route the highway in their favor."

She fixed the flashlight beam back on his face. "Here's what we are going to do. You sit tight. I'll run home and get Pumpkin."

He wrinkled his brow. "Pumpkin?"

"My car! I'm driving you home at least."

He tried shaking his head, but winced. "I'm good. My bike is parked at the office."

Stubborn man. She dusted off her hands and strode to the open window, a plan forming in her mind. "I might have given you a concussion. If you think that I'm letting you hop on a bike and drive down a country road populated by deer and freaking armadillos, then you are seriously mistaken, my friend."

"What's that supposed to mean?" he asked with no small suspicion.

"It means I'm going to take you home." And while the words came out casually enough, the heat igniting in her belly made her wonder if she was about to take them out of the frying pan and straight into the fire.

Chapter Eighteen

"There." Tuesday plumped the goose-down pillow behind Beau's head as he reclined on the black leather couch in Belle Mont's den. "Better?"

"Feels the same as the last three times you did it," he said gruffly. The scent of bubble-gum-flavored lip gloss hung in the air. It took almost five minutes before a name could be attached to the feeling warming his chest. Comfort.

Strange, considering she'd caused the injury in the first place. But with Jacqueline it had felt like there was only room in their relationship for one person to ever be taken care of. He was the man, the rock, the dependable one, and cool in a crisis. The truth was that role came naturally to him. Still, every so often it felt damn nice knowing someone in the world cared whether or not you got home okay.

"Refill?"

He gestured toward the full glass of water with cut lemon on the coffee table. "I've got plenty, thank you."

"Fresh bag of ice for the noggin?"

He slid the frozen bag of broccoli off his head and set it to one side. "How about taking a seat? You're making me nervous with all that hovering."

"I feel terrible about hurting you," she said.

He knew she was being honest. For the last half hour he'd dutifully swallowed two ibuprofens and allowed himself to be subjected to her battery of concussion tests, the ones she'd looked up on her phone.

His pupils had dilated in response to the flashlight that she insisted on beaming into his face. No. He didn't feel nauseous. No. He had no amnesia around the events from the accident. On the contrary, he remembered the details in clearer imagery than he'd like. Every two-by-four thwack was tattooed in his brain. He did have a lingering headache, and that made Tuesday insist on sticking around for further observation.

"And just what are you hoping to observe?" he asked.

She sank into his great-great-grandmother's carved rocking chair. "It's just a little something I hear on TV shows. Nurse?" She affected an official doctor-sounding voice. "Ensure the patient is kept under observation." She giggled and tucked her knees to her chest, wrapping her arms around her shins and setting her chin on her knees. "Want to know a secret? Once I tried out to be on a hospital daytime soap. I even made it to callbacks, but I never got the part."

He stretched out his sore back. "Too bad. You are a natural." He meant it, too.

She crouched beside him. "No sleeping."

"For how long?" Not that he was planning on crashing anytime soon. In fact, between the adrenaline from the accident and the fact Tuesday Knight was in his house, he felt hot-wired and hyperaware.

"I'm not sure. But a while." She glanced around the large room stuffed with furniture and animal heads on the wall. "Cheerful room," she said, gesturing to the frowning ancestor over the mantel. "How many bedrooms are in this place anyway? Four hundred?"

"Eight. Plus the carriage house."

"Good gravy. I bet I could stand up straight in your fireplace, too." Her eyes were as round as her parted lips. "What's it like living in an honest-to-goodness mansion?"

He bit back the word "lonely" and cleared his throat. "I keep most of it shut up. Saves on housecleaning."

"Want to watch a movie?" She seemed to understand not to press the issue.

"Guess so. I don't watch much TV."

"But look at the sheer size of that beast." She pointed toward the large flat-screen mounted over the fireplace mantel. "And those." She waved to the surround-sound speakers in the room corners.

"I do watch the news."

"Please tell me this is your valiant attempt at humor."

"Don't forget about the city council meetings on Public Television if I miss a meeting for some unusual reason."

"Sorry, did you say something?" she said, pretending to wake up from a deep sleep.

"Very funny."

"That is, honest to God, the single most boring reason to own a beautiful TV like that that I have ever heard." She gawked like he was a mystery she could decipher if only she peered hard enough into the depth. "Go on. Call out the last movie you've seen."

"I don't have time for stories." He studied her face, his mouth quirking in the corner. "There's a but in there, isn't there?"

"But..." She smiled. "Stories are how we learn who we are, our place in the world, how people live, and how they react. We find our truths in them, figure out the world."

She was like this beautiful, perfect window into thoughts and ideas that he never had.

"Fine. Let's just say—hypothetically—that I agree to a movie." He grabbed the ice pack and placed it back on his head. "Are you going to suggest some chick flick?"

"Now, that depends." She arched a brow. "Would you prefer a prick flick?"

He burst out laughing. When was the last time he'd done that?

"I mean, we could watch some gross-out comedy about hot tubs and time machines, and hangovers in Vegas, or a horror about chain-saw murders, or maybe superdepressing people sitting around and being superdepressing? Me? I happen to enjoy romances. Why not choose hope? Root for a happy ending."

She had a point.

"All right, then. Pick something, anything. No, wait. Pick your favorite." He was curious.

"Careful what you say." She frowned. "I'm not sure you'll like my favorite."

"You went through a great deal of trouble defending what makes for important watching, so put your money where your mouth is."

"But if you don't enjoy it, I'll never get over it."

"You see me backing down?"

"All right, so we're doing this."

He went to the bathroom, and when he came out the screen was filled with black-and-white images of couples dancing provocatively. Tuesday was singing, "Be My Baby."

He took a seat. "What's this?"

She side-eyed him, brows mashed together. "Please tell me you're kidding."

"Nope."

"Stop." She shook her head. "You don't know what this is?"

"It looks from the eighties? *Flashdance*?"

She pressed her palms together in prayer. "Stop speaking before I start wishing I'd hit you harder."

"Is it good?"

She squeaked in outrage. "Pineapple and ham on pizza is good. This is great."

"I don't do pineapple on pizza."

She tipped her head back and groaned at the ceiling. "You don't like pineapple on pizza and don't know what movie this is?"

He wasn't sure if he should nod or shake his head.

"Here's a hint: I carried a watermelon." She waited expectantly.

"It's about a picnic?"

"I can't tell whether you're trying to be funny or kill me." She slapped her forehead. "It's *Dirty Dancing*, only the single best love story of the late eighties. Forget about the new version. This is the one that counts."

He shrugged. "I've heard of it."

"Heard, not seen? Jesus, take the wheel." She sucked in an audible breath. "Where to even begin? Let's see. Okay, so this wealthy girl named Baby goes on vacation at this summer camp with her family, where she meets a dance instructor named Johnny Castle, a hottie from the wrong side of the tracks. They're from two different worlds but are perfect together." She gave a happy sigh.

Tuesday had many talents, but film criticism wasn't one. Still, the movie wasn't half bad. Even better was studying Tuesday from the corner of his eye, her face rapt as she soaked in every detail, her body swaying to the music. It was clear that she loved every second, and he loved every second watching her happiness.

At the dramatic finale, she sniffled. He started. "Why are you crying?"

"It happens every time. I love love. No shame." She wiped her eyes and beamed at him. "Wasn't that the best?"

"Yeah," he murmured, and he wasn't lying.

But he also wasn't talking about the movie.

* * *

"There's no need to stay over," Beau said as she turned off the screen. "I'm a big boy."

She glanced at the door. Going home would be the easier option, give her some much-needed distance from this man and, more to the point, whatever *this* was, the tension stretching between them, so thick as to be almost visible. And yet...

"I'd never forgive myself if something happened to you." She dropped all pretext and allowed honesty to creep into her tone, because while it would be easier to run, the way she always did from problems, a new desire rose within her—small but insistent. A little voice urging her to be brave.

He narrowed his eyes as if trying to see her better. "In that case, let me make up one of the spare bedrooms."

"No, please, don't go to any trouble," she said hastily. Bravery had its limits after all. And the idea of sleeping in a bed knowing Beau Marino was on the other side of the wall, well…It was hard to know if that situation would give her sweet dreams or frustrated nightmares. "I'll crash on the couch. I do all the time at home."

"If you sleep at Belle Mont, you get a bed. That's just good manners." He ignored the hand she offered to help him up.

His grimace was so slight as to be almost imperceptible, at least to anyone who hadn't become an expert in the finer points of his many subtle facial gestures.

"Slow down, Emily Post." Worry was making her a little snappish. "What's wrong? Are you dizzy?"

He stood with a wince, rolling his shoulder. "Tired more than anything. I had a long day at work. I went into the office at six this morning, and it's what, almost one?"

"You know what they say about all work and no play?"

"A person gets a lot done?"

"Ha-ha." She noticed the box on the mantelpiece. "What's this?" She walked over and studied the gold coin. "This is old, isn't it?"

"Looks like it." He joined her. "Found it the summer I turned ten, down in the river bottoms." His gaze grew distant. "Man, I wanted to believe the gold was real."

"Wait." A thrill *zing*ed through her. "You discovered pirate gold? The Redbeard legend is real? Not just a town tall tale?"

"I spent the better part of that summer scouring the banks afterward. Mama called me treasure crazy."

"I don't blame you. And you never found anything?"

"Not a trace." He shrugged. "It either doesn't exist, or it's been hidden so well that nobody's ever going to find it."

"Never say never," Tuesday said. "Have you shown this coin to Cedric Swift?"

His brows knit. "The English historian?"

"The treasure is his part-time hobby."

He snorted.

"He believes it's real."

"You know him well?"

That was a jealous tone. "If I said yes would it bother you?"

"No, of course not," he sputtered. "In fact, I have a date. This week."

The grandfather clock chimed over her stunned silence. He had what now?

"I emailed her," he said after taking in her thunderstruck expression. "She wrote back."

"Let me get this straight. You are going on a date with someone you have never met, never even spoken to?"

"Yes."

"Well, that sounds nice." No, it didn't. It sounded terrible with a capital *T*. Why couldn't he get through that thick but sexy head that she was right there and not repulsive and single and attracted.

Which was a problem.

A big problem.

Better not get involved with a guy she found irresistible. It would no doubt cloud her better judgment.

"It's late," he said at last. "We have to sleep."

Their gazes locked and her pulse turned turbulent. She

refocused on the portrait of a glum man with a walrus-sized mustache. There wasn't a faint resemblance to the brooder before her. And yet behind Beau's frown, she sensed the determined little boy inside him, the one audacious enough to believe not only in buried treasure, but that after three hundred years he'd be the one to discover it.

"Only one room has sheets on the bed," he said.

"Which one is that?" she whispered, knowing the answer.

"Mine. But I'll make you a deal. Clothes stay on. No touching. And I won't get under the covers."

She studied his face for intent. "Okay, I'm in. As long as that's as far as this will go."

"Between getting clobbered upside the head and watching my first movie in years, this evening has been exciting enough." He reached as if to brush her cheek, but balled a fist and punched his hip. "Want to know a secret?"

"Always."

"If it took a two-by-four for us to hang out, it will have been worth it." He rocked on his heels. "I had fun tonight."

"Me too."

"Does this mean we're friends, of a sort?"

"Of a sort." She curtsied, and five minutes later was on his bed, her actual head resting on one of his actual pillows. It was a masculine room, painted light gray, with a black and white color scheme, with giant windows that he told her looked out over the river bluffs. She'd have to take him at his word until the sun rose.

"It's weird, isn't it?" she announced to the dark, once she was situated and unable to bear the intimate silence. "Us here together? Kinda, sorta having fun?"

"Strange." His voice was husky with sleep.

"Want to know something else strange?" She paused for maximum effect. "I love popcorn-flavored Jelly Bellies."

A pause. "No one eats those."

"My favorite."

"Would you believe me if I said you're the strangest person I've ever met?" He chuckled drowsily, rolling over.

And the inexplicable thing was that sleeping together didn't feel strange. In fact, as her eyes closed, the late hour weighing down her bones, it felt like the most natural thing she'd done in a long time.

Chapter Nineteen

The next afternoon Beau sauntered into Chez Louis, Everland's finest dining establishment. The hostess took his name with a discreet nod, walking him back to an intimate ivy-walled courtyard. A woman, her dark hair pulled into an elegant chignon, sat at a bistro table tapping away on a cell phone.

"Hello, uh, Meredith?"

"Wait." She lifted a single manicured finger. "I just need to get this offer out before noon and then...yup, we're done." She fixed on his face with a straightforward gaze. "My goodness, aren't you the spitting image of Rhett's description?" She stuck out a hand. "Wonderful to meet you in person, Mr. Mayor."

"Likewise." He slid into the opposite chair. "And how exactly did Valentine describe me?"

"That you're the male version of me?" She pointed to the phone clutched in his hand. "How many e-mails did you read on the walk over?"

"You got me." He gave a surprised bark of laughter as the truth hit home. "Six."

"Not bad." She inclined her head. "And city hall is, what, two blocks?"

Competition flared. "I also checked the mayoral Twitter and Facebook accounts."

"Oh, cute. You're still on that stuff?"

He frowned at her dismissive nod. "Our senior population has embraced technology and rank among my most loyal followers."

"That's sweet." She gave a superior smirk. "I checked twenty-four messages and finalized another offer in the parking lot."

He shook out his napkin and set it across his lap. Rhett had done exactly as promised. Found a woman who would be for all intents and purposes his perfect match.

But while he liked her, there wasn't even a spark. And from the way her longing gaze kept sliding to her phone, the feeling seemed mutual.

Strange. He frowned to himself. He'd always imagined it would be easier to date the female version of himself. That similarities would make everything easier.

But instead it felt a little dull, like looking in a mirror and already knowing the view. No surprises. No excitement.

No spark.

"How are you settling into Everland?" he asked, trying to think of anything to say.

"Keeping busy." She fiddled with a bracelet. "Come to think of it, you live out near the bluff? In that Greek Revival mansion with the magnolias and pecan grove, am I right?" She leaned in on her elbows. "That's an awful lot of square footage for one man."

For a horrified moment he thought she was proposition-ing him before they'd put in an order—already measuring the drapes. But then she launched into a spiel on how the housing market was hot, especially for sellers. She was scheming, all right, but the focus was on getting him to be a client.

"Thanks for the tips, but I'm staying put," he said with enough resolve to douse the gleam in her eyes. "Belle Mont's been in my mama's family a long time."

To her credit, she attempted a smile. "How refreshing to see someone so invested in family history."

The elevator-style background music seemed to increase in volume as the seconds ticked on, until finally growing un-comfortable.

There was no babbling. No inappropriate observations or nosy questions. This was a civilized adult lunch date.

And boring.

So. Fucking. Boring.

The server appeared, and they ordered the same thing, salade niçoise and mineral water with a lemon slice.

Beau scooted his fork to be level with the knife and spoon. Time to try again. Search for any flicker of interest. "Tell me more about yourself. What movies do you like?"

"Movies?" Her laugh was incredulous. "I can't think of the last time I watched anything."

His gaze slid to his fork again. A sudden desire hit him, not one of romance, but to pick the utensil up and stab it in his eye, end this misery. "Okay, any hobbies?"

She cast another glance at her phone. "Who has time?"

He tipped his head back and studied the patch of blue sky. "Music?"

"Don't get me wrong. I like it. I just don't... listen to it."

He'd had dentist visits more fun than this conversation. "How about food? You like to eat?"

"Now we're talking. I've never met a pizza I didn't like."

Progress. "What're your thoughts on pineapple toppings?"

Her eyes went to the size of saucers. "Wait. Oh dear. *You* like pineapple on pizza?"

"No. I just met someone who did." And finally he gave a name to the unfamiliar feeling coursing through his veins.

He missed Tuesday.

He blew out a swift breath.

Yes. That was it, dammit. The ugly truth was that he missed Tuesday.

The way she rambled about things that he didn't fully understand.

Her spontaneous crazy.

Her strange taste buds.

Had she whacked his head harder than he thought? Because she didn't make sense. A woman like Meredith Rogers did. The two of them could sit on the couch, faces lit blue from laptop screens, breaking the silence to comment on a project or ask for advice on phrasing an e-mail. And when he went to official functions, she'd be on hand to say the right thing and behave in a way that didn't offend any sensibilities. She was safe, and he'd be bored.

God, he'd be so bored.

By the time the salads arrived, two things were as clear as their crystal glassware. One, he liked the new Realtor fine. But she deserved someone who found her fascinating. Two, it turned out that what he was craving wasn't simply female companionship, but a real connection. The elusive, mysterious spark.

By the end of the date, neither pretended. He didn't mind Meredith's disinterest any more than she seemed to mind his. With a businesslike handshake they were off, heading in opposite directions before the Chez Louis front door slammed.

He strode toward city hall, slowing his usual brisk pace to check the weather report. Sunny and seventy on the coast. What if he took the afternoon off? First time for everything. He loosened his tie, pausing before tearing the damn thing off, shoving it in his pocket, and veering toward his bike, parked under the sign that said, RESERVED FOR THE MAYOR. The *Calypso* needed a new spark plug in the outboard motor, and he needed to recalibrate.

Fifteen minutes later, he pulled into Buccaneer's Marina. Rhett's truck was parked in its usual spot. Beau tore off his helmet with more force than required, his fleeting good mood fading fast. The last thing he felt like was confessing that his first date had been an all-out disaster. Worse, that Rhett had been right and probably had known all along he'd be right. Smug bastard.

He strolled onto the dock, waving at a few people on their boats. Some were getting ready to go out, others just coming back. Four slips down from the *Calypso*, the singing started, an unfamiliar tune, but the voice came straight from his dreams.

Despite the day's heat, goose bumps erupted across his lower back.

Tuesday?

And there she was, platinum hair pinned in loose waves around her face, wearing oversize circular sunglasses and a red-and-white polka-dot bathing suit. Her sexy lips were painted a matching cherry color.

"Thought you had big plans." Rhett came from behind, carrying a gas tank.

"Those plans went back to her office." Beau shoved his hands in his pockets. "You were right. We did have a lot in common."

Rhett grinned. "Something tells me there is a 'but' buried in there."

"But it's not going to work out."

"Huh. Imagine that."

Yep. Smug bastard.

"Go on. Say it," Beau muttered. "Say it and get it over with."

Tuesday quit singing. Now she wandered up on the bow, holding out a vial of nail polish over a kid dressed in all black. Beau couldn't quite see what color she'd chosen, but he bet it matched that suit.

"So what's the plan? You heading out, or what?" he asked.

Rhett blew a frustrated breath before reaching for a fishing pole. "I want to, but Tuesday's afraid of the water." Rhett smiled and waved as Pepper emerged from below-decks, her hair wrapped in a scarf. "My lovely fiancée has ordered me on pain of no sex for a week not to push the subject."

"What do you mean?"

"Tuesday doesn't like the water. She's afraid of it."

"But she's on a boat."

"She thought she was coming out to sunbathe. And now Pepper is saying that we can't force her. I guess she got caught in a dinghy out in a storm as a kid. I can't put the pressure on. Celibacy and I aren't friends."

Beau shook his head. "Maybe you can't, but I sure as hell

can." Before Rhett could say anything else, he'd jumped on the boat.

Tuesday made a show of ignoring him. "You're blocking my sun, Mr. Mayor." Whatever strange intimacy they'd shared in the night had burned away in the harsh light of day.

"Not for long. We're taking the boat out."

She lowered her shades while snapping her gum. "That's fine. I'll get my things and wait for you back at the marina's clubhouse."

"What?" The kid next to her visibly perked up. "I want to go out."

"But, Flick, honey, we have music here," Tuesday said, reaching for sunscreen. "And magazines. And lounge chairs."

"You're coming," Beau said softly.

"I can't sail," Tuesday snapped. "I do not like it, Sam I am."

"Oh, please, oh, please. I really want to go," the girl said, presumably Flick.

"When is the last time you've been on one?" he asked.

She didn't answer for a moment. "I was nine, on White-fish Lake."

"Now you're what, twenty-six?"

"Twenty-five."

"And this is the Atlantic."

"The ocean is way deeper than some Podunk lake in Northern Maine."

He dropped into a squat. "Trust me. You'll have fun."

Her gaze traveled his face, as if seeking something. "I mean it. I'm...terrified on water." She held up a hand as though nipping any rebuttal from him in the bud. "I know

I have a habit of exaggerating things, embellishing details. But no crying wolf, this time I mean it. The only reason that I came down here at all is because they assured me I wouldn't get pressured."

He could tell her words weren't hyperbole. There wasn't so much as a flicker of her usual humor in her eyes. Instead they were wide, a little glassy. And while he didn't want to scare her, he did want to push her. "I made no such promise. And besides, I know you." And the thing was that he did. Tuesday would enjoy the hell out of herself on this boat if she'd relax. "Trust me," he said, pausing to clear his throat.

"Trust you?" She spoke the words slowly, as if mulling the taste, finding the flavor unfamiliar.

"For a woman who gets no small enjoyment out of pushing others from their comfort zones, maybe you should try it for a change." As much as he knew he was laying it on thick, he didn't intend to back down. He didn't want to be an overbearing dick, but the weather was perfect, the sea calm. Ideal conditions to take a nervous beginner out on the water.

"Come on," Flick pleaded. "Maybe there'll be sharks. I love sharks. They're my favorite animal."

"And here I thought I was supposed to be the one who lobbied *you*." Tuesday looked as if she might flatly refuse, except for the fact she'd tugged her lower lip between her two front teeth. "You challenge me, Beau Marino."

"Likewise," he said, unable to resist a smile. She was going to give it a shot because he'd asked. She trusted him, and he meant to be worthy of that gift.

* * *

"You sure you're up to this?" Pepper asked, setting a hand on Tuesday's shoulder and giving her a concerned look. "I know you aren't a big fan of the water."

Understatement.

Tuesday detested the water.

Okay, that wasn't exactly true. She loved lingering in a bubble bath, bonus points if the water was infused with lavender or ylang-ylang. But water that went overhead? Nope. No likey. And yet here she was bobbing on a small yacht with Flick, her sister, her sister's fiancé, and the most frustrating man she had ever known, motoring out of Buccaneer's Marina and turning into the mid-Atlantic.

Waves crashed against the break wall, and her heart responded in kind. A seagull swooped low with an angry call, and it sent her ducking.

"You are wound up," Flick said.

"Tuesday! I'm serious." Pepper whipped off her sunglasses "I can tell Beau to turn this boat right around."

"That won't be necessary." Beau stood at the wheel, calm and in control, hands at ten and two. In that white shirt with the sleeves rolled and well-fitting khaki pants, he was the epitome of preppy maritime style. Tuesday was hit with a wave of something that she preferred to attribute to seasickness because what was the alternative? That she was nursing a big, fat, honking crush on a man who couldn't be more different from herself?

Yeah, yeah, it was true opposites attracted. But at some point couldn't two people be so different that they'd sooner kill than kiss the other? Where was that line between her and Beau? And would finding out land her in federal prison on second-degree murder charges?

"Having fun yet?" he called.

"Reminds me of this one time I got a splinter."

Rhett stepped forward. "Flick, want to come practice steering?"

"Sure!" She jumped up and tore to the wheel.

Beau took a seat beside Tuesday.

"You can do this. Keeping looking at the line where the ocean meets the sky."

For a split second she felt more settled, but he had to go and slide his hand closer. As his pinky hooked hers, all bets were off. Her chest squeezed. Her stomach didn't feel as if it held butterflies. No, her stomach behaved as if it had become a butterfly. Sweat beaded her upper lip.

Rhett gave Flick a basic sailing lesson, and to Tuesday's everlasting relief, they didn't venture too far away from land. Rather, they hopped between coves, lagoons, and hollows common on the islands around them. After an hour they dropped anchor in a pretty half-moon-shaped bay.

"This is lovely!" Pepper exclaimed, turning over one shoulder while gathering her medium-length hair into a short ponytail.

And for a couple of seconds, Tuesday really did feel good. Better than that. She could even see why someone would have fun doing it. Except she made the fatal mistake of peeking over the side. The yawning pits of hell couldn't have appeared more sinisterly fathomless.

"I...I...I have to go below for a moment." She offered a silent prayer of gratitude for her oversize Marilyn Monroe sunglasses. Pepper and Rhett were sharing a tender look as Flick gripped the wheel, steely gaze leveled to the horizon. They wouldn't notice she had vanished.

Before Beau could ask a question, she rose. "I need the little girls' room."

Chapter Twenty

Tuesday lurched down the companionway in faltering micro steps. Solid ground was an illusion. Beneath the hull waited an abyss, while the ceiling was low enough to make her duck into the galley kitchen. She braced herself against the dinette table as she paused, letting her eyes adjust to the gloomy light. Ahead, through an accordion-type door, a V-berth bed nestled into the boat's bow.

She stumbled to the sink and cupped her hand under the tap, taking frantic sips of water.

"Tuesday?"

She choked.

Beau peered from halfway down the stairs. "I'll tell Rhett to head back. I shouldn't have forced you to come out."

"Please. Not another word. Flick is having the best time." The bow rose on the crest of a wave, rolling side to side as it came down. "I've got to get horizontal," she muttered.

"Seasick?" He skipped the bottom step.

"Fear always settles in my stomach. I used to throw up after auditions. People on the subway must have thought I kept vodka in my water bottle."

He squeezed into the galley, opened a drawer, and removed a dish towel, running it under the faucet. After squeezing out the excess water, he handed it over. "Hold this to your forehead. My mama used to do that for me as a boy."

She removed her sunglasses and did as instructed while sitting on the edge of the berth. "I swear I didn't know you'd be here," she whispered. "I overheard Rhett mentioning to Pepper that you had a date with some hotshot real estate agent?"

He sat beside her. "I can explain—"

She held up a hand. "It's fine. Good, even. I'm happy for you." The last thing she wanted to hear trapped in this floating coffin was an awkward letdown. "You don't owe me an explanation."

"Don't I?" His voice held a husky edge.

The boat rolled again, the hull creaking. This time she barely registered the motion. A body could hold only so much emotion. The gaze locked on her face was making her want to scream.

"What do you want?" she whispered.

He made a helpless gesture and leaned forward as if to stand, then snapped his head back.

"This." He grabbed her in his arms, and his mouth found hers right as the boat rolled on another breaker. They went flying back onto the mattress.

His lips tasted like butterscotch, and he braced his weight, holding himself over her like a shelter. She got an overwhelming feeling of safety even as his kisses were more dangerous by the second.

"I can't be near you and not do this," he growled into her mouth.

But she'd as soon explain quantum physics than unravel the mystery that unfolded here in this dark, tight space where the world contracted to urgent fumbling and uncertain hands entwining.

His fingers laced with hers, and as he drew them up and over her head, she arched her back. Her bathing suit was a vintage one-piece. When she'd fallen, her legs had splayed, and he was there between them. The flimsy material of her suit wasn't doing much to mask his need.

He shifted, deepening the kiss in a way that got her responding on instinct.

"I have to stop," he ground out. "Or in another three seconds I'm going to have you out of that suit while there are three people above deck."

Tuesday's stomach coiled. Her thighs clenched. Her ancient fight-or-flight response was short-circuited by an even more ancient "fuck me now" primal reaction.

She needed to manage this mad desire for Beau. She also needed to set up auto-bill pays and start going to bed at a more reasonable time.

She'd get on top of all that...tomorrow.

They had to stop. He was right. She had to stop. Otherwise they'd get caught, and neither one of them wanted to face interrogation about whatever was between them.

Because then it would be real.

But...

Right now she wanted to be nothing more than the woman in the red-and-white polka-dot bathing suit getting ravished on a boat. Every part of her body, down to a cellular level, hungered for more.

She worked his shirt from his pants. He sucked in as she explored the hard planes of muscle so different from her own soft landscape. A whorl of thick hair trailed to his navel. She dragged a finger over it, savoring the coarseness.

He broke the kiss and looked down, filling her vision, his belly trembling. She kept exploring. *Good Lord.* No sign of give anywhere on these abs.

"You aren't ticklish?" Her batted eyes matched her teasing tone.

"Not there." He toyed with the strap to her suit. Not yanking it down, just a subtle tug, a reminder that he could.

"Tuesday! Tuesday!" Flick called from the stairs. "Look! Come look! You have to see! It's amazing!"

Beau was off of her so fast it was as if she'd hallucinated the whole thing except her palms were still warm from his heat.

She sat and reached for her glasses. They'd come off the top of her head and were lying on the bed. "Coming!"

His neck muscles corded. "I'll need a minute."

She returned to the deck, smoothing the muss from her hair, and did her best to ignore Pepper's questioning stare and Rhett's secretive smile.

"Hurry! Hurry!" Flick jumped up and down as a dolphin pod skimmed the bow wave. Their silver fins knifed the water, and she'd put her hand on a Bible and swear they were smiling.

Her gaze connected with Flick's just as a dolphin breached and sent a spray of water directly into the girl's face.

"Oh my gosh," Pepper said, passing over a beach towel. "You're soaked."

"It's all good." Flick wiped her face. Most of her thick eye makeup came off, and without it she looked younger, like a regular kid.

"What did I miss?" Beau took in Flick's drenched condition. His playful tone did a good job of not sounding forced.

The girl responded by giggling and swatting him with a towel.

"You did not just do that." He opened a seat bench and pulled out a Super Soaker water gun. "Do you know who you are messing with?"

"Arm yourself." Rhett tossed Flick a water gun of her own, and the two of them went at it, scampering around the boat taking potshots.

A pelican flock dipped into view, their V-line formation kissing the horizon, which Tuesday didn't need to focus on as she no longer felt sick. Instead, with her lips swollen from kisses and the wind teasing her hair, Flick had gotten it right.

Everything *was* all good.

Chapter Twenty-One

⌒

Toots looked up from what appeared to be reheated biscuits and gravy in the Happily Ever After staff break room. "How's lobbying going, Princess?"

"The Letter to the Editor booth we installed for the visitors is making an impression in the *Examiner*," she said. "It's good to open a dialogue. Conversations have the power to change the world." At least according to the dog-eared library books she was reading.

"Talk's cheap. Do we have a new lease? No." Mean Gene shoved an overstuffed tuna salad sandwich into his mouth, answering his rhetorical question with a grim finality.

"Have you guys heard about the norovirus outbreak in South Carolina?" Lettie Sue held up a copy of yesterday's paper. "It says Georgia is at risk."

"We're always at risk for something." Z-Man plucked off his red rubber nose and reclined in his seat, clasped his hands over his polka-dot chest, and closed his eyes. Within five seconds his breathing changed. Seriously. Was it really possible to fall asleep like that?

"Have you had more face time with Mayor Marino?" Gil asked.

Tuesday clamped her throat to prevent a nervous giggle. *Sucking-face time.*

So she had a kissing problem with Beau. So what?

So she was supposed to be a professional and these people were counting on her to save not only their livelihood but also their quirky way of life. And kissing wasn't going to get Beau to take her seriously. Nope. Kissing was a surefire way to send him running in the opposite direction. Frustration tightened her jaw. What if she was messing up everything, getting into bed with the potential enemy—literally?

These people trusted her. They needed her to be more than a princess kissing frogs, indulging in romance.

Except Beau didn't feel like a frog. Nope. Not even remotely amphibian. Her heart thudded extra hard on the next beat. In fact, the mayor seemed to live up to his reputation as the Prince of Everland.

But this was the real world, not a fairy tale, and while she was in the business of playing make-believe, she needed to be a realist.

"You can bend his ear at the Fall Ball tonight," Caroline said.

"The ball?" Tuesday stared around the table at their expectant expressions. "Should I be going to this ball?"

Their faces collectively fell. Mean Gene muttered something about this being amateur hour, but his mouth was too full of food to make clear sense.

"It's an event. Scratch that. It's *the* event of the season." Toots blotted her lips with a napkin. "All the Everland movers and shakers go to the Fall Ball. It's held every year at the Ye Olde Carriage House over on Forever Lane."

"And I'm supposed to be moving and shaking?"

"In fairness, tickets are harder to come by than hens' teeth," Lettie Sue said, folding the paper.

"You can bet Discount-Mart will have a rep there." Gil's expression twisted with worry.

"Count on it," Mean Gene muttered.

Tuesday ground her knees beneath her voluminous skirts. Gene was right; she was an amateur scouring library books in the hopes of figuring out how to be a lobbyist. She was a joke, except when she failed no one would be laughing.

It wasn't funny that Happily Ever After counted on her.

"Well, even if I did manage to magically procure a ticket from a hat, I have nothing to wear." She plucked at her dress with a self-deprecating laugh. "The under-ten crowd might think this look is fancy, but it's not going to impress actual bigwigs."

"I possess a ticket." A quavering accent broke through the chatter. All heads turned in unison to regard Madam Magna in the doorway.

"You?" Tuesday asked. "How?"

Madam Magna flicked away the question with a twist of her gnarled hand. "I give it to you on one condition."

"What's that?" Tuesday asked.

"Clever girl." Madam Magna smiled. "Never agree to anything before hearing terms." She shuffled closer. "I give you ticket, but only if you wear this." She reached into her robes and removed a gold chain, the emerald stone winking in the light. "Is lucky charm." Magna set down her necklace and the ticket. "But get no ideas. You return it to me tomorrow."

"How did you of all people finagle a ticket?" Mean Gene asked.

Madam Magna shrugged, privately amused. "I know people who know people."

"Well, hot digging dog!" Gil slapped the table. "Our princess is off to the ball."

"Wait. There's still the small matter of my wardrobe deficit?" Tuesday said. "I own sundresses, not dressy gowns."

"Why, I know just the thing." Lettie Sue piped up. "I was a bridesmaid a few years back for my cousin in Virginia Beach, a real fancy affair. You're taller, but we look about the same size. I'm sure the dress will fit you."

"And I'm a whiz at hair," Toots said.

"We've got ourselves a plan," Gil said.

There was a *thud* and a snort as Z-Man startled awake, his front chair legs hitting the linoleum. "What did I miss?"

Mean Gene picked up his rubber nose and lobbed it square between his eyes.

And so, after a busy day at work, Tuesday ended up in Toots's well-kept mobile home surrounded by the other park staff.

"You sure I don't look like an eggplant?" she asked, flouncing the plum-colored skirt. She could play an amusement-park princess, but a calm, cool lobbyist was a whole new role and no fake British accent would help lend her credibility.

Her coworkers stared. If they laughed, she'd call the whole thing off.

"You look beautiful," Gil said. "You're going to charm the pants off everyone there."

Tuesday resisted the urge to bite her nails. To add fuel to the fire, Beau Marino would certainly be in attendance, and the idea of him without pants made her one part excited and two parts house-on-fire panicked.

"I hope I make you guys proud," she whispered. She didn't feel elegant or smart or capable of witty banter. She wasn't even sure if she'd know anyone there. Pepper and Rhett had gone on a romantic sailing getaway off the Carolina coast for the weekend. This meant it was she alone, on her own two legs, to sink or swim. Everyone counted on her, and there was no fairy godmother or friendly woodland animals waiting in the wings to help her out in a pinch. She could win the day or be an epic fail.

Her stomach muscles squeezed. Apparently responsibility was a nauseous feeling.

"The green from the necklace brings out the rosy color in your cheeks," Lettie Sue said before two furrows appeared between her brows. "Or do you have a fever? Is there a thermometer in here, Toots?"

"I'm fine, but late. I need to go." Tuesday reached for her purse. Waiting only increased her nerves. "Hey, and lucky me." She pointed through the bay window to her car parked out front. "I already own a Pumpkin."

As she exited the trailer, she squeezed Madam Magna's necklace while offering up a small prayer that the old woman's mumbo jumbo was grounded in some sort of reality.

In the absence of fairy dust, she'd need any luck that fate could scrape together.

Chapter Twenty-Two

~

Beau's shoulders flexed in his grandfather's classic fifties-era tuxedo. Hard to derive pleasure from the simple, elegant cut tonight. Not while the top of Humph's shiny bald head kept popping up around the venue like a damn Whac-A-Mole game. It looked like Miller had secured three Fall Ball tickets for Discount-Mart associates, and together they'd worked the room like circling sharks. There wasn't a hand that remained unshaken.

Donna from the Tourism Commission was here, too, and the trick was keeping the two camps apart. All he needed was for Humph and his pals to discuss reneging the park lease and throwing up discount chains and bargain outlets as he tried to talk up the town's historic commitment. He straddled the fence here, but there was no telling which way the wind would blow, and he needed to ensure Everland sailed smoothly through any choppy waters.

The noise in the room dropped a few decibels. Beau

glanced around, not seeing a reason for the hush until his gaze swung to the stairs and vertigo took hold.

Tuesday.

His heart threatened to make a hasty exit from his chest. She looked…There weren't words.

Damn. A realization crashed through him. This woman might be unsuitable, but she was it for him. He wanted to know everything about her, from her favorite color to food to song. He'd watch every romantic comedy ever made if it meant sitting beside her on the couch. He would never eat the popcorn-flavored Jelly Bellies, but he'd pick them out of the jar and feed them to her one by one, regretting nothing.

She caught his awestruck stare, and the same heat that flushed across her cheeks spread down his ribs.

"Excuse me," he said to whoever he'd been speaking to. It didn't matter. Nothing mattered except getting closer to Tuesday.

Which proved extraordinarily difficult because the crowd ebbed and flowed, blocking her from view. Everywhere he went people wanted to have a moment of her time. Ask a question or share a joke or suggestion. As soon as he got close to her, she was whisked someplace else.

Everyone wanted to talk to her, to compliment her dress, her hair. The women wanted to be her, and the men—shit, from the covetous look in their eyes, they wanted to be *in* her.

Gunner from Mad Dawgs monopolized her for a second dance. His hand crept down her back like a reverse Itsy Bitsy Spider. Beau's fingers twitched with the urge to stride over and tie the dude's arms into pretzel-like knots.

What the hell? He'd never been one to 'roid rage or puff

up like an alpha dog and fight. He preferred to keep his unshakable cool, calm demeanor, and found it wielded a more effective power.

"Lovely, isn't she?" A soft voice penetrated his mental fog.

Beau glanced down, and there was Donna smiling like a silver-haired elf. The top of her head barely reached his biceps.

She inclined her head toward Tuesday. "You haven't taken your eyes off her since she entered the ballroom."

"I..." He had nothing. She'd busted him fair and square.

"Moving on is hard," she told him. "A man from church asked me to coffee last week, and instead I drove to the cemetery and cried for an hour. But even as I did, some part of me recognized that I won't say no forever. We're human, and need companionship. It's a basic need, like air or water. You won't be betraying your wife's memory."

Guilt steamrolled his lungs, made breathing a joke. This kindhearted woman intended nothing but sympathy. She thought they were equals, compatriots in grief. She didn't know the last words Jacqueline had said to him.

Staying in this marriage would be worse than death. I hate you.

He'd never wanted her to get her wish. But he couldn't change what happened next.

He hadn't stopped her from leaving. He'd watched coldhearted as she'd climbed off his boat, swinging her small red suitcase. He hadn't known she was already packing off to a new lover, but if he had, he wouldn't have cared. His heart had broken long before that deceptively cheerful sunny day.

Not even Rhett knew the whole toxic tale of his marriage because the details were fucking awful and the dead shouldn't be held accountable to the worst version of themselves. So he'd played the role of the mourning husband at her funeral, sitting shoulder to shoulder with her parents. They'd never questioned why she was with another man. He knew they knew. They knew he knew.

What more was there to say? And in those weeks and months after her death, he'd been so fucking shut down that he'd never challenged the version of events that had spread through the town like wildfire. By the time he stepped out of the fog, a sanitized version of the story had become real. Everyone wanted him to live the lie; it was easier for them that way. He hooked a hand around the back of his neck, kneading corded muscles.

But he hadn't gotten off easy. While the world might give him sympathy, at night the parting words of his wife clanged through his skull like a malicious bell.

I hate you.

I hate you.

I hate you.

He couldn't tell that truth, and so the silence had grown and grown like a thick wall of thorns, until he'd been choked from the light. Then Tuesday had lit up his world with the megawatt intensity of the Las Vegas power grid, a fireball, a solar flare. When he closed his eyes, she remained imprinted on the back of his lids.

He knew he wanted that woman more than his next breath. But he'd tried being with someone so different before. And how did it end?

I hate you.

I. Hate. You.

But once upon a time, long, long ago, there had been love, or at least infatuation, and a fascination over their mutual differences. But the edges where they were different had never snapped together. Instead, they'd rubbed and rubbed, grating the other until they were both left cut, raw, and bloody.

A glass pressed into his hand. He glanced down at the sweet tea Donna offered.

"You're peaked. Drink." She used the same tone Mama did at times. The one that didn't allow for a lick of dissent.

He took a polite gulp.

"There, that's better." Donna nodded in satisfaction. "I know you don't know me from Adam, but I like you, Beau Marino. I think you're a good man."

You're a type A, workaholic bore.

Jacqueline's complaints had grown so familiar he had stopped hearing them.

"I know you've asked me here in a professional capacity, but if you ever need to bend an ear, a friendly ear that can understand, I want you to know that I'm here."

He managed a nod.

"Now, if I might overstep myself a mite further, I want you to know Marvin had a saying he was fond of. It gets me out of bed the mornings that it seems impossible. 'Life is for the living.' And he's right. We need to live."

"And what do you do?" He took a deep swallow. "To live?"

"I'm thinking how to rebuild my life. The old version doesn't fit anymore." She smiled. "I might get a dog. Or a cat. Or a dog *and* a cat. Marvin was allergic. He was also a homebody. So maybe I'll finally go see Europe. I've always had a hankering to sip wine and stare at the Eiffel Tower."

"You're a remarkable woman," he said with complete and utter honesty. She had been dealt a terrible hand and was playing it in a way that left him humbled.

"What about you, Mr. Mayor?"

He turned the glass in his hands. "My situation is different. My marriage . . . well, let's just say that it wasn't happy." A muscle ticked in his jaw. What the hell? Had he just given voice to his greatest secret, coaxed free by an empathetic expression?

She set down her drink on a side table and touched his shoulder. "It's okay, son. You can breathe."

"I don't talk about the past."

Her look was knowing. "You need to someday. But tonight there's a ball. It's a full moon, and love is in the air. Who knows? Maybe some of the magic is dusting off on you." She nudged him. "Why not ask a pretty woman to dance? That tuxedo isn't meant to be lurking in corners."

Tuesday's laughter pealed from the dance floor. The room had made a semicircle around her, and she was . . . tap-dancing? Good Lord, was there anything this woman couldn't do?

"There's a pretty woman right there."

Pretty? That was a pale, weak word, and Tuesday was everything red, gold, and vibrant. "I'm not like her."

"You don't have to be."

"I attracted an opposite before. It was a recipe for disaster."

"Ah, yes. I think I see what you're getting at." She nodded sagely. "But are all the ingredients the same this time around? Is she"—she jutted her chin at Tuesday—"like your wife?"

He frowned. Tuesday was confident, and so was Jac-

queline. They were both funny, entertaining, and flattering. But Jacqueline's shiny package had hidden patholog-
ical lying, self-serving manipulation. It wasn't until after
they were married that he'd noticed her habit of kissing up
and kicking down. She was nice to people whose respect
she wanted and borderline cruel with those who didn't
matter in her eyes.

He'd fallen for her young, barely twenty, and she'd
pulled the wool over his eyes so hard that he didn't quite realize things weren't right until his grandma's diamond was
firmly on her finger.

Her mother had approached him at the wedding reception with relief in her eyes. "She's your responsibility now.
Good luck."

At the time he'd bristled at the notion, thinking Jacqueline had been right; her parents were horrible people. Who
referred to their daughter in such a way?

But Beau didn't realize he hadn't fallen in love with the
real Jacqueline. He'd fallen in love with her mask.

And when she started to take it off, she could slip it back
on so fast that he almost didn't notice. But as the years went
on, she left it off more and more, until some days he felt like
he was going crazy.

He'd look at her at a party, dazzling the room, and think,
*Is that the same woman who just spent our grocery money
on shoes and then blamed me for not looking after her?*

Did Tuesday wear masks to the world?

As if she could hear his thoughts, she spun in his
direction, her cheeks bright, her hair falling over her
shoulders like spun gold. Her lips parted and her eyes
glowed.

For an instant it was as if they weren't two separate

people. They didn't see each other; it was deeper, more profound. Then she blinked, turning to giggle at a joke someone said, and the moment was gone, but his whole body thrummed with possibility.

"No, she's nothing like her."

Chapter Twenty-Three

The band struck up a slow, romantic tune. Couples began pairing off and stepping onto the dance floor to sway beneath the soft mood lighting. "May I have this dance, Miss Knight?" The smooth-as-whiskey drawl spread delicious heat through Tuesday's middle.

"Mayor Marino." She fastened on a wry grin before turning to face her unexpected petitioner. "Now, here's a surprise. I didn't peg you for a dancer."

"What did you peg me for?" His wicked smirk made her breath catch in her throat. Was his tone friendly or flirting? His gaze locked on hers, making it impossible to stare back without turning three shades of red.

His smile. His magnetic eyes. His powerful, masculine build. The trifecta of secret fantasies. Heat bloomed between her legs.

"I'm going to let you in on a little-known fact. One that I don't go sharing with just anyone."

"Phew." She studied a potted fern like it was a wonder of the known world. "Good thing I'm not just anyone."

Wow, great comeback, Captain Zing. Good Lord, sometimes her life felt like one long awkward moment broken up by snacks and napping.

"No." His face grew more serious than normal. "You're definitely not just anyone."

"Okay, dish." Could he hear her galloping heart over the orchestra? The music started, Tchaikovsky's *Swan Lake*.

"You've piqued my interest." He'd actually piqued quite a few things, mostly in her good bits.

"In junior high, my mama made me a deal. I got a Red Ryder BB Gun if I attended youth ballroom summer camp."

Couples whirled past on the carriage house's polished dance floor as she frowned, brow knitting. "What's the big punch line?"

He grimaced. "That wasn't a joke. I can waltz, fox-trot, samba, and quickstep."

She tried to process this unexpected fact, but her internal hard drive short-circuited. "How did you fail to fess up on the night we watched *Dirty Dancing*?"

"It didn't seem applicable."

She honestly didn't know if he was putting her on or if he was serious. "You went to ballroom dance camp?"

"For one entire week. I told Rhett that I was going to tennis camp, and he made fun of me enough for that. Mama isn't one for being stuffy, but she said a real man knows his way around the ballroom floor."

"That's fantastic." Her laugh was nervous. The

prospect of Beau in that perfectly fitting tux knowing how to lead was rather swoon-inducing. Fine, absolutely swoon-inducing.

"I don't know about fantastic." He gathered her close, his hand spanning her shoulder blades as he guided her into an effortless waltz. "But I do always aim to make my mama proud. It's the Southern-boy way."

He kept to the rhythm, never stepping on her toes, and adding small flairs to their turns. He wasn't just competent. He was good. Really good.

She had been in the ensemble for *The King and I* and made sure to add her own panache. "People are staring at you," she whispered after they rounded the floor a second time.

"No. They're watching you." His gaze traveled her face. "You're beautiful. A real princess."

He wasn't the first man to ever call her beautiful, but never in all her twenty-five years had someone studied her every last feature with awe.

"You're acting unusual tonight," she said breathlessly. Normally he kept up an indefinable guard, as if he were surrounded by an invisible wall.

Tonight was different. He was different. She was different.

"There's something magical in the air." Garlands of gold-painted autumn leaves lined the room. Votive candles flickered from tables between mason jars brimming with hydrangeas, dahlias, orange calla lilies, thistle, and garden roses. Tiny fairy lights twinkled over white-painted pumpkins artfully arranged on hay bales.

When the music finally ended, she moved to take a step away, not wanting to monopolize him, but he held on. Not with any force, just a supreme reluctance.

"Go another round?" he rumbled.

"For luck?" she assented.

The music started, and he leaned in until his lips were in shiver-inducing proximity to her ear. "I do feel lucky."

"Why's that?" she murmured, subtly tracing a thumb over his arm muscle.

"Every single guy in this room would trade his front teeth to be in my position."

He was transforming their odd friendship into a sort of flirtationship. "I'm not even certain that you like me half the time."

"The truth is that I haven't known what to make of you."

"And you like putting people in boxes? Assigning them neat labels?" She couldn't help baiting him. This is how they always acted. It was their shtick. Now he was changing the rules with his open admiration, and she didn't know how to play along.

"I've lived compartmentalized for a long time." He traced the underside of her jaw. It was nothing but a fleeting gesture, but one intoxicating enough to enter her bloodstream as if she'd just chugged a glass of champagne. She was two seconds away from inviting him out onto the balcony for a little uninhibited lip-biting, neck-sucking, ass-grabbing, up-against-the-wall fun.

She cleared her throat. "How's that working out for you?"

He unleashed a low, gravelly laugh. "Sometimes I get so damn bored that I imagine doing wheelies down Main Street in my underwear."

"Boxers or briefs?" She was being terrible, but it was too much damn fun to resist.

He looked so adorably scandalized that she almost couldn't stand it. He leaned closer, his bottom lip grazing the shell of her outer ear, giving her the most delicious case of the shivers. "Who says I wear either?"

Oh. Mah. Gravy. She jerked so hard at the frank admission that her necklace swung, the chain heavy over her chest.

The necklace. She covered the emerald pendant with her hand, snuffing her good mood.

She'd assumed Madam Magna's promises of irresistibility were nothing more than a bippity-boppity-boo pep talk, a real-life version of giving Dumbo a feather and encouraging him to fly.

Except Madam Magna never broke character. Not even peeing. Tuesday had once stumbled upon her in the staff bathroom and the older woman hadn't given a single sign that her act was anything other than the real deal.

What if the necklace had been enchanted with some magical power? What if Beau's captivation was due to the necklace?

"I have to make a confession," she murmured as the last chords of Strauss's "Blue Danube" faded away. How was she going to say this? *Hey, yeah, so I'm wearing a necklace that might be enchanted and we should leave it here before it goes any further and you require a sexorcism.*

Hmmm. How exactly does one lead in on that particular conversation?

"I'm crazy about you."

She swallowed a groan, half elated and half guilt stricken. All she needed to do was suggest they get some air. They could remove themselves to somewhere more private, where she could dazzle him with her six-part talking points she'd jotted down from her library books and then let him kiss her until the sun rose.

But it wouldn't be fair.

"It's not me you're crazy about," she whispered. It was this enhanced version of her. The blond princess mask. The woman who entertained a crowd and had competent dancing abilities. Even if the necklace wasn't magic, it didn't hide the fact that everything captivating him was the glossy exterior. The best shiny parts of herself. But what would he do when confronted by one of her less-than-stellar parts? The woman who slept in past her alarm? Who was easily distracted. Who could start a conversation about wanting to eat less meat and end up discussing Bob Saget. Nothing about her was linear.

She and Beau might be attracted to each other, but that wasn't everything. He also was town mayor and the best friend of her future brother-in-law. That made for terrible fling material. If she gave in now, they'd see each other over and over. At supper club. On the boat. At the house. In the paper. At any and all Everland town events.

She wanted him more than her next breath. Her whole body inclined toward him like a plant seeking the sun. But she was supposed to have played a professional tonight. People counted on her to be professional. Instead, here she was, royally screwing things up as per usual. This necklace was dangerous. Desire was dangerous. She knew this from hard-won firsthand experience.

Her life wasn't a fairy tale of frolicking with happy woodland animals, and she couldn't ever forget it. And if she screwed this up, she wouldn't be the only person hurt this time. All of her friends at the park would suffer, too.

"I have to go."

"What?" he asked.

"I'm leaving." The music stopped, and they'd ended their dance near to the main entrance.

She took a step away. And another. Sourness flooded her mouth. She'd gotten so caught up in Beau's flirting that she hadn't even lobbied him. And everyone at the park was counting on her.

She'd blown it. Mixed business and pleasure and—

"There you are!" A stout woman engulfed her in a rib-cracking hug.

"Mrs. Boyle?" Tuesday wheezed at the steely-haired woman clinging to her with barnacle intensity.

"Debbie. Please. Call me Debbie." The woman beamed. "You've no idea how much fun Flick had on the boat ride you took her on. Since that day I've heard of nothing else except 'Tuesday said this, and Tuesday likes that.' I just want to say thank you."

"I'd love to see her again soon," she told Mrs. Boyle. Her instincts were screaming at her to run out the door. Get away from Beau, who was still close, too close. But she'd screwed up so much tonight that she didn't want to mess up Flick, too. "We got along great."

"Yes, please. The poor thing needs true friends, bless her heart, and a positive young female role model to look up to. I've had my hands full with the kids I've got under my care at the moment. Flick gets so depressed over the adoptions. Little Rowan found a forever family last week. No one wants to consider someone her age. After she went sailing, I saw her first real smile."

"Let's get her some more," Tuesday said, taking the woman's hands in hers, her throat scratchy and tight even as her heart filled close to bursting. "Let's make sure she has a smile every day."

"You're a good woman." Mrs. Boyle hugged her again before beaming to Beau. "And you're a lucky man to have this one, Mr. Mayor."

Tuesday couldn't bear to face him after that comment. She counted in her head as the woman turned and walked toward the appetizer table. *One...two...three...*

Run.

Her feet flew over the polished oak floorboards. She gathered up her skirts and sprinted like she was back on that Moose Bottom Softball team, bottom of the ninth and she had to get home. Yes, this was a stupid, immature reaction, just like the idea that this necklace was responsible for Beau's seemingly magical interest, but that didn't mean she needed to escape any less.

The clock rang out, twelve peals. How was it already midnight?

Footsteps echoed down the stairs behind her. Beau closed in. And if he spoke he would say something perfect and then all her common sense and planning would fly out the window.

She flew into the parking lot and hooked a sharp right, turning around. No one.

Good, she'd lost him.

Wait, where was her purse?

That was bad, because she wouldn't go back inside. And now she didn't even have a Pumpkin to take her home.

Some fairy-tale ending.

She'd have to go on foot, in these heels. She'd darted up Forever Lane when a realization hit her with enough force to make her stop in her tracks, wide-eyed and gasping. No matter how fast she went, she could never outrun herself.

Chapter Twenty-Four

$\sim$

Beau banged through the banquet hall's double doors and into the sultry night. He swiveled his gaze left and right, scanning the sidewalk. Nothing. Damn. Tuesday had moved like quicksilver. He clutched her beaded purse, the one she'd forgotten on a cocktail table. It had been unzipped, and as he'd taken the stairs two at a time, the contents had spilled. Precious seconds were wasted chasing scattered coins, a red crayon, four tubes of lip gloss, and a set of car keys with a *Grease* logo.

It was too late. She was lost to him, swallowed by the night. His heart twisted in his chest. Maybe this was for the best. After all, they were nothing alike. But he'd been running, too, for a long time, running scared from any chance of ever being hurt. But what if the parts where he and Tuesday differed were what made them fit together, like matching pieces?

He raked a hand over his head and sucked in a breath.

He had her car keys. She was traveling by foot, and the most direct way home was up Forever Lane.

"Mayor!" Councilman Merryfox barreled around the corner, brandishing a cigar. "I stepped out for a smoke. Care to join me? I wanted to hear your thoughts on the proposed vacation rental ordinance and—"

"Call Karen." Beau strode to his motorcycle. "We can face-to-face next week."

"Next week? But this is urgent." The older man's jowls shook with indignation.

"No." Beau slung his leg over the seat, dropped the purse in the pannier, and fired the engine. "*This* is urgent."

And he tore into the dark.

His headlights hit her after six blocks. He pulled to the curb and turned off the ignition. "I'm taking it as a positive that you didn't dive into those bushes." He nodded at the hedgerow. No doubt she'd heard him coming. Without the headlights, it was impossible to decipher her expression. No moon tonight, but that only made the stars shine brighter.

"You probably think I'm crazy," she muttered.

"Let's be clear." He removed his helmet. "I definitely think you're crazy. But here's the important thing. I think I like it."

"Wait." She lifted a hand, her voice veering toward shrill. "Hear me out before you say another word."

He slid off the seat and stood, hands digging into his pockets.

"Do you mind stepping under the streetlight?" she asked.

He complied, freezing at her drawn-out groan.

"In that tux you've got such a James Bond look going on. Let me stand here a moment and soak up the view." At last she heaved a sigh. "Thanks. Now, where was I?"

"I'm not supposed to be saying a word."

"Right." She stepped forward, close enough to reveal the small furrow between her brows. "Okay, so here's the deal. You are bewitched."

"I agree." He reached and took her hand, resting his thumb on her wrist. Her accelerated pulse hammered his skin.

"For real." She tried to pull back from his inexorable grasp. "I'm dead serious."

"Me too." Instead, he wrapped his other hand around her waist with gentle force. She was close, but not nearly close enough. He wanted her skin to skin, to slide into her secrets, to know her inside and out.

"Don't dismiss me." Her hands splayed on his chest, not exactly pushing him off, but not inviting him closer.

"I wouldn't dare." A dark rumble rolled through his chest.

"I'm trying to tell you the truth. There's a small but real chance that you aren't of sound mind." She fisted the ornate necklace and dangled it under his nose. "You're probably under a magical spell. I'm sorry. Madam Magna said it would make me irresistible, and I wanted to talk to you about the park. That's the whole reason why I came tonight. But then you had to go and be nice. And you had to go and look..." She dropped the necklace and tweaked his bow tie. "All of that. But I don't want to enchant you into anything more. There. I know I sound silly, but my conscience is clear."

"Let me get this straight." He pulled her the last inch closer, the speed to the motion making her gasp. "That necklace you're wearing is magical and it's the reason I'm standing here?"

"Maybe. Maybe not. Oh, I don't know!" she cried. "Go on. Tell me this is the dumbest thing you've ever heard and ride off back to your life."

His jaw tensed. "Can't do that."

A pause. "So you think it *is* magic?"

"Fuck the necklace. You're the magic."

Her mouth parted in surprise, and he used it to his advantage. Her lips were cool and slightly sweet, hints of plum and juniper. He groaned, dipping back ever so slightly to settle her weight on his. Her breasts strained against his chest, and her hands laced at the base of his neck. He moved with slow intent to her cheek. Her neck. Her ear. Their breath grew more and more ragged. Never did he ever want to be anywhere but here, on the corner of Forever and Always. Here the future was bright. Here the best days of his life still waited.

"Someone will see us," she gasped.

"Don't care." Let Janice make a video and send the file "reply all" to every city department. Let the *Back Fence* put a snapshot on a ten-foot billboard on the Everland outskirts.

"There's got to be statute about public decency, and I'd hate to break it with the mayor in the middle of the historic district."

She had a point. Because at the rate they were going, he was going to have her naked and up against the stop sign.

"Come home with me," he rumbled.

"Is that wise?"

"Sounds genius." He grazed the sides of her dress, teasing her soft breasts. No bra. Fuck. The satin feel to her skin killed him without even trying.

She shivered. "But what about the necklace? What I said..."

He took her face between his hands. "Do you wear that necklace every hour of every day?"

"Madam M loaned it for tonight. Who knows where she got it? It's some heirloom—"

"Stop." He nipped her lower lip. "Take a breath. If you haven't been wearing that necklace since you arrived in town, then there's no magic. Because since the first moment I saw you, it's been impossible to think of anything else."

Her lids fluttered as she absorbed the impact of his words. "If we go, we won't stop at kissing."

"We'll go as fast or as slow as *you* want. And I've got to say, I hope you pick slow." His circled that silky skin with his thumbs, grinning at her muffled moan. He wanted to take his time. Use every hour of the night. Then he got an idea. "Tell you what. I do want you to come home. But on a date."

"Date?"

"I'm baking you the world's best chocolate soufflé."

"At midnight?" She arched a brow.

"That crazy enough for you?"

Her grin stretched ear to ear. "You know what? I think it just might be."

Chapter Twenty-Five

Beau helped Tuesday off his bike. Her dress was held up by two straps, each tied together with a tight knot. His Eagle Scout training could serve a purpose tonight. It would take short work to peel off that scrap of silk. No alchemy of starlight was responsible for the soft glow across her face, but his carriage house security lights. Still, the effect wasn't rendered any less magical.

She held on to his hand, her fingers grazing his tux jacket. "What tricks do you have up your sleeve, Mr. Mayor?"

He spun her in a twirl, and instead of feeling like an idiot, he found himself laughing. Christ, he was drunk on the balmy night air and his proximity to this beguiling woman. They danced a moment to invisible music before he whispered, "I'm not one for tricks or secrets."

She paused, resting her face on his cheek with a sage expression. "Oh, come on. I'm sure you have a few skeletons in that impeccably ordered closet of yours. I'll show you one or two of mine if you show me yours."

Her strap slipped a fraction down her shoulder, and he bit the inside of his bottom lip. He could think of plenty he wanted her to show him.

"I'll go first." She scrunched up her face, concentrating intently.

He took advantage of her closed eyes, drinking in every detail of her beautiful face. Normally, he spent so much time trying *not* to look that this unexpected opportunity was like staring at the sun. Afterward her face would be imprinted on everything.

"Okay! Oh my God, I've got a real doozy. Ready?"

He chuckled, smoothing an errant hair from her cheek. "I'm braced for anything from highway robbery to the fact you are an actual princess from a lost realm." A muscle twitched in his jaw. When the fuck was the last time he had been whimsical? Maybe never.

She took a deep breath and let it out through her nose. "When I was six I tried to kill a man."

Beau choked. "Beg your pardon?" This woman would keep him on his toes forever.

"Don't run." She gripped him tighter. "I'm exaggerating."

"Good. I was starting to worry. Especially after our run-in at the Roxy."

"He wasn't a man; he was a kid from a nearby property. Ernest Bloom." She spoke his name like a true nemesis.

He arched a brow. "That's another joke, right?"

"Oh no." She shook her head with mock gravitas. "He used to try to kiss my sister on the school bus. She *hated* it and the grown-ups just shook it off like 'boys will be boys.'

Anyway, Ernest followed her everywhere, and one day I had had enough and found a rock on the playground, a big fat stone, and balanced it up on the monkey bars. Then I taunted him to chase me. I decided that I would swing up and push it onto his dumb head. He took the bait and I did. Except it missed."

"Jesus Christ. Remind me not to get on your bad side."

"Just don't mess with the people I love." She drifted off, looking thoughtful. "I didn't really understand what it meant. 'Killing a man' was an expression that I heard about from the country-western movies my father watched. Glad I didn't succeed though. Black and white stripes would not be a good look on me."

"Did he ever mess with Pepper again?"

She grinned. "Last I heard he was at the seminary training to be a priest."

He whistled. "Impressive."

"Scared him straight." She dusted her hands. "Okay, your turn."

"This might be hard to believe, but I was a wound-up kid."

"Shocking." She giggled.

"One summer we spent in Bermuda, at my gran's place in Hamilton. I used to not be able to walk down the sidewalk without stopping and tracing my finger over every crack. Got so bad Gran didn't want to take me anywhere. And if she did, she kept her handbag ready to give me a smack."

"That's terrible!" She pursed her lips in sympathy, all humor eclipsed. "How old were you?"

"Probably the same age you were when trying to send Ernest Bloom into an untimely grave. I think it was the change. This might come as a shock to you, but I'm not so good with change."

Tuesday slapped her cheeks, eyes wide with feigned astonishment.

He turned to take in the vast home. "Mama had talked about selling this place. Moving us to the island forever. I missed Georgia, I guess. Home. Everland. Rhett was like a brother to me."

"No brothers and sisters?"

"Mama had three miscarriages. I stuck. I'm tenacious like that."

"You love her a lot." It wasn't a question.

"I do. But..." He threaded his fingers together. They had been still so long the security light switched off. The darkness made talking easier. "Guess this is a secret too. I'm not sure how much room there was in her and Dad's relationship for me, if that makes sense? I know they love me. Hell, they even like me, and not because they're supposed to. Except they're a tight unit and there's not always room for another person. It's weird, being the third wheel in your own family." He shook his head, walking again. The light flicked back on. "Nah. Don't listen to me. I'm being stupid."

"No!" Tuesday stamped her heel on the path. "Stop it right there, mister! There is no apologizing during secret sharing. That's the first rule."

"And here I thought you weren't big on rules."

"Ha! Look at you perking up," Tuesday said in a teasing tone. "My life's not total anarchy. Of course there're rules. And here's one more. You don't share what you learn in secret sharing. No sharing and no apologizing. Look. I have two rules."

"I'm impressed. Plus I'm still scared of you and that rock."

"Just don't kiss my sister and you will be safe."

"No way will I piss off you *and* Rhett." An idea occurred to him and he took off his bow tie. "I want to blindfold you before we get inside."

She chewed her top lip. "Do secrets bring out your kinky side?"

Good thing the night hid the heat staining his ears. "It's been a long time since I've been on a date with a woman that I'm interested in. I want to do it right. Be romantic."

She allowed him to cover her eyes. Her mouth quirked. "Just saying, kinky can be romantic."

And when he stepped back, taking in her curls, that dress, the curve to her shoulders, the dip to her waist, his fantasies whorled through his mind in one disorienting kaleidoscope. And he knew she was right.

* * *

"Okay. You can remove the bow tie."

Tuesday blinked at the kitchen counter. The stainless-steel mixer gleamed in the glow of the hanging barn light. A bag of flour. Bittersweet chocolate. Eggs. Sugar. Whole milk. "You weren't kidding."

Beau shook his head gravely, turning the oven to 375 degrees. "I never kid about my chocolate soufflé."

"Lesson learned." Clearly he didn't know she and kitchens tended not to mix. She eyed his fine ass as he bent to retrieve a pot from the cabinet. It took all her willpower not to bite her knuckles.

He grinned, a sudden smile that hit her like an unexpected rainstorm. "As much as I'd like to sit back and take in the moment that Miss Tuesday Knight admits she was incorrect on something, in this case, I want to work together."

"Baking a soufflé? Isn't that like taking a beginner skier down a double black diamond?"

He shrugged. "Wouldn't know. Not a snow fan."

"Stop the presses! I think we found something we have in common. Wait, two things." She picked up the bar of bittersweet chocolate. "I do love middle-of-the-night desserts."

"Maybe we should quit while we're ahead."

"Wait! There is a third. Kissing. We both like kissing."

His left eyebrow rose slightly higher than his right. That was the tell. He kept his face such a careful study. Except that eyebrow always went a few millimeters up when he was uncertain. The fact warmed her head to toe.

"Yeah. You heard me." It was easier to tease than be serious. Admit something real and heavy flowed beneath the light undercurrent of banter. "We're good at this."

"We are." His voice was husky. "Experts even."

The space between them charged. It would take three steps, four max, to close the difference. See if they could kiss well here, too. And they were alone. It wouldn't have to stop there.

"I'm nervous." The tightness in his tone backed up the muscles bunching near the hinge in his jaw. And the simple, honest admission did something to her that no amount of flirtatious back-and-forth ever would.

"So am I." She began buttering the dish. "Who taught you how to cook?"

He stirred the chocolate in the double boiler, hands clenching the spoon. "Mama used to say that a man needed to know three things: how to fix a dessert, iron his own shirt, and sew a button. That someday future women would thank her."

"Smart lady." Tuesday laughed, grateful for a moment to recalibrate, to slow her racing heart. "I suck at ironing, by the way."

Beau gave her a resolute stare. "I make my own starch."

"Stop." She nearly dropped the dish towel. "No, you don't."

"One tablespoon of cornstarch in two cups of water."

Her gaze fixed on the rare smile tugging the corner of his mouth. The revelation was oddly endearing. "I'm not sure whether to be impressed or terrified."

"Your mama didn't teach you these things?"

Tuesday thought. "We grew up in small-town Maine."

"Sounds cold."

"So, so cold. So much snow. So much cold. Beautiful though."

"I'd like to check it out, in summer."

"Yeah, good idea. My dad ran a maple sugar bush farm, made homemade maple syrup. Mom was his opposite. He loved being outdoors. She liked being inside. I guess they were opposites. They must have attracted at some point, but over time they repelled each other, pushed each other further and further away. She left when I was in high school. Moved down to New Hampshire, where she was from, and met a banker. They live in the suburbs. She has a housekeeper now."

"She abandoned your family?"

"I...you know, I don't know. My sister thinks so. I was the baby. My mom used to love to style my hair. She could do so many intricate braids. We didn't have much money, but she'd shop at thrift stores and garage sales and find me cute dresses. Sometimes I'd find her sad and I'd try to cheer her up. I'd ask her to brush my hair and she would, even though sometimes I could hear her sniffling and I knew if I turned around I'd see her crying."

Tears sprang to her eyes and she ground her fists into them. "Wow. Hello! Where'd these come from?" God, way to keep things light. Her inconvenient emotions would probably sink the night.

"I'm sorry that happened."

"Me too." She took a breath. Then another. "Can we return to the regularly scheduled programming? Chocolate is always the cure."

Beau looked like he might press forward but changed his mind at the last moment. "My mama taught me how to separate yolks from whites. Can I show you?"

"I won't pretend that I have skills. Instruct away."

"Okay, pick an egg, any egg."

She selected a brown one and he stepped behind her, her back heating against his chest. His arms slid over hers. "Now, what you do is give it a tap to open the shell. No! Not so big, just a little one." His hand engulfed hers, guiding the movement. "Good. That's real good. Now let the yolk settle in one side. That's it. Now you start to transfer the egg back and forth and back and forth, let the white run out like that until voilà! All you have left is the yolk."

Tuesday gawked at the golden yolk in the shell. "Martha Stewart, eat your heart out."

He checked the chocolate and milk; it had melted down into a decadent pool.

"Can we eat that as is? I'm sure the soufflé is amazing and all, but hey, a bowl of melted warm chocolate is going to do me fine."

His laugh was just as decadently rich. "Haven't you ever heard that good things come to those who wait?"

"Sure, by people waiting," she quipped. "They need something to tell themselves."

That really got him going, his deep laugh rich as sun-warmed molasses. "Let me make you a deal."

"I'm not agreeing until I hear the terms."

"Smart woman. When you have this dessert, you are going to say it's better than the best sex you've ever had."

She set her hands on her hips. "You have a low opinion of my sex life."

"Nah." He winked. "Just a very high opinion of my soufflé."

She arched a brow. "You're on."

Standing behind her he continued to help guide her effortlessly through measurements and pouring, mixing and stirring. He didn't grind on her or get perverted, not that she'd have minded. Chocolate was meant to be an aphrodisiac, and she'd never experienced anything so sexily mundane as chatting over nothings in the kitchen with a man who didn't try to cop a feel. He appreciated and even savored her for who she was and what she offered, which right now was fully dressed, fairly polite company.

In fifteen minutes he opened the oven and slid the soufflé in.

"And now?"

"We wait," he answered. "Until it's puffed on top and jiggly in the center."

"You have a way of making cooking sexy."

"Do I? I guess that helps even the field."

"How so?"

"You make breathing look sexy." His gaze lingered on

hers for a few beats before he turned and began to wash the dishes.

She stared at the back of his head, his broad shoulders, his narrow hips, blinking in surprise. He seemed wholly unaware that he'd broken her heart and put it back together, refashioned it into something new, stronger, and brighter.

Chapter Twenty-Six

"**H**ey! Back away slowly." Beau spun around, hands covered in dish suds.

Tuesday sprang back from the oven door. "You sure it's not done?"

He dried his hands. "Five more minutes."

"Smells like heaven." She inhaled deeply. "If heaven were made of chocolate." Her small breasts rose and fell in her dress. They fascinated him. Those perfectly proportioned pale orbs. Her skin was so fair, almost translucent along the undersides of her arms. Is that how her skin would be, peaking into two pale nipples? He imagined taking one into his mouth, worshipping it while she gripped his hair and rocked back her head. Sucking until she lost that challenging smile. Until she begged for mercy. And he wouldn't stop until—

The timer beeped.

"Ready!" She clapped her hands in delight.

"Ready," he echoed thickly, swallowing to rid his body of the hoarse need. Christ. It had been seven years since he'd touched a woman. Who was he kidding? There was a good chance that he wouldn't last long enough to get his pants off his hips.

"Look at that. You made that," she said as he pulled it out. "That's Instagram worthy." He sliced a piece and smothered it with whipped cream, dotting a dollop on her lip.

"Hashtag, winning at food. You like whipped cream? I should have asked."

"Everything is better with whipped cream."

He felt her naughty wink deep in his dick.

She licked her lips clean with a groan that made him rock hard. "Hashtag, Is this dessert better than the best sex I've ever had?"

He watched, captivated, as she dipped fork prongs into the rich crust, scooped a bite, and brought it to her lips. When her mouth parted, there was a glimpse of tongue.

"So what's the verdict?" he asked huskily.

"Good." She dabbed her lips with the side of her index fingers, wiping away invisible crumbs. "The best thing my mouth has ever tasted."

"Better than sex?"

"I have to say yes, but with a caveat." She pretended to consider, pursing her lips into a mock pout. "Better than any sex I've had...yet."

* * *

Tuesday licked her dry lips. They'd shared kisses before. But this was different. Them. Alone. No one in the world knew where they were, and the night stretched out with end-less possibilities.

"Is this what you want?" he asked. "I'm not taking this any further unless you say yes."

Did she want him?

He watched her behind the invisible line that separated friend from enemy, man from lover, want from need.

She'd wanted men in the past, and when she'd gotten them, it hadn't been healthy. This wasn't wanting. Wanting meant never being full or whole. She didn't want him to forget herself. She wanted to kiss him to remember the old magic, the fairy-tale promise she'd held in the deepest part of her. She couldn't tell him that. That was her place, her small hidden castle, but maybe tonight could help take her back there. This was less about wanting and more about be-lieving.

How do you say that to someone? You can't, but you can show them.

"I need you."

He shook his head. "Needs are about surviving. Want?" He raised his hand and grazed his knuckles over her clavi-cle. "Wants are living. Wants are pleasure. Do you want to live, Tuesday? Do you want pleasure?"

"Who'd say no?"

"You might. I don't just want to touch you here." His hand dropped, skimming the side of her breast. "I want to touch you here." He rested a hand on her heart.

"You already have," she whispered.

The first kisses were slow, soft, no more than a whisper, a brush, a promise. Such a slight touch, and yet she shivered because, oh God, those lips were made to kiss a woman, and tonight she was it. Their kiss meshed and melded.

She wound her arms around his broad shoulders, knotting her fingers behind his neck as he bracketed her waist, his thumbs flirting with her hip bones. Strength coiled inside him, powerful, commanding.

Maybe even.

She wasn't sure what that meant...the maybe even. She didn't want to think about it for fear it would pop faster than a soap bubble.

Instead, she rolled her pelvis up, a fraction, a small grinding flirt.

His voice was barely a whisper. "Tuesday. Christ. I love what you're doing to me."

"And we haven't even gotten started." Her nipples were hard and hot beneath her light dress.

"Oh, we're started, babe. We got started the minute I first set eyes on you. There is nothing sexier than a woman who isn't afraid to be herself." He dipped beneath her skirt, his fingers sliding to the crease at the bottom of her ass, playing with the lacy ruffle. "You are fearsome."

"You're pretty fierce yourself."

He pinned her with his heavy-lidded gaze. She was addicted to the color of his eyes, the icy blue almost Arctic except for the depth and warmth. A wonder she ever found them cold.

When his mouth covered hers again, his tongue tangled with hers, and she was filled with a sweetness that had nothing to do with chocolate. She barely had time to process before he was probing, nipping, and sucking her in.

And this was only his mouth. Imagine what the rest of him could do.

She rocked her hips into his again, and he lifted her off the ground. Her feet had nowhere to go except around his waist as he carried her through the kitchen, down the hall, and into his bedroom.

Except they didn't move to the bed. He walked her straight into the wall. Never in her wildest fantasies had she imagined Beau Marino dropping to his knees for her. Her palms splayed the plaster while he massaged her inner thighs, urging her to widen, to open, licking the crease on either side of where she wanted him most. No. He didn't lick her there. He didn't even kiss her. Instead he breathed on her sensitive skin. Slow, hot caresses that who knew could feel so good, almost as good as, and then there it was. The first kiss. The big lick. There was absolutely nothing tentative about it. Slow and ruthlessly steady. From his groan of approval, he savored every second.

She stared into the pitch-black, giving herself over to sensations that she hadn't wanted to let herself believe were real. Guys had done this before. Sometimes it had felt good. But this. This wasn't good. He sucked deeply and good Lord, he owned her in this moment. Her legs shook, quivering from thigh to ankle. Then he had them over his shoulders and this couldn't be happening, except it was.

No part of her touched the ground. His mouth meshed to her body as if she were something rare and delicious, demanding she give in. Give over to pleasure. And so she gave up need and want and simply became, rocking against his face in a building frenzy until he slipped a finger inside her, then another, and pressed forward in a come-hither gesture, and she obeyed. As he sucked and nibbled, his hands migrated to her ass, and he carried her to the bed at last.

She unbuttoned his shirt—well, that was a fancy word for "tore it apart." A few buttons might have been sacrificed, but he didn't even seem to notice. He could do her like that, lit from the hall's diffuse light, which seemed to capture the gleam in his pale eyes. This whole suit thing really worked for her. She sat up. "My turn." And before he could argue, her mouth was on his nipple, the hard, flat point, and oh God, those muscles. She needed to worship the muscles. The salty sea air imbedded in his skin.

He had gotten a condom on, and they knelt across from each other, breathing hard.

"Tue—shit. It's been so long. I might not last."

"If I don't feel you in me, I'm going to start begging," she said.

"I think that's something I'd enjoy. But not tonight." He pushed her back on the bed and was above her, his strong shoulders flexed, his belly against her, hard and rippled and sheened in sweat. There was a faint sucking sound as he angled himself into place, and he pushed slowly, excruciatingly, tenderly slowly, a few inches inside.

"More," she begged. "More."

"You feel magical," he ground out. Then he went deeper and deeper until there was nowhere else to go. He filled her utterly and stared. She closed her eyes, and even still he could feel his eyes looking at her, taking her in, and there was nowhere to hide anymore, no part to play except for herself. She wasn't the sex kitten or the innocent. She wasn't acting in a specific way to turn a guy on. She was just Tuesday, and from the feeling of the thick, hot stretch between her legs, he seemed to like that just fine. He withdrew a few inches and came home again. More than fine. She let him do that a few times before she gathered up the courage to open her eyes. To look back. And what she saw there took her breath away.

He appeared full of wonder. Amazed. And she wasn't the

only one who couldn't believe this. She let out a whimper. "Like that?" he asked.

"So much."

He appeared determined to get her to make the sound again. Which she did. Many times over.

His movements lost their control, took on a desperate rhythm, and soon her legs draped his shoulders. Their skin slapped as their breath came short and fast.

"I can't. I can't. I can't hold on," he ground out.

"You don't have to," she cried. Because somehow she was there, too, ahead of him, dropping off a cliff. His fingers knotted with hers, and they went in tandem. Down they fell, crying out, capturing each other's moans. The mattress squeaked as he dug his knees in to get better purchase, to go further, and he got there, and for one infinitesimal moment they were bare to each other, naked in need, offering themselves at their most basic, at their core, and for the hot, pulsing moment, it was more than enough. It was pure magic.

Chapter Twenty-Seven

Beau blinked in the dim dawn light. Tuesday talked in her sleep. No complete sentences, but in the past five minutes she had said the words "golf ball," "agreed," and "nozzle." What was she dreaming about? And "nozzle"? She'd fallen asleep in his arms, cheek resting on his chest. He'd held her close, not wanting to speak, not wanting to break the strange magic that hung in the space. And before he knew it, her breathing had deepened, and here she was, twitching and dreaming.

What must it be like to be Tuesday Knight? To give herself over to experiences? To trust so deeply. Here she was when he'd given her reasons to doubt, and she trusted him enough to fall asleep with him. To give him the secrets of her day. He knew she had been with other men. But tonight he knew she let him in somewhere private. He knew because he'd done the same.

She nestled in deeper, releasing a happy sigh as he

settled a hand on her waist, her ass soft against his groin.

He sucked in a breath, not wanting to wake her up with a pushy erection. It took a moment to realize she rocked back and forth in a subtle shimmy—tormenting him on purpose.

"You're asking for trouble." He reached for a breast, the nipple tip already stiff across his palm. Add "responsiveness" to the long list of things he was starting to love about Tuesday Knight.

"Not asking." She rolled to face him. Her fingers traced his happy trail down, down, down, until he turned to granite in her hand. "Begging."

"That a fact?"

"Uh-huh." She rose, cheeks flushed. "How do you want me? On my knees begging?" She hooked one leg over his waist, straddling him with an unselfconsciously playful grin. No scurrying off to fix hair or add makeup.

"Sounds good to me." Nothing sexier than a woman comfortable in her skin. And what skin it was, creamy silk he couldn't quit touching. Each caress unlocked a new secret, led to a new mystery. Would she moan if he stroked the curving flesh of her inner thigh? Gasp if he peppered the concave plane of her stomach with gentle kisses? Buck if he took her ass in a firm grip? Sigh if he slid his tongue between her soft intimate folds and sucked in her sweet nub?

"I am supposed to be pleasing you," she protested after a groaning moan. "That's why I hopped up here."

"You think this doesn't give me pleasure?" He gave another slow, savoring lick.

"This seems selfish."

"This is me at my most selfish." He swirled and kissed, thrusted and sucked. There was nothing better. He slid a finger into her heat, pressing hard until she came apart.

He got on a new condom and she slid down, sheathing herself in one grinding rock. Their bodies joined like the easiest thing in the world. The dawn light spilled through the partially closed curtain, catching the gold chain on her neck, the gold burnishing her hair. Hope flooded him. This was what he'd been looking for, and here he'd found it in the most unexpected place. Easy and perfect. Perfect and easy. He sank into heaven. He braced his hand on her waist, guiding her to the tempo, letting her set the rhythm.

Fuck, he loved this. Watching her find pleasure. It was so easy, the way their bodies moved together.

Her head flung back, and together they soared.

When he opened his eyes again, it was noon. He blinked. No. Impossible. He blinked again, but the alarm clock on the nightstand didn't change. The numbers "12:00" shone back.

Shit. He scrambled to sitting and checked for his phone. It wasn't there. Double shit. He must have left it in the kitchen. Today was a conference call with the Tourism Commission. He had the PowerPoint pitch prepared.

He threw on his boxers. Tuesday was nowhere to be seen.

He ran down the stairs and wrinkled his nose, assaulted by the smell of something burning. Then the fire alarm went off.

"Shit," she yelped after a *bang*. He quickened his pace.

Tuesday stood in his tuxedo shirt on a kitchen chair, banging at the fire alarm with a broom handle.

"Sorry," she called as the alarm stopped. "I couldn't reach."

The kitchen was a mess. Cracked eggshells lined the table, as well as grated cheese and some badly chopped mushrooms. "What's going on?"

"I made you breakfast in bed. Or at least that was the plan. I have eaten enough omelets in my day that I didn't think it was going to be hard. Turns out I was wrong."

"I admire the sentiment," he said, and he did. His kitchen was a disaster zone, but who cared? He could clean it later. There were more pressing concerns.

"My alarm clock didn't go off." He buttoned his shirt. "I never sleep in. There's a meeting and I'm late."

"Oh, the alarm," she trailed, her expression guilty. "I might have turned it off."

"What?"

"You looked like you could use more sleep. Plus, we were up, you know, all night long. Are you mad?"

"Of course not." He bent his lips in a smile, but his frown remained hidden on the inside. Who turned off alarms without checking? "Just not used to having other people here." And she didn't know his schedule. What today meant for him.

"I can't offer you a omelet for the road, but I can fix you peanut butter and toast. The breakfast—or lunch—for any champion."

"Sounds good."

"Good." She leaned to kiss him and he tried to snuff out the flicker of doubt. She hadn't meant to do anything wrong, but that didn't change that his day had just gotten a lot fucking harder.

Easy? Had he really thought being with Tuesday would be easy?

Because it might be anything but.

* * *

She kept her arms wrapped around Beau as they passed the WELCOME TO EVERLAND sign on his Ducati. He slowed to the school speed limit, and she took the opportunity to shout, "What's that?" pointing to the over-the-street banner: HARVEST FESTIVAL THIS WEEKEND: PIE BAKE-OFF, SPELLING BEE, QUILT AUCTION, AND MORE."

"Isn't it self-explanatory?"

It was actually. She could fill in the blank with what would be in the "more" category, but dammit, he'd barely said a word since breakfast.

"You can drop me at my house."

He turned on Forever Lane, and in the light of day it looked like a street, a pretty street full of old houses tiered like wedding cakes, but nothing particularly magical. And there was the corner of Always. "Mother, Father," she muttered. Pepper and Rhett stood there with Kitty and the three golden retrievers that she could never quite tell apart.

One peed on a hydrant to extinguish every last hope of a potential romantic reenactment moment.

They glanced up at the sound of the bike. Pepper's eyes went as wide as her mouth. Rhett looked at her. She looked at him. And Tuesday decided nothing had ever been as interesting as the back of Beau's head. They hadn't gone ten seconds before she felt her phone vibrate in her bodice, because yes, she was still wearing her ball gown.

She could see the text now. OMG WHAT HAVE YOU DONE? OR SHOULD I SAY…WHO HAVE YOU DONE?

Talk about a bike of shame.

When they pulled onto Love Street, of course Miss Ida May stood in the middle of her driveway, and because bad luck comes in threes, she was flanked by her two partners in crime, Phaedra and Lucille.

So much for any hope of a quiet good-bye kiss. These three biddies were going to make this situation front-page news on their blog before lunch.

"This isn't good," she said as he killed the engine.

"Not really," he answered.

She couldn't get a look at his eyes in those damn Ray-Ban sunglasses. Her own face reflected back, and as she unbuckled the helmet he'd provided for her, it became obvious she had a serious case of bed head. Less polite folk might even be tempted to refer to the look as freshly fucked.

"I have got to go. I'm running late, and Karen is going to have to reschedule the call if I don't—"

"Of course, go! Please. You don't owe me an explanation," she said. But what did he owe her…and what did she owe him?

He nodded toward the trio currently gaping as if Santa Claus and the Easter Bunny had appeared, but he held her gaze. "Good luck handling that."

She didn't really have a choice. "Thanks," she said. The word left a strange taste.

"I'll call you," he said distractedly, and then he was gone.

That's when she realized the flavor; it was bitterness.

Of course Beau had somewhere he had to be, but he'd

also spent the night with her, and sometimes, given the situation, plans could be adjusted. And not only had he dropped her off like a special-order delivery, but he'd done it in plain view of the three biggest gossips in town.

And had he stayed to smooth things over?

No. No, he hadn't.

Her sister rounded the corner, although as she held the leashes for three dogs, it was hard to tell who was walking who. Rhett came up behind with another.

Phaedra, Lucille, and Miss Ida May huddled together. She couldn't hear what they were saying, but all outbursts of "law law" and "I declare" suggested high emotions were involved.

All she had to do was paste on a smile, flounce her skirt, and be her brightest, shiniest, most princessy self. She could concoct a silly story about how she was locked out of her car and Beau offered to take her home, but then he'd simply had to show her something or other at Belle Mont and one thing led to another and she fell asleep on his couch.

No one would want to believe it, so by feeding them a story, she gave them an out.

Let them play pretend.

Except, you know what? She didn't want to. She didn't have it in her.

She had had the best night of her life and somehow had woken up from the dream to find herself in, not a nightmare, not quite, but in one of those dreams where you walk and walk and never end up anywhere.

Beau had slept and scrammed. And she felt scammed. And right now all she wanted to do was get out of this dress, get in the shower, and have a good long cry.

So she didn't pretend to smile. She didn't wave at the neighbors. She didn't even wait for her sister.

She turned around, walked into the empty house, and locked the door, but it didn't make a difference. The vase of fresh cut daisies on her coffee table mocked her. No point destroying a perfectly pretty flower when she already knew the answer.

He loved her not.

Chapter Twenty-Eight

Ma Hogg rocked in her porch swing perusing the paper. The *Hogg Jaw Herald*'s headline took up half the page: TEN THINGS TO KNOW ABOUT THE NOROVIRUS. A cloud of dust kicked up the road, slowing near her mailbox. What fool would interrupt her when Southern Woman's Gospel Hour was on Everland Radio?

Everland Radio.

"Ha!" She snorted before taking a slow sip of sweet tea. Once she was finished it would be Hogg Jaw Radio. Soon, so soon, her town would get its due and those Everland snobs would be stuck crying into their peach pie.

She raised her bifocals from the silver chain around her neck. Humph Miller's Cadillac bounced down her driveway. He drove too fast, kicking stones into her flower beds. "There's a man I'd unplug from life support to charge my phone," she muttered to her hens while reaching for the .22

perched against the railing. The warning shot struck off the front bumper.

A grinding filled the air, the sound of brakes locking. "Son of a biscuit." Humph Miller jumped out of the driver's side door. "Are you crazy? You just shot me."

"Heavens to Betsy, *this* is shooting at you." She fired again, this time taking out his front wheel. "That's for blasphemy, and for being a numbnut."

"You know what? You're crazy as a pet coon under a red wagon." His nose matched the shade of a fresh-boiled beet. "Yeah. I finally said it. Someone needs to lock you away from the decent people."

She set her sights and took aim again. "Tell me, is that what you are, Humphrey Miller? A decent person?" The bullet took off his passenger-side mirror.

Humphrey made a strangled sound. "I love this car like it's one of my own kids."

"And I loved my daddy. He's the one who taught me how to shoot cans off the fence post when I was knee-high to a grasshopper. You know what else? He taught me that a man should respect a woman. Did you get the mayor to sign off on condemning the park last night?"

"What? No." He frowned in confusion.

She raised the gun again. "That's 'ma'am' to you, boy."

"No, ma'am," he ground out. "He left before we had a chance to corner him."

"Who'd he leave with?"

"Sounds like you already know." He grimaced, forcing out the word. "Ma'am."

"I want to hear you say it." Her tone was deadlier than her aim.

"With that Happily Ever After Land princess. The pretty

blond Joe Wilcox asked to work as a lobbyist. Mayor Marino chased after her on his motorcycle."

"And before he ran off to be...lobbied...who else was he engaged in conversation with?"

Humph looked flummoxed by her game of Twenty Questions. "No one of importance comes to mind."

"That's because while Beau Marino and the head of the Georgia Tourism Commission were locked in a deep and meaningful conversation, you played 'Sink the Sausage' in the coatroom with your intern."

His eyes bugged. "How did you—"

"You ever wonder why I gave you a shot at the big leagues?"

He opened his mouth.

"This was a rhetorical question, Monkey Breath. Look up the word when you get home." She sat back, savoring the moment. "Oh, on second thought, you don't have a home. Not anymore."

"What did you do?" His underbite became more pronounced.

"You got a shot at locking up the Discount-Mart deal because your long-suffering saint of a wife's granny hailed from these parts. LaWanda Foster sang in the Halfway Baptist Choir for fifty years, the star of the soprano section. Now"—she frowned, momentarily losing her trail of thought—"where was I?"

He opened his mouth again.

"I said, don't speak. The whole point of a rhetorical question is to make a statement, not elicit information." She lowered the gun. "The Fosters have been in Hogg Jaw nearly as long as the Hoggs. LaWanda, God rest her soul, requested I try to help you before she passed last month. I wasn't sure, and warned you not to make a mess of things. And what did you go and do?"

A pause.

"Go on, then. This time I'm not being rhetorical."

"I tried to do—"

"Aw, forget it." Ma Hogg waved her hand in derision. "Quit your yapping."

"I did my best." He twisted his hands. "I'm telling you, I did my best."

"Yes. Bless your heart." She clicked her tongue. "And more's the pity, because it wasn't nearly good enough, sugar. Not twenty minutes ago I called your long-suffering wife."

He went so white he could blind an angel. "You did what?"

"Have I developed a stutter? Merris now knows all about how you've played your tiny blue-veined piccolo all over town. Now get out of my sight." She picked up the shotgun and leveled it again. "Last I heard, your better half was about to have one hell of a bonfire with your golf clubs."

"Please." Humph swayed, forehead sheened in sweat. "Where am I supposed to go?"

"You think that's something I have time to concern myself with? I'm busy; you're ugly. Have a nice life."

After Humph rolled off in his ruined car, Ma Hogg rose, slung the gun over one shoulder, and eyed the old apple tree near her house. It had been planted not long after her wedding day. Her mother-in-law, the old bat, had sworn back and forth and every way sideways that apple trees couldn't grow in this climate, not in the coastal humidity. That she'd proven the ornery woman wrong brought no end to her satisfaction. The tree was gnarled and stunted, but grow it did, even bearing fruit. Bitter, puny apples only good for baking, but...

"Wait a cotton-pickin' second." She hoisted the .22 and shuffled closer. "Only good for baking, eh?"

Good thing no neighbors lived for nearabouts half a mile, so no one could hear her cackle.

One didn't become the largest crime boss in the county by letting half-wits do their dirty deeds. No, if she wanted Hogg Jaw to beat out Everland as a Coastal Jewel, she'd have to roll up her sleeves and double down on playing dirty.

But first she had a newspaper to read.

Chapter Twenty-Nine

It had been a long morning. Beau's Tourism Commission phone presentation went well, but Everland wasn't out of the woods. They were competing for the last of two small-towns slots to secure the coveted Coastal Jewel designation. The problem was that the other town was Hogg Jaw.

The conversation had kept circling back to the Roxy Theater. Donna Summer and Angie Robert in particular wanted more detailed plans, ones that he fudged, but fudging made him uneasy. He preferred to deal in cold, hard facts, to provide concise information unobscured by flowery language.

As he hung up, Karen, who'd sat opposite his desk taking notes, flashed a disbelieving look.

"Think I blew it?" He removed his headset.

"Not the call." Her tone was aghast.

"What's up?"

"You abandoned the poor girl on the street?"

"Who?" He glanced at the window. There was nothing in sight but green lawn and trees exploding in autumn red-gold. A coolness spread through him, his old invisible armor. The one that protected him through all kinds of shit.

Karen shook her head, her eyes slits. "For being a so-called prince, you're a real dunce."

He swiveled back, her words finding a chink, and their meaning stung. "Can you stop speaking in riddles?"

"The *Back Fence*," she all but shouted. "I checked your e-mail during the call wrap-up and saw an alert. The article just came out."

"Article? What article?"

She rose, clutching her pen and paper. "Go on the blog yourself. You can't miss it."

He grabbed his mouse, and the movement woke his desktop. A quick search for the blog got the site. He gaped at the headline: KICKED TO THE CURB: PRINCESS DITCHED AFTER LANDING A ONE-NIGHT STAND WITH EVERLAND'S PRINCE.

There was an out-of-focus image. Tuesday stood beside his bike in her ball gown, their faces close, not actually kissing, but about to or just had.

He cursed under his breath.

Karen mashed her lips, opening her mouth twice to speak before finally seeming to find the words she sought. "Tell me you didn't sleep with that poor girl and then drop her off like so much trash."

"I had the meeting," he said flatly.

"A meeting?" Karen spread on the sarcasm. "Oh, phooey. You think that couldn't have been rescheduled?"

"It was important."

"And last night wasn't?" She frowned, crossing and re-crossing her legs. "I don't mean to tell tales out of school, Mr. Mayor, but I have seen that young woman in this office and it's clear that she wasn't just a pretty face."

"It happened fast. Too fast," he murmured. Kissing Tuesday had been bad enough. Sex? He might as well kiss common sense good-bye. Forever.

"When has love ever followed an assigned speed limit?"

"Whoa, whoa, whoa. Who said anything about love?"

"I did, you big bully. And kindly don't raise your voice at me. I went to school with your mama and can remember when you wet the bed."

"I didn't mean to cause her trouble." He'd felt uncomfortable this morning, but that wasn't fair. All through the conference call about the Roxy Theater he'd regretted his rushed exit. He'd wanted to get a little breathing space, but instead he'd ended up unmoored, drifting aimless within himself.

"Don't dodge the bullet. Part of being a real man is owning your mistakes, and this one is a doozy."

He hadn't meant to sell Tuesday out. But the road to hell was paved with good intentions.

"I have to go."

"You do. And remember, women love flowers."

He didn't stop for any of that, too focused on getting to Love Street. When he pulled up in front of her cottage, he heaved a sigh. A light shone from her bedroom.

But no one answered the door.

He knocked again, hearing her dog scratching the wood.

"Tuesday?" he murmured.

"Go away," she called.

Karen had been right. "I'm not going anywhere."

"Ha." She opened the door, the security chain latched. "Big words. Until you have another meeting."

"Guess I deserved that." He'd give up a lot in life never to see pain in Tuesday's gaze. Worse, it was a hurt he was responsible for putting there. He'd fucked up, broken her trust. But the question remained, had he broken everything between them as well?

"Guess so." She regarded him for a minute, wounded humiliation stamped on her face. It made his insides churn.

"You know, I didn't expect you to spend the day with me."

"But I should've gotten off the damn bike and walked you to the house."

The admission earned a small smile. "It ain't rocket science, just good manners."

"Would you like to come with me?" he said. "I have somewhere I want to take you."

She studied him a moment. "First, I want an apology."

He cleared his throat. "I'm sorry that I ran out of here and left you alone with the *Back Fence* biddies and your sister. I did have a full schedule, but to tell you the truth, I panicked."

"Makes sense." She glanced down at her faded THEATER KIDS DO IT BETTER T-shirt. "I am pretty frightening."

He looked around. A curtain twitched in Miss Ida May's house. "I haven't been with a woman since my wife died," he murmured. "And before she passed we'd been estranged."

Her hand went to the latch, undoing it with a turn. "I've heard a little of this."

"Not from me," he said firmly. "And while I don't like

to make a habit out of speaking ill of the dead, you need to know a few things."

She studied him. "You've intrigued me. Let's go."

A few minutes later he parked in front of the Roxy Theater.

"You didn't bring me here to hit you again, did you?"

He snorted. "No, although I'm also not saying that I don't deserve it."

The side door was opened courtesy of the fire marshal. He'd put in a call and despite misgivings had been granted access with a caveat that the floor might be unstable.

He didn't let on that he'd been in the premises recently.

They walked in, and Tuesday gasped. The hall was shadowy. Shafts of light seeped around the borders of the boarded-up windows and through cracks in the walls. "It's even prettier in the daylight. Look!" She ran up the stage stairs and took in the ceiling fresco, painted a midnight blue pinpricked by gold foil stars.

"Do you miss it?"

"Miss what?" She hummed a tune under her breath, her gaze turned to the empty seats, wistful and unfocused.

"Being onstage."

That got her attention. "Only about every five minutes or so."

"Everland is as different from New York City as it's possible to be. There're no bright lights or star-studded marquees. But how would you feel about helping to restore this old place?"

Twin lines appeared between her brows. "How?"

"What if you founded a community theater?"

"Me? Found a community theater?" She repeated it blankly.

"As a key part of the strategy that could get us over the line with the Coastal Jewel program."

"You. Over the line." Any enthusiasm had drained from her. She wasn't being overly dramatic or stamping her feet, but there was a seismic shift. Her shoulders slumped as if something vital leached from her.

He didn't know how to stop the leak.

"You don't have to." Frowning, he flipped back through their conversation, unable to pinpoint where he'd gone wrong. Somewhere he'd fucked up. "I figured you'd appreciate the career upgrade."

"Upgrade." Her eyes darkened to the color of a sea squall.

How many times had he planned dates or gifts for Jacqueline only to be met with scorn? He must have an invisible sucker tattoo on his forehead. "Will you stop parroting me and say something?"

She lost the glazed look to her eyes. "I'm happy plodding along in my life at the park. Happy enough anyway. Responsibility has a way of biting me in the butt. So I guess I'm saying thank you, but no thanks."

He'd thought she'd jump at the theater with both feet. This was supposed to make her happy. He was offering her a chance to do what she loved, and her face looked like he'd drop-kicked a puppy.

She took a deep breath. "Anyway. What did you want to tell me about your wife?"

Coldness flooded him. He'd wanted a true connection, to share his history, but how could she expect him to be open when she wouldn't do the same?

So he pretended to get a text. "It's Karen," he said, fishing out his phone to stare at the blank screen. "There's an emergency back at the office."

She didn't move. Or lift her head. "Thank you," she whispered. "Your offer was nice."

Nice? She might have well have said "meh." He gave a nod and walked toward the exit, frustration crushing his windpipe. He'd gotten so close to closing the gap with another person. Last night he'd felt a connection more than the obvious. But his confidence was shrinking by the moment.

How would he make Tuesday happy? Their edges didn't fit. And if they didn't match up, how could it work?

* * *

Tuesday listened to "Beauty School Dropout" on repeat for the next few days, her least favorite song in the entire *Grease* soundtrack. Now she got Frenchy on a deeper level. It's hard not to know what to do next, to take a chance on a dream only to crash and burn.

Beau meant well. She knew it. Earnestness had been stamped all over his face when he'd spoken the words "community theater." She loved musical theater. When she was a kid, all she'd done was belt out *The Sound of Music* around the house.

She turned off the music app and eyed her mason jar salad. The idea had looked cute on Pinterest. In reality, it was wilted lettuce stuck to rice with a few sad carrot shavings. She eyed the microwave in the corner while plucking the tiara off her head. "My kingdom for a freaking Hot Pocket?" She needed to eat her feelings, and salad wasn't going to cut it. After Beau offered her the chance to organize the community theater, it was all she could do not to burst into tears on the spot. It wasn't that it was a bad idea. In many ways it made sense, was even flattering, but that was the problem.

Her dreams had never made sense, but that's what made them so wonderful. She'd been a little girl from Moose Bottom, Maine, who was good at softball and could hold a note. She'd gotten audacious. Decided to hell with graduating high school and scooping ice cream while taking community college classes. She'd set her sights on Broadway and declared that is where she'd end up.

She didn't expect to land a Broadway show on the first try or get her Actors' Equity card. She was prepared to pay her dues through grit and hard work. She cheered every time a friend landed a national tour, and after getting drinks with another friend living to do regional work, she'd go home, look in the mirror, and remind herself that everyone had their own artistic journey. While her path was uncertain, that didn't mean it was a bad thing. She'd always done things her own way.

But in the end she'd failed. She'd taken a chance and crashed and burned her entire career.

"You feel as if you've gone in a wrong direction?" Where had Madam Magna come from?

"I'm a little lost," Tuesday admitted to the woman at the end of the table. "I tried and failed as an actress. No one said it would be easy. I had all these big goals and knew it would take hard work to make it, to live my dream. The trouble was there are others with the same one, and up at the top of the mountain there is only so much room. And not everyone can fit. After New York, I guess I lost confidence in having a place up there."

"This isn't New York," the older woman said.

"Obviously," Tuesday snapped before gesturing to the salad. "I'm sorry. I brought rabbit food for lunch. I thought that eating healthier might cheer me up, but I'd murder somebody for carbs and cheese."

Madam Magna walked to the freezer and pulled out a frozen burrito. "You like?"

"Get out of town—you eat that stuff?"

She inclined her head, her earrings making a tinkling sound. "There are times when nothing else will do."

Tuesday held up a hand. "Can I get an 'amen'?"

Madam Magna frowned and moved to the microwave rather than reciprocate the gesture.

"So what am I going to do?"

"About what?"

"My life," Tuesday said impatiently. "Isn't that your job?"

Madam Magna appeared nonplussed. "I tell people the truths they don't see."

"Okay, clue me in."

"You already know what to do."

"I do?"

"Listen to your heart; it's telling you."

"No offense, but that's the best you've got? Listen to your heart? What if my heart stays quiet and my spleen gets noisy? Or my gallbladder wants to weigh in? I let down Beau." Because she was scared. But she didn't know how to stop being scared. Or how to survive messing up in another job.

Madam Magna didn't so much as crack a smile. Tough crowd.

The microwave *ding*ed. Madam Magna removed the burrito and set it on a paper plate. "You think you are funny, girl. But when you are ready to listen, you will know what to do."

And with that she flung the lunch on the table and strode out of the room.

Chapter Thirty

—◠—

Beau muted the Falcons game and stilled, head cocked. The only sound was the soft whirl of the den's ceiling fan. His ears must have played a trick, imagined car wheels rumbling up the driveway. No one was expected, and his stern personality never invited unannounced visits.

Shaking his head, he got up and stretched his lower back before padding to the kitchen to refill his water bottle. The back door was wide open. He froze, focusing all of his senses, fighting for cool calm despite the hot surge of trepidation. It had been shut an hour ago when he'd gone in to fix a club sandwich. He remembered because he'd debated texting Tuesday and instead had chosen to step out to the home gym on the side porch for a punishing round of pull-ups. He distinctly recalled turning the lock as he'd come back inside.

An unfamiliar red car was parked by the carriage house. His heart pounded as his mind raced. "Cocksucker," he muttered, flexing his hand into a fist. Guess his hearing had been right on after all. Someone was here.

Someone was in his fucking house.

"You kiss your mama with that mouth?" a deep voice boomed before a strong forearm gripped him in a headlock.

"Hold him, Charlie. I'm grabbing the Dial," a female snapped.

He opened his mouth to holler and choked as half a bar of soap slid through his lips. The choke hold released and he landed on his knees, clawing the soap from his mouth, fumbling for his dropped water bottle to rinse out the bitter alkaline taste.

"Mama?" He blinked at the elfin woman frowning down at him, folded arms slammed across her nautical striped shirt, her ashy ponytail bobbing in disapproval. Wendy Marino was a miniature steel magnolia with the temper of a short-tailed shrew if provoked, and bad language ranked next to "chewing with your mouth open" on her list of intolerable offenses.

He might be thirty-five, but some things never changed.

"Dad?" He glanced at his father, biceps bulging beneath his skull-and-crossbones tank top. Neat gray dreads hit his chin, while a goatee framed his broad smile.

"Hey, son." His accent was a familiar blend of British, South American, and Caribbean.

"Why didn't you guys come to the front door like normal people?"

"Normal?" Mama glanced at Dad, her customary humorous expression returning. "Who does he think we are? Besides, we have a key. We're not company. We're family."

"Look at him down there cutting-de-eyes at us." Dad offered a hand up.

"Thought you'd like a surprise." Mama tackle-hugged him as he stood. "My, you've grown another inch."

Beau chuckled. "Not since I was nineteen. Maybe you're shrinking."

"There's a scary thought." Mama stared down at her pint-sized frame.

"I didn't know you were off the rock." He used his father's slang for the island. "It's been a while since you've come stateside."

"For days," Dad agreed, Bermuda slang for "a very long time." He studied the kitchen, his expression carefully neutral. "Still looks the same."

Not for the first time, Beau fleetingly wondered if his laid-back father had ever felt out of place in a classic Southern plantation house. If so, he'd never let on.

"It was high time we saw our favorite child," his mama announced.

"Your only child." He grinned as he spoke the familiar response.

"Toe-may-toe, toe-mah-toe." She rose on her tiptoes and tugged him down to plant an affectionate smack on his face.

"First you choke me, now you kiss me? What gives, woman?" He feigned an annoyed tone, wiping his cheek. This is what they did. They doted on him. He pretended it annoyed him.

He wasn't fooling anyone.

"I'll take our bags upstairs and then fix us a drink." His dad hadn't worked as a bartender in years, but that didn't mean Charlie Marino had forgotten his way around a cocktail shaker.

"And I'll powder my nose." Mama never wore makeup, but it was her long-standing euphemism for the ladies' room. She might have sailed from Everland years ago, but you could never fully take the Southern charm from her.

Beau headed into the living room, clicked off the blaring television, and gathered the stack of dirty dishes and food boxes. The long formal drapes were drawn tight despite the beautiful afternoon, and the air held a musty feeling. His stomach lurched. The place looked like shit, as if some sad sack had been holed up and wallowing away from the world.

This wasn't the picture he wanted to paint. He'd gotten himself more or less patched back together these last years.

Mama and Dad had never said a cross word about Jacqueline. They hadn't needed to. He'd noticed the worried way they'd watch him when she was around. How Mama would give an extra hug every time she left. The way Dad clapped his shoulder with a reminder that he was there if Beau ever needed anything. Anytime. All he had to do was ask.

But the words "I'm lost" and "I can't do this anymore" always formed a logjam in his throat.

That Mama had never gotten along with Jacqueline should have been a sign right off the bat. She was a woman who could befriend most everyone...like Tuesday in a way.

He stared at his pool table, pounded momentarily by a shore break of longing, dragged by a rip current of regret. Not for his ex-wife, but for the woman who'd seemed poised to be his tomorrow.

But tomorrow is promised to no man.

"I scarce believe. You've met someone?" Mama stood in the doorway, a hand pressed to her chest, staring as if she could see all the Tuesday memories tattooed in his brain.

Her laugh. Her sigh. The way she'd spun his world off its axis and left him adrift in a strange new orbit.

"How in the he...ck?" He managed to amend his language at the last moment. He set the dishes back down. "What are you talking about?"

"There are panties," she stage whispered. "In your sock drawer."

All the blood drained from his face. He wished he could join it, let the floor open into a whirlpool, suck him down. Tuesday's thong. He'd kept it in his drawer, never sure what to do with it. Seemed a waste to throw it away, but it would have been too awkward to return it.

"You had a pile of laundry on your bed. I thought I'd help put it away, but—"

"Don't worry about it."

"Worry about what?" Dad entered the room.

"Our son has found a girlfriend," Mama announced, relief plain on her face.

"No. Not a girlfriend," Beau bit back. He didn't know what she was. He was angry, at her, at himself, at the fact that they were so close to something so damn good, but they couldn't get there.

She knit her brow. "When I discovered—you know—I assumed. So, a lover, then."

He almost wished it had been violent intruders who'd broken into the house. He glanced between them, their arms casually slung around each other. "Anyway, who wants a drink again?"

His parents frowned at his deflection, but they would never understand. They fit together perfectly. A human jigsaw. The rhyme in a poem. Like milk to the cereal. Not everyone had it easy or got so lucky. And when it came to their only son and love, he couldn't be more different. He was raw, jagged edges, a discordant verse—a piece of burnt fucking toast.

* * *

Tuesday ground fists in her eyes, frowning at the time on her phone. Six thirty in the morning? Who'd ring the doorbell at such an ungodly hour? Alarm thrummed through her veins as her feet hit the carpet.

Maybe someone had gotten hurt. Maybe Pepper had tripped over one of the dogs and cracked her head against a dresser. Or maybe Miss Ida May had impaled herself on a rosebush thorn.

She stumbled faster, hand skimming the hallway wall, and reached the living room in a time that would place her on the podium in a fifty-meter-dash event.

Throwing open the screen, she stared around the empty porch. No one was there. Her wind chime tinkled in the wind. The *Everland Examiner* sat halfway up the walkway. Had some local tweens had a sleepover and decided to celebrate staying up all night with a game of Ding-Dong Ditch?

Tugging her robe closed, she stepped on the new NICE UNDERWEAR welcome mat for a better look at the side yard. Her toes bumped a wooden crate, a box brimming with red apples.

"That's random." She picked it up and looked around the empty street one last time before bringing it inside. She'd hefted the apples onto the kitchen counter and was getting out a box of cereal when there was another knock.

This place was busier than Grand Central Station.

"What now? A pail of peaches?" she muttered to Tony the Tiger.

This time someone was there. Flick stood on the porch, no black makeup smeared over her eyes, and her hair tied in a tight braid. She looked smaller, younger, and more vulnerable.

"May I come in?" she asked in an unfamiliar, subdued voice.

"Of course. Of course you can, honey," Tuesday said, closing the door behind her. "Hey, did you bring me apples a couple minutes ago?"

"Huh?"

"Never mind."

"Sorry to bother you." Flick's gaze darted around the living room as if unwilling to settle anywhere long. Her small body was wound tight. Tuesday had a sense that a single touch would fling her across the room like a shot rubber band.

"Come in the kitchen. I'll make coffee. Wait." She froze, shaking her head. "Not coffee. Um, hot milk?"

Flick snorted. "Sometimes the only thing in the cupboard was my mom's instant coffee. I learned to boil water by six years old."

The casual comment turned Tuesday's stomach. "Well, in my house you don't get it until you're old enough to drive. How about settling for a hot cocoa?"

Flick gave her a strange look. "You care what I drink?"

"Um, yes?"

"Do you have whipped cream?"

Tuesday resisted a smile. Now she was getting somewhere. "As if I'd offer you hot cocoa and not have whipped cream. And what say you to an extra-fancy peppermint stir stick? I bought a bag from What-a-Treat."

Flick grinned. "You're on."

It wasn't until she was halfway through the cocoa that Tuesday finally pressed.

"What's going on?"

"Harriet got to go back to her family yesterday." Flick twirled the peppermint stick around and around the mug. "Her mama got custody back."

"This news doesn't make you happy?"

"Of course. I'm not a monster." She broke the candy in half. "Her mom wanted her, so she cleaned up her act and jumped through every hoop."

"When did you last talk to yours?"

The girl rolled her eyes. "That woman doesn't talk. If she has anything to say, she screams it. Besides, Mrs. Boyle was talking this morning to her daughter. I heard her whispering that my mom is voluntarily terminating her rights."

"What does that mean?"

"She's giving me up." She broke the peppermint between her teeth, crunching loudly. "She doesn't want me back. Guess absence doesn't always make a heart grow fonder."

"What about your dad?"

"Good question. No clue." She pushed her empty mug away. "Mama said I look like her, and I guess she's right, 'cept I don't want to. Who wants to wake up every morning to see the face of the person who wishes that they were never born?" A strangled sound escaped. The refusal of a cry. She wouldn't give in to the impulse, because if she did she might drown.

Life didn't always have a simple beginning, middle, and end. Sometimes the story was a big, honking mess.

"Your mother is an idiot," Tuesday announced. "A donkey stuck in a pile of stupid."

Flick stared, eyes wide.

"That's right, I said it," Tuesday slammed her hands on her hips. "She'd have to be not to notice how awesome you are."

A tiny smile pulled on Flick's lips. "A donkey, huh?"

"Actually, no, because that's insulting donkeys. She's like a donkey patty."

"Poop?" Flick giggled. "You're weird."

"But you're wonderful."

Flick blushed to her roots. "Why is she throwing me away, then? What's wrong with me? Should I have acted different? Read more? Told jokes. Kept my room cleaner? Complained less? What did I need to do?"

"You're perfect the way you are." Tuesday stopped smiling. "I mean that. If she can't see how special you are, you don't have to change. You don't need to be perfect to be lovable. She has to be whacked out not to recognize how special you are, and maybe that should mean that I feel sorry for her, but I don't. I just feel mad. Because I'm on your side. Yours. Not hers."

Flick's lower lip trembled. "You make good hot chocolate."

"I know." Tuesday winked. "Maybe I should be more modest, but if you have a gift you might as well own it."

Flick took a shuddering breath and regrouped. "What are those apples doing?"

"Not much," Tuesday shot back.

"You know what? We should make a pie," Flick said.

"We should?"

"Today's the Harvest Festival Pie Contest. I saw the sign on my way over."

"That's right." And Beau would be a judge. Maybe this unexpected gift could be a peace offering.

Tuesday wagged her finger. "Has anyone ever told you you're smart?"

"Not enough."

"Well, grab an apron, Miss Smarty-Pants. Time to get baking. How hard can it be?"

Chapter Thirty-One

◠

Tuesday entered the Sweet Brew Coffee Shop for a quick pick-me-up pit stop. Today would be the first time she'd see Beau since their disastrous conversation at the Roxy Theater. Hopefully flooding her system with caffeine would kick-start her courage. Outside the picture window, Everland Plaza was abuzz with activity. Townswomen busily covered rows of folding tables with white plastic cloths while Miss Ida May stood on the gazebo steps and directed the pie arrivals under a banner that read, A SLICE OF EVERLAND: 49TH ANNUAL HARVEST FESTIVAL PIE COMPETITION.

"How can I help you this morning?" Delfi asked from behind the counter. She wore a wine-colored crocheted dress that looked like it had last been worn during the Summer of Love. A silver hoop winked in her eyebrow, while a few feather extensions peeked through her hair. The barista had a friendly if aloof demeanor, as if she were in the medical profession and her customers were patients under her care. She treated them with compassion and speed, always keeping the line moving.

"Double espresso," Tuesday replied automatically before pausing. "Wait. No. Sorry. Hang on. I want to try something different."

Delfi nodded solemnly, as if she understood the gravity of the moment.

She searched the hanging chalkboard menu, seeking the furthest thing possible from a double espresso. Softly jangling music pumped through the shop's sound system, all cryptic lyrics and intricate harmonies. The bell over the front door tinkled. More people got into line. The pressure built. "How about a…a…iced salted caramel mocha?"

"Very good." Delfi rang her up. "That's going to be…"

"On me." A familiar voice spoke behind her left shoulder. Only one man sounded like he'd coated his vocal cords in honey and then rolled around in gravel.

Tuesday's eyelids slammed shut. Her arms went heavy, her knees weak. She'd spent enough on improv classes; why not pretend to be in one? The audience is tossing out possible reactions. *Eager Beaver! Cold and Wounded!* She dug deep but found that, incredibly, all she wanted to do was err on the side of truth.

Cautiously Optimistic.

She turned and caught Beau peeking at her legs, exposed beneath her very flirty, very flouncy skirt. Slowly, he raised his eyes, and they bored into her, the intense expression making her girlie bits go off like a Roman candle. Tingles exploded into new tingles.

"Long time no see." Code for *I missed you.*

He blinked, swiping a hand over the top of his head, and

turned his attention to the community bulletin board. "It's been busy the last few days."

Heat suffused her cheeks. "Ah. I see." So that's how he was going to play it. She'd been around the block enough to know a thing or two. Namely, if a guy wants to see you, he finds a way.

"I'm serious." He dug out his wallet and handed Delfi a bill. The barista rang up the order, pretending she wasn't listening to every single word. "My folks are in town." He motioned out to where a petite, angular woman with an ashy-brown ponytail stood across the street, resting her head against the arm of an attractive fifty-something biracial man.

"What's the occasion?" They looked nice enough, although much more casual than Beau. She could never imagine him in a pair of flip-flops or board shorts.

His gaze returned to her face, resting for a fraction of a second. "My birthday."

Her lips parted. "When's that?"

"Next week."

"Oh." A beat. "I didn't know that."

He shrugged. "Why would you?"

Because, you idiot, when people are in a relationship, this is the type of information that is generally shared. But she wouldn't say that. Nor would she be desperate, smother herself in frosting and sprinkles and invite him to make a wish.

"It's not exactly an official day of town celebration."

She hoisted a pie. "But I could have made another of these bad boys." She froze, gripping the pan. So much for her "no desperate acts of approval" rule.

Bur she didn't want to play games, or a role.

She forced her shoulders back, spine straight. His big hands flexed and her skin pebbled. She wanted to be real, and what she really wanted was to fall. Whenever they shared the same air space, her body grew taut, ready to leap.

But would he want to catch her? She wasn't perfect: she slept in, could sing the entire soundtrack to *Oklahoma!* but routinely forgot her account passwords, was genetically incapable of making it anywhere on time, and tended to overshare. She was a tangle of controversy and contradiction. The Hot Mess Express.

Could he handle her occasional trips to Chaos Town, or would she spend her days apologizing for being who she was?

"Whipped cream on the mocha?" Delfi asked over the grind of the beans.

At least that question had an easy answer.

"I love whipped cream." She refused to break his gaze.

Only a slight pupil dilation, the smallest hint of a nostril flare showed how her coy statement affected him.

Oh, he was good.

And she was ready to rise to the challenge.

"I can never resist whipped cream. Don't you agree, Mr. Mayor?"

The vein in his temple became more pronounced.

Why not be wicked?

Last week she'd kissed her way across his sweat-slicked chest, felt the hard pound of his heart vibrate into her lips. So many nights were the same. Here was someone who could have meant something—everything.

She sucked in a frustrated breath. They had stood at the corner of Forever and Always, so how had they ended up detouring to What Might Have Been Cul-de-Sac?

He eyed the flaky butter crust. "You made that?"

"Yes. Well, Flick helped me." All morning as they'd rolled dough and stewed apples, she'd told herself that she'd done the right thing in turning down the community theater idea.

That was *his* dream, not hers.

The trouble was that she didn't know what she wanted. Since leaving New York, life had ceased to be a nightmare, but it was nowhere close to a dream come true.

It takes a lot of setbacks and self-sabotage to be this chaotic. Right now there was a fifty-fifty chance her underwear was on inside out. And there were enough crumbs at the bottom of her purse to qualify for a meal, or at least a hearty midmorning snack.

She focused on the crust with a prayer that the fat tear plopping into the filling went unnoticed. If there were questions, she'd blame allergies. Better to appear in need of a Benadryl than be outed as a full-fledged basket case. "It took me two tries to weave the lattice crust. I don't know if my pie will tip the scales in favor of Everland, but here's hoping. The apples are some sort of magical."

He raised his brows. "Magic?"

"Mocha on the bar," Delfi called.

He turned to the register. "What happened to double espressos?"

"You know me." She forced a blithe grin. "Always trying something new." She picked up the cup and popped the lid. Wow. Delfi hadn't held back on the whipped cream. If she took a sip, there was a strong likelihood this might make a mess. But so what? Sometimes a girl got a little whipped cream on the tip of her nose. If Beau didn't approve, he could add it to his list of "Reasons Tuesday Wasn't a Suitable Girlfriend."

She took a careful sip.

"Good?" He opened the shop door and they crossed the street, heading into the Plaza.

"Sweet." Tuesday liked Delfi enough not to want to insult her by tossing the beverage into the trash in full public view. But this was too sugary, even for her.

What if her judgment was fundamentally broken?

He waved at a silver car pulling up to the curb. Donna and Angie from the Tourism Commission emerged.

"Think they're going to come through for Everland?" she murmured.

"With any luck." He held her gaze with unnerving directness, his eyes brighter than the noonday sky. "I want to thank you for the part you've played."

"Oh geez." She wrinkled her nose, fidgeting with one of her rings. "It was nothing."

"Don't sell yourself short." He jammed a hand in his pocket. "You hosted a great tour that day at the park. Karen has been clipping impassioned letters from visitors from the *Examiner* and scrapbooking them as proof. You were behind that, Tuesday."

Hearing him speak her name with that grave intensity and Georgia lilt worked a peculiar effect on her body. Some parts went limp, warm, and languid. Others tightened, tensing into a keen ache.

"Is it enough?" She drew a hard breath. *Am I enough?* The unspoken question felt like it hung over her head with all the subtlety of a pop-art word bubble.

And just like that his eyes went to a dark, wicked indigo.

"Guess we'll see," he answered after a drawn-out pause, as if answering her hidden question.

"Hey!" Tuesday leaped out of her skin as a pair of skinny arms engulfed her waist.

"Flick, hi," she said, setting the pie on the table, giving the girl a distracted smile. "You okay? You look pale." That was an understatement. The kid could camouflage herself in a snowstorm.

"My stomach hurts. Probably from scarfing half of that first pie." She turned to Beau. "The first one we made burned because *somebody* was too busy singing songs from *Phantom of the Opera* to notice the timer."

"I was teaching this one the chorus to 'Angel of Music.'"

"Anyway, guess what?" The kid jabbered on, not sensing the tension. "I talked to Mrs. Boyle, and she said that if you agreed, you could be my foster mom. Isn't that great?"

"You?" Beau got there first, his lips setting in a thin line. "A foster mom?"

"Me?" Tuesday's voice chimed in, hollow and empty. "What do you mean me?"

The smile on Flick's face dimmed to a low wattage. She settled a hand on her lower stomach. "Obviously you don't have to. It's not a big deal. I just thought that when you said..." She glanced between them with a little laugh. "Ha, I got you good, huh? You should see your faces. Like I'd live with *you*. You can barely cook. I'd end up in the kitchen trying to feed us both."

Tuesday cracked a smile as relief sank in. "You'd be my own personal Cinderella. How are you at mopping floors? Cleaning toilets?"

"Hardy-har-har," she said. "Hey, I got to go, though."

"Mrs. Boyle looking for you?"

"Ha, yeah, something like that."

Beau waited until Flick had run off. "She was being serious."

"What do you mean?" Tuesday picked up the knife, unable to remain still. "How should I cut this? Into eighths, or sixteenths?" Her insides were unsteady, like she was on a boat in the open ocean.

"About you fostering her. She tried to play it off as a joke, but did you get a look at her eyes? She meant it."

"No way." Tuesday snorted, trying to shake her unease. "She's been around me enough to know that I can barely take care of my dog. You heard her. It took me two tries to get this pie right, and she had to help me make the crust because when I did it, the batter ran loose."

"You like to say that you aren't capable of responsibility, but it's not true. It's why I nominated you for the role in spearheading the Roxy."

She glanced up, and his face was dead serious, no bullshit. He didn't want to force her to be someone else, or ruin her dreams. He believed in her. He thought she could do it, but what if she couldn't? What if she was incapable? Tried and failed? Panic nearly suffocated her. She set down the knife and wiped her damp palms on the apple-embroidered apron she'd bought for the occasion.

"I'm not cut out for that sort of thing. Or for being anyone's guardian."

"Not cut out or plain don't want to?" he asked with low menace. "See, there's a big difference."

"What do we have here? Apple pie? Thank heavens. If I ate another bite of peach, I declare I'd go batty. I've had peaches and cream, peaches and crumble, peaches and caramel, and peaches with sour cream." Donna stood before them, holding an empty plate and wearing a name tag that read JUDGE.

Another woman with red hair and the same name tag stood behind her. "And I'm allergic to peaches. And dairy. This means yours is the only entry I can judge."

"Donna, Angie. Lovely to see you both." Beau used his grave formal mayor intonation. Nothing at all like the chastising timbre he'd used a moment before.

Tuesday cut into the pie, preoccupied, and passed it over.

"I'm not sure I can handle this." Donna poked at the pie. "Even if it smells amazing, and it does, I just saw a child getting sick in some bushes. When I see someone sick, then I feel sick, and ugh, it's a chain reaction."

"Good thing I saw nothing," the redhead interjected. "Anyway, doesn't matter. My stomach is more steel than flesh." She wolfed down the pie sampler in four bites. "My word. That's good stuff."

"Shhh. Don't let the competition hear you," Tuesday said with a smile. "On second thought, let them hear it and shiver in their boots."

She held on to that smile until they walked away, then glanced back at Beau.

"I'm not what you think that I am," she blurted. "And as much as you might want me to be something different, I'm not that girl. So you either take me as I am or you don't take me at all."

"You know what I see?" He took a deep breath. "I see a woman who is hiding from her potential. One who could take the world by the tail, but is afraid."

"Afraid?" Her dander went up. "I'm not afraid."

"Really? Because I think you're so scared it's hard for you to breathe. I think you're so scared of being successful you'll do anything to sabotage it. Even if that means turning down a position you'd be damn good for, even if that means telling a little girl who thinks you're the greatest thing since the invention of sliced bread that you don't want her when it's plain to me and anyone around you that you adore the kid."

"Stop talking."

"Or what? What will you do? Quit the act and get real. Who is the real Tuesday? Hell, I don't even know why your parents called you Tuesday."

A small group was beginning to draw close. "They didn't," she whispered.

"They didn't what?"

"They didn't call me Tuesday, okay? Tuesday isn't my real name."

He gave a half snort, shaking his head. "You're kidding."

"It's a nickname. I never liked my real name."

"If you wear a mask long enough, it stops being a disguise and becomes who you are."

She stared ahead, unseeing.

At last he whispered, his plea barely an audible breath, "Look at me."

Looking meant seeing, and what would he find if she dared? "No," she choked.

"Tuesday Knight, or whatever the hell your damn name is, you look me in the eye or I am walking away and that will be it."

He didn't understand. It wasn't that she wouldn't look at him. She couldn't. Because what if all he saw was…her? Just Tuesday. No act. No mask.

And what if after that he looked away?

"Three…"

Her stomach muscles tightened. It wasn't fair, asking this of her. If he really had feelings, he wouldn't be doing this.

"Two…"

He wasn't going to catch her if she took a chance and jumped. He was pushing. Pushing. Pushing. And she wouldn't fall again. Couldn't fall again.

"One."

"Knock it off!" She picked up the pie and threw it, and the problem with being the star hitter of the Moose Bottom Mavericks was that the talent didn't extend to throwing. Her aim went wide. Instead of hitting Beau, she nailed Miss Ida May in the face as the woman was busy taking notes on the entire encounter.

"Tuesday, Tuesday!" Mrs. Boyle broke through the crowd. "Is Flick with you?"

"Tuesday's not even her real name," Lucille Munro cried, causing a momentarily hushed silence before everyone began speaking at once.

Tuesday pressed her temples with the heels of her hands. She'd lost it, dropped the princess act, the lobbyist role, even the acting-decent act. And worse, the Georgia Tourism Commission judges had watched the whole thing. So much for being a princess kicking dragon tail. She'd single-handedly spoiled Everland's chances for the whole town. Happily Ever After Land staff had counted on her and she'd ruined everything. She could feel helpless, defeated tears building.

"For shame," Phaedra hissed. "You stay where you are until we call the police for assault. This will be going in the police blotter. You can be sure of it sure as I am looking at you."

"I'll help clean up." Tuesday grabbed at napkins next

to the plate, wanting—needing—to do something, however small, to try to put this right.

"You've done enough." Lucille blocked her path, arms crossing over her formidable bosom.wwe

"What's this about Flick?" Beau said in a clipped, tight voice.

"I can't find her." Mrs. Boyle wrung her hands, deep worry lines grooving the corners of her mouth. "Someone said they saw her getting sick by a parking meter."

Donna from the Tourism Commission stepped forward, her brow furrowed in concern. "Is she a young girl, wearing a T-shirt that said, 'I Wanted Pizza—'"

"'Not Your Opinion!'" Beau interrupted.

"Last I saw that poor chile, she was with her." Phaedra pointed at Tuesday.

"And she's not to be trusted," Lucille said. "We've been digging around, ever since poor Mayor Marino was seen with her at the Fall Ball."

"We uncovered the truth." Miss Ida May swiped the crust from her face and reset her straw hat. "We know what *really* happened in New York City."

Tuesday's knees wobbled as the air left her lungs in one long whoosh. The world seemed plunged underwater. Time slowed. Sounds distorted.

"She had an affair with a married man," Miss Ida May announced, pausing dramatically before adding, "Her director."

"For shame," Toots snapped. "The *Back Fence* now starts fires if there isn't enough smoke. Our princess would never do a thing like that."

"Never." Even Mean Gene had her back. "Y'all are lying like a no-legged dog."

Tuesday glanced around the group, her friends and co-workers. Even Pepper and Rhett stood on the edge of the crowd. This was a nightmare, one where you walk into a public place and realize you're naked. That was a sweet dream compared to this moment.

"I also agree." Beau's voice was unwavering. "Whatever our differences, I vouch for her."

Horror sank into her bones. He vouched for her.

Even when she couldn't give him what he wanted, he stood by her.

And that's why letting him down hurt so much.

She met his gaze one last time, wanting to memorize the expression there, one not tinged with bitter judgment and anger. "I'm sorry," she whispered. It took a moment for those two little words to find their mark.

Then he registered their meaning and the park exploded.

Chapter Thirty-Two

～

Some days deserve to be erased from memory. After Tuesday dropped her bombshell, the Everland Plaza exploded. Turned out she wasn't lying about being a terrible cook either. Note to self, if a woman shares a fact, believe her.

The trouble started right before noon, with Angie Robert saying she didn't feel well enough to continue judging the pie competition. Miss Ida May, Phaedra, and Lucille followed suit.

"It was the flying pie." Miss Ida May slumped beside a tree. Her purple hat with the net trim had gone cockeyed, and her floral-print dress hiked above the thick bands of her knee-high stockings. Two women from the quilting bee fanned her as she pressed a lace-trimmed hankie to her mouth. "Tuesday's pie did this."

"Or whatever her name is." Lucille moaned from a few feet away.

Beau passed around bottles of water as the sick waited for friends or family to see them safely home. He passed Toots and Mean Gene, assembled with other Happily Ever After Land staff, in a solemn half circle around Mr. Wilcox. "I'd never have believed she would do something like that, never in a million years," the older man was saying. "Not our princess."

"An affair with a married man, or poisoning the pies?" Gene quipped before Toots smacked him in the chest.

Donna passed into view, leading a hunched-over Angie in the direction of the Hill House B&B, where they were spending the night. Beau swallowed a groan, his shoulders stiff. Goddammit. Looked like Everland could kiss the Coastal Jewel designation good-bye and settle for Coastal Contamination. But the pain in Tuesday's eyes as she'd fled had cut deep. As much as he was angry at the situation, he couldn't find the heart to be angry with *her.* He raked a hand over his head and barked a frustrated laugh.

Tuesday Knight had him tied up in knots as usual.

"Can I interest you in some hand sanitizer, Mayor?" Lettie Sue popped in front of him waving a gallon-sized bottle under his nose. "There have been norovirus outbreaks all over the county lately. Can't be too careful."

He gave an absent nod and stuck out a palm for a dollop. Too bad he couldn't cleanse away the whole morning. All he'd wanted was a low-drama, quiet affair. An easy relationship. Instead, he'd gotten mixed up with a big-city adulteress who'd gotten half the town sick.

"The crisis has inspired me to do armchair research on preventative folk remedies. It appears as though elderberry can make a difference. Know where to get any of those?"

"Elderberries? Not outside of a Monty Python sketch," he quipped.

She stared blankly.

"Oh, come on. You know what I'm talking about. 'Your mother smells of hamsters and—'"

"I'll thank you not to bring my mama into this. I was only trying to be of help." She flounced off without a backward look.

Once those infected were cleared from the park and the nonsick sanitized, thanks to Lettie Sue (who kept shooting him dirty looks), there was nothing left to do but get on his bike and ride home to Belle Mont.

After parking next to his parents' rental car, he checked his phone. Three new text messages waited from Discount-Mart. Their offer—a lowball—on the Happily Ever After Land property was their last and best offer. They hadn't wasted time.

"We won't be as generous tomorrow," the last note had hinted ominously.

Tomorrow. After the pie news got out.

No new e-mails except for a Google Alert connected to his name. His stomach sank. The *Back Fence* already had a headline: THE PRODIGAL PIE: A PESTIFEROUS PRANK OF POISON AND POOR TASTE.

He lowered the phone, unable to read past the heavy-handed alliteration. Miss Ida May might be ill, but that hadn't subdued her indignation.

As mayor he possessed the executive authority to condemn the amusement park. The idea made him want to hit something, but people in this town needed jobs and opportunities closer to home. He couldn't put dinner on the tables or shoes on kids' feet. But his policies could.

"Drink?" The Belle Mont screen door slammed, and his mom came down the front stairs and handed him a beer.

"You've heard?"

"This is Everland," she said with a small smile.

"Of course." He scrubbed his face. "Why'd I bother asking?"

"Feeling okay?"

"I haven't gotten sick since that time Rhett gave me chicken pox in the third grade. Don't intend to start today."

Mama cocked her head. "That's not what I mean. The girl at the center of this, she's the one, isn't she? Miss Fanny Floss."

"Mama."

She pressed a hand to her neck. "Rats. Too bad I haven't worn your grandma's string of pearls for a decade. I'd be tempted to clutch them."

"It wasn't like you thought." He walked into the kitchen, grabbed a beer, and came back out.

She waited until he popped the cap. "I'm curious. What do you think I think?"

"Is this a trick question to get me to talk about my feelings?"

"Maybe." Mama arched her brows. "Lord knows I have to get crafty to get a clue what goes on in that handsome head of yours."

"Trust me. You wouldn't understand." He flopped onto the step and loosened his tie. "You and Dad have had it easy when it comes to love."

"Have we, now?"

"No drama."

"Give me a sip of that." She plucked the beer out of his

hands and took a long swallow. Then she handed it back and slapped him upside the head.

"Ow." He rubbed his hot ear. "What was that for?"

"Your father and I didn't raise you to be a fool." She walked down onto the grass. "Come on, walk with me." She took off at a fast clip, and he had no choice but to follow.

"Charlie and I had it easy, huh?" She veered off the driveway onto the lawn, walking toward Seaview Hill, the highest point for miles on the eastern edge of the property. "No drama?"

"How can I answer without you hitting me again?"

"I owe you an apology."

That was unexpected. "What for?"

"Beau Marino, I'm your mama. That means that even though I'm fifty-five, I still see you as my little boy. But I've protected you long enough. And sometimes the past deserves to be ancient history and bygones become bygones because there's no sense doing anything else but moving on, and if there is one thing I am good at, it's moving on."

"Did all the women in my life join forces today and decide to become cryptic?"

"How old was I when I had you?"

"Twenty?"

"Twenty years old. And just how proud do you think that made my mama and father? Their only daughter unmarried and pregnant before becoming a full-fledged adult?"

He'd always known Mama had had him young. That's part of what made her Mama. But it was a minor detail. She was also fun, up for anything.

"I'd gone sailing alone and gotten myself knocked up by a Bermudan bartender. An Afro-Bermudan bartender." She paused as the words sank in.

"Grandma and Grandpa didn't approve of Dad?" He couldn't remember much about his mother's parents. They'd retired to the Blue Ridge Mountains before he started school and he'd seen little of them after. He'd never wondered why. That was just how they were. Old. Frowning. Disinterested. His daddy's parents, on the other hand, were loving and high-energy enough that it paled out anything else.

"That's the G-rated version."

"They didn't like that I wasn't pure lily-white," he said slowly. The full weight of his statement hit hard and heavy.

"Honey, you were never half of anything. Just wholly you. Perfect. Beautiful. So I chose to redefine my family." Mama didn't move a muscle, but he felt enveloped in a hug. "You and Charlie are my people. And his beautiful sisters and your late grandparents, bless their souls. I wanted more children, but that wasn't meant to be, and *you* were enough." She gave a rueful grin. "But the world isn't black-and-white. And neither was the situation. I didn't want any of that ugliness rubbing off on you. I had to follow my heart and be with the man who made me happy regardless of my family's approval. But when you say there was no drama with your father and me, I have to laugh, because when people refer to World War III as something down the road, they don't realize that it happened right here, in that big house, when I made it clear that I intended to raise my son in my hometown, head held high."

"What did they do?" His heart ached for her.

"Moved full-time to their condo in Boco." But her laugh still carried a twinge of pain. "It was their quiet way out of having to love my husband and child. They said they tried their best, but you know what? It wasn't enough. In fact, it was nowhere near enough. You and Charlie aren't someone to be tolerated; you are the loves of my life."

"Get over here." He grabbed his tiny mother and squeezed her tight.

She clung back, fierce and strong, before sniffing loudly and pushing him back. "My. That's quite enough of all that, now. What I want to know is what is happening with that girl, Miss—"

"Please don't say her name. I'm sure you have read the *Back Fence* by now, and everything that happened at the Harvest Festival after you left. She was with a married man? How can I be with someone like that? Not after…"

His mother gave him an MRI-level stare, taking in everything he'd never admit. "She's like Jacqueline, then?" Only Mama wasn't afraid to say his dead wife's name to his face.

He kicked at the ground. "She's blond."

"So was I before all this gray." She ran a hand over her hair. "What else you got…?"

"Apparently a cheater," he said weakly.

"Have you asked her?"

"No." He glanced at his beer, already empty.

"Son, are you saying you're taking the word of Miss Ida May and the Biddy Brigade at face value? Bless their hearts, if those women ran their feet as hard as their mouths, they'd be winning every marathon on the Eastern Seaboard."

"It's not easy between me and Tuesday," he protested. "We aren't that much alike."

"And love has to be easy in your mind?" She smacked him upside the head again.

"Ow, Mama. You keep doing that and I'm going to end up in the emergency room with a concussion."

"Then let's get on home so I can clean out your ears.

Love is work, every day a worksite, and you build it together, brick by brick."

"What?"

"A life."

Beau stared out at the line of blue in the distance. The horizon. The ocean. The possibilities stretching.

"If you feel as strongly about the girl as I sense you do, then don't be a dummy. Go for it. See if she's worth the fuss." She touched the center of his back, twirling her fingers in small concentric circles the way she used to do when he was a small boy and afraid of monsters under the bed. "I don't know all that went on between you and Jacqueline behind closed doors, but remember you don't know what goes on behind anyone else's doors. What you see on the outside isn't always what's real. It's scary to try again, but there's a bright side."

"There is?"

She blew a kiss in the direction of his skeptical scowl. "I didn't raise a coward."

Chapter Thirty-Three

"Abandon all hope, ye who enter here," Tuesday mumbled into her pillow.

"How did you know I'd come in?" Pepper peeked beneath the elaborate blanket fort taking up most of the living room. "I let myself in through the kitchen."

"I'm gifted with omniscient psychic powers. Oh wait. If that were true then I'd never have gotten out of bed today. You stepped on one of J. K. Growling's squeaky toys in the backyard."

Pepper crawled inside. "You plan on hiding here all day?"

"All day?" Tuesday sniffed. "That's for amateurs. I'm an expert at avoidance. I've got enough food to survive a week. After that I might scoop my life savings from the change jar and see if I can afford a bus ticket to Phoenix. Catch up with Dad's road trip. I can stand on sidewalks around the country and sing in front of a hat, busk for Airstream gas money. I'd be an asset."

"I don't think Dad's that hard up. And I don't think they really want a third wheel. You know they're hitting up the nudist colonies in every state, right?"

Tuesday gagged. "Not my favorite kind of full moon."

Pepper shuddered. "I am a little sad that I even went there. The mental image…it burns. It burns."

"Let me replace it with another one." Tuesday rolled over and used a movie trailer announcer's exaggeratedly deep voice. "It looked like an average Southern small town. Quiet. Peaceful. Uneventful. Until the day *she* moved in."

"Knock it off."

"She brought with her bad morals, and that's not all…" She dropped the voice and groaned loud and long. "Somehow the pie was infected with norovirus. How did that even happen? I swear I washed my hands. I'm like patient zero here."

"Norovirus is so contagious. You could have picked it up around the park."

"There hasn't been a single case here until today."

"No, I know. But we were bound to get it. I heard it had gotten as far as Hogg Jaw." Pepper's brow furrowed. "Huh. Hogg Jaw."

"You know you sound like Velma from *Scooby-Doo* right now."

"Very funny, Shaggy. It's just Hogg Jaw is in the finals to become a Coastal Jewel, too, right?"

"Apparently. It's a little weird because it's not as close to the ocean, but whatever." She stretched and burrowed back into her pillow. "It's upriver, though I guess it's close enough. Back to my hibernation. Wake me when the town quits hating my guts."

"Hogg Jaw might be desperate."

"What are you saying? Bioterrorism?"

"That town has a reputation for sabotage." Pepper shrugged. "Remember how Judge Hogg tried to pry off the Davy Jones statue this summer?"

"That was crazy. He wouldn't be back for more, though, would he?"

"I don't think so. Like I said, it must have just been something you picked up at work, or maybe you bought bad fruit."

Tuesday frowned. "I didn't buy the fruit."

"You picked the apples? I didn't even know there were orchards outside of North Georgia."

She sat up, wide-eyed. "I didn't pick them. They were left in a basket at my front door."

"By who?"

"Who knows? I assumed it was some do-gooder. One of those random acts of small-town kindness, like sharing cups of sugar and stuff."

"Can you run this past me again?"

"Someone left me a basket of apples and I baked them into a pie and . . ." The bottom fell out of her stomach. "Holy crap. Was I set up?"

"Who'd have reason?" Pepper tapped her bottom lip, deep in thought. "Miss Ida May seems like she was gunning for you."

"She doesn't think I belong with Beau, but it couldn't have been her. After I accidentally threw the pie in her face, she got sick. So did the other *Back Fence* ladies. They wouldn't have wanted to ruin the pie competition."

"Who would?"

"The Georgia Tourism Commission were guest judging and—"

"If they made the contest look bad...Hogg Jaw would win."

They traded uneasy stares. "I could ask Beau. Oh wait, scratch that. He hates me."

"Stop being so dramatic. Beau Marino is head-over-heels crazy about you."

"Correction." Tuesday shook her head. "I make him crazy. But it's a two-way street. He makes me crazy, too. You should have heard him trying to boss me about working at the Roxy."

"The closed-down theater?"

"He was trying to secure funding to open it back up and thought I should run it. Me, in charge."

"That doesn't sound the least bit bossy. It sounds like he knows you perfectly."

"Me, in charge?" She feigned a laugh. "I'd make it a disaster. Plus, I'm not sure a town of our size could support regular productions. It might be better suited as a half-time education-extension program. Then you could pair up with dance teachers, and music teachers, make it a hub for creative kids' stuff."

"Um, did you hear yourself? That idea was genius. A kids' creative art center? The entire area would get behind that! I've been chasing grants for the shelter for months now, and do you know how many opportunities there are for kids' education? Lots. I could help you. The Knight sisters, we'd be unstoppable."

"Except the part where I said no. Turned him down flat."

Pepper's brows mashed together. "You what?"

She covered her face with her hands. What had she done? "I really am an idiot."

"In this case, I am not arguing. You have to go find him.

Tell him your idea. It doesn't sound like he was trying to boss you. He just knew that you could take the place and run with it, and I know you could if you'd just believe in yourself."

"But you heard those terrible things Miss Ida May accused me of."

Pepper blinked. "I did."

"And it was true." The words tasted bitter, made it hard to swallow. "I did have an affair with a married man. She wasn't lying."

"Was that the whole story?"

"Of course not. She skipped out the part where he'd told me he was divorced. Why are you even asking?"

"Because I know you. And I know you'd never do something like that. And after you left, I looked up the article she'd posted on the *Back Fence* and found the jerk's name. And so I looked that up, and there was an entire section of Auditions.com devoted to what a skeezeball he was."

"You really are a super sleuth."

"I know my sister. And to know you is to love you. But if you're going to live here, I want you to be happy. Beau's a good guy and he's offering a path."

"I was too scared to see it."

"You want him." Not a question.

"More than anything."

"So why are you still here talking to me? Go get him."

A motorcycle roared up the street, the engine cutting off in front of her house.

Pepper crawled from the blanket fort to the window and peered through a gap in the curtains. "Looks like he beat you to the punch."

Tuesday gripped the closest quilt. "What am I going to do?"

"Be honest. The real question is what am *I* going to do? I don't want to stick around here for any makeup sex."

"You really think we'll make up?"

"Yes, and now I have to go hop the fence. I'm sneaking out the back door and climbing up on your garbage can. If you hear something, it's not a raccoon on steroids."

"Wait…"

The doorbell rang.

"Bye." Pepper was gone in a blink.

Tuesday crawled out, took a deep breath, and opened the door.

"I have to tell you something," Beau said abruptly. His chest rose and fell in an erratic tempo, his eyes wild.

"I wasn't sure you were ever going to speak to me again. I can go first if you like. I wanted to say that—"

He raised a hand, silencing her. "Flick is missing."

Chapter Thirty-Four

⌐

"What do you mean missing?" Tuesday's brown eyes were wide with shock.

"She hasn't been seen since the Harvest Festival, and according to police, she left a letter saying she was leaving for good." He'd been en route here when he was flagged down by a deputy. "A search party is being assembled. She was last seen getting sick near the Kissing Bridge."

"She ate the poisoned pie, too!"

Beau's chest tightened as Tuesday filled him in on the pie theory. It was outlandish, devious, and contemptible. That was Hogg Jaw, all right. "You've been spending more and more time together lately. Can you think of anywhere she might be?"

"She loves the library."

"They've checked there."

"The bus stop?"

"There too." Thunder rumbled in the distance. "It's supposed to storm tonight."

"This is all my fault." Tuesday swayed. "If anything happens to her, I'm never going to forgive myself. Wait!" She gripped the door frame. "If she was last seen by the bridge, she might have gone up the river."

He nodded slowly. "Lots of nooks and crannies to hide."

"Or get trapped." She ripped a hair elastic off her wrist and gathered her long hair into a bun. "I don't know how, but I *know* that is where she is. Will you take me?"

He took her hand. "I won't stop until she is safe."

It didn't take long to get on Beau's bike and head to the river. They parked at a lookout near the state park, upstream from the bridge. The clouds were getting darker and darker. Fogged rolled in.

Tuesday leaped from the seat and tore to the ravine's edge, cupping her hands to her mouth. "Flick! Flick!"

Beau hunted the underbrush until he found what he was looking for, an old, almost overgrown fishermen footpath that led to the water's edge. "This way. This is how I used to go as a boy."

They hiked up the river as the rain increased, the ground growing steadily more muddy and slippery underfoot.

"What time is it?" Tuesday gave the gloomy sky a dubious look.

"We have another hour until total darkness."

She brushed a branch from her face. "Will we find her?" Dead leaves crowned Tuesday's hair, and she had dirt on her forehead.

"Yes." He cast a glance at the deep water with a silent prayer that when they did find her, she'd be okay.

They walked in silence for a few minutes.

"Listen, there's something I have to tell you. From earlier. I had sex with a married man."

He forced himself to hold his gaze. This was what he wanted after all. Clear the air. No more secrets. Hear the truth from her, raw and unfiltered.

"I didn't know. Isn't that stupid? I didn't know he was married. I knew he had been, of course. But I had thought the divorce was finalized, except it wasn't. It wasn't even in process. I was this...pawn." She spat the word. "The two of them had a messed-up relationship, and somehow I became the frosting in their twisted Oreo. I ended things as soon as I found out, but he was cruel. He liked...hurting me. That's when I heard that he told everyone I'd seduced him. That I'd hounded him relentlessly. Called him after auditions. Showed up at restaurants. As if I even had the money to be hanging out in the kind of places he frequented."

Her words came quicker, as if once unleashed they were unable to be contained.

"At first he invited me to his brownstone. Said he wanted to talk about a part. I was too flattered at the attention to think anything of it. I was so sure that this was my chance. That I'd worked hard. Paid enough dues. At last I'd made it." Her laugh sounded like something wounded. "All he wanted was to use me."

Beau's jaw clenched. "He forced you."

"No. I made it easy. I didn't realize what had happened at first. He was so romantic and charming. Then he started with the insults. Not many, just chosen with exquisite care. He made me feel unlovable. And yet he loved me. And I got so messed up in the head that I believed him. The spell didn't break until one afternoon when we were, you know, and I looked up and his wife was there, in the living room, watching us, holding a suitcase, home from a work trip."

"That's..."

"Terrible. Idiotic. Disgusting. Trust me. There's isn't a word you can say that I haven't used."

"Repulsive."

"Well, okay, there you go. I'll add it to my list."

"I meant him."

Her mouth opened and closed. Her shoulders slumped a fraction. "I guess I thought he was right, that I was unlovable. My mom, she left us. I can remember the day she packed her bags. Pepper cleaned the kitchen...refused to say a word. My father went hunting. I was the one who went upstairs, into her room, and begged. I got down on my knees, and she stepped around me on her way out the door.

"Later, after she moved to New Hampshire and remarried, she tried to apologize about it once. But it's a hard thing to get over, your own mom walking past you and choosing another life. Maybe that's why I chose so many bad men. They just kept feeding my internal script, the one that told me that no matter what I did or promised, I wasn't worth it. That it was all I deserved."

He hooked a hand around the back of his neck. "And I thought that a relationship was supposed to be easy if it was real. But it's work, even with the right person."

"The best kind of work?"

"Yeah, the best."

He froze, pointing down at the trail. "See that?" Small footsteps were embedded in the mud surrounding a large puddle.

"Flick!" Tuesday called, and he joined in.

The only answer was the pitter-patter of rain.

"Flick!" Her voice cracked. "Flick, can you hear us? Come on, honey."

"Wait." Beau grabbed her arm. "Do you hear that? There it is again." A muffled shriek, as if came from beneath the ground.

"Where?" Tuesday swiveled her head, staring around at the fallen boulders. "How do we figure out how she got under us?"

"By working together." Beau cupped his hands to his mouth. "Flick, if you can hear my voice, keep yelling." He and Tuesday followed the answering cries, playing a game of hot and cold, until they found a spot where the gully opened into a small marsh, a cove surrounded by sandstone on three sides.

"Help! Help!" The girl's voice grew louder, increasing in clarity.

"This way." Beau scrambled over loose rocks into a small cove set back from the main river, Tuesday at his heels.

"Help! I can't get out. I'm stuck down here."

Beau maneuvered between two boulders, bent, and peered into a small opening, fishing out the small flashlight stuck on his key chain.

Flick's tear-stained face peered up from the shadows.

He helped Tuesday ease down the four-foot drop and followed her. The sobbing girl had tried to take shelter from the storm and had slid in, twisting her ankle. He shone the light around to check out the structural integrity of the cave, and the light hit a flash. Then another. And another. He gave a slow shake of his head, a smile spreading over his face. "I can't believe it." Gold. Piles of it. Every direction.

"You did it." Tuesday hugged the sniffling girl. "You found it, the lost treasure."

"I was dizzy and wanted to lie down out of the storm," Flick explained through hiccups. "I thought I could crouch under an overhang, when I saw the hole." She rubbed her eyes and buried her face in Tuesday's shoulder. "Last night Mrs. Boyle was on the phone talking to a friend, and she said that she was so tired. That fostering was more work than she expected and she wasn't as young as she used to be. All I could think was what would happen if she didn't want me? Would I go to a group home? Never have a family? So I wondered if I was really good and tried hard, what if I could live with you instead? But you didn't want me. No one wants me."

"Hush, darling. That's not true." Tuesday was patting her head, pushing the hair from the girl's tear-streaked face. "You are so wanted. You are so special."

Beau kept the beam from Flick's eyes but noticed her lips looked dry. "You've been sick, haven't you?"

"A few times." She nodded. "I'm thirsty."

Beau set the light between his teeth and ripped off his jacket. "It's a cool evening, and soon it will be a cold night. We're going to get you warm."

Tuesday pulled out her phone. "I don't have any reception in here. I'm going to call in search and rescue. It's better they come to us, and help keep her dry."

"I can walk," Flick protested weakly. "I don't need a fuss."

"I'll go out and get a signal," Beau said. "You hold her."

Tuesday nodded. "It's all going to be okay. Just put your head right here in my lap and take a snooze." She sank next to a chest, and coins crunched underfoot. She drew Flick onto her lap, holding her as if she were a much younger girl.

Beau hauled himself halfway up the gully before he got a bar. He called 911 and described their location. When he got back to the cave, Flick was dozing, arms clinging to Tuesday's neck.

Beau crouched and stroked her hair. "You know, we did make a good team."

"We did. Thank God we found her." She glanced around at the bounty. "And all this. I can hardly believe it's real, can you? Imagine, all this time Redbeard's treasure really existed, right below Everland."

He ran the flashlight beam over the rocky wall. There were chests overflowing with goblets, necklaces, diadems, and coins. "When I was a kid, I used to believe that there was something more than just waking up each morning and going to work or school."

Tuesday nodded slowly. "I can remember how I cried and cried on my eleventh birthday when I didn't get a letter from Hogwarts."

He looked at her intently. "What if magic exists, but it's not the version from the storybooks? What if it's baking a cake in the middle of the night?"

Her smile was soft. "Or hearing a song lyric you've listened to a thousand times and finally understanding what it's really trying to tell you."

"Or kissing on a boat."

"The corner of Forever and Always."

"A cave filled with treasure."

"Maybe magic is all around us all the time if we're brave enough to look."

He crawled behind her and held her against him. She was

being strong for Flick, and someone needed to be there for her.

She kissed the girl's head and tucked his jacket closer around her shoulders. "It's these moments that hold the true magic in life—the moments when you're inexplicably happy. We so often overlook them, take them for granted, that we fail to see them for what they really are. This is our real magic, and I'd take it over Hogwarts any day."

"I love you, Tuesday." There. He said it, the words that had been dancing on his tongue for too long, waiting for him to get the balls.

"I love you, too." She leaned back into him, and he felt her body melt into his, as if all the tension released in a long exhale.

What had he been so afraid of? Loving Tuesday was like breathing, a vital function, part of his physical makeup and necessary to his survival.

"And it's Grace," she added with a cringe. "Grace is my real name."

"Grace?" He tried it out. "It's pretty, but not you. How did you get to Tuesday?" He wanted to know, plus talking seemed to calm her down.

"In my bedroom back in Moose Bottom there was a needlepoint that said 'Tuesday's child is full of grace.' I think it had been my grandmother's. One day I woke up and decided that I liked Tuesday for a name better. I was five and my parents were good sports. They went along with it and it stuck, even though I was really born on a Friday."

"A Tuesday born on a Friday." He chuckled, shaking his head. "Got to say, it suits you."

Shouts filtered through the cave opening. Followed by dogs barking.

He picked up a coin and held it in front of them. "I wonder what will happen to the treasure."

"You know what? I have an idea." She adjusted Flick in her arms. "Two, actually. Do you trust me?"

He kissed her head, breathed in her sweet scent. "Always."

And the magical thing was that he meant it.

Chapter Thirty-Five

It didn't take long for word to spread about Flick's rescue and her inadvertent discovery of Redbeard's lost treasure. By the next morning the entire town was abuzz with the news.

"I say, but there's a right-sized crowd gathering outside. National news trucks, the whole bit. You're a hero." Cedric Swift ruffled Flick's head. "The magnitude of the treasure exceeds my wildest dreams. It's going to take months to catalog the findings."

Tuesday's throat caught as the girl beamed. She placed Beau's phone on the hospital counter. The *Back Fence* had posted a full retraction to their character-assassination story. The biddies went so far as to offer a genuine apology and an invitation to join the Everland Ladies Quilt Guild.

"Knock, knock. Hope I'm not disturbing." Donna Summer poked her head through the hospital door.

"Not at all. Please come in." Tuesday jumped out of her

seat and motioned to the empty space. "I know the last twenty-four hours have been...strange...to say the least. But before you give Hogg Jaw the Coastal Jewels designation, please, please hear me out."

"No! First hear us out!" Pepper burst into the room, followed by Toots, Mean Gene, Lettie Sue, Gil, Robbie, Caroline, and Madam Magna.

"We have fire codes here." A frowning nurse bustled in. "Out, out! All of you, out! My word, this is like trying to herd cats."

"Shove a sock in it, Irene." Toots planted her feet. "We'll be out of your hair in two shakes, but first Madam Magna has something to say."

The old woman shuffled forward. Today's turban was dandelion yellow and garnished with a diamond made up of tiny silver sequins. "The apples were poisoned by an old witch."

A hush fell over the room.

"Well, technically that's an exaggeration." Pepper jumped in with her no-nonsense tone. "But nevertheless, the apples for the pie Tuesday baked *were* knowingly tampered with—"

Beau wrapped his arm around Tuesday's waist, pulling her in close. She leaned into his quiet strength, relishing the sound of his protective rumble. "Who'd do such a thing?" He sounded ready to crack a can of whoop ass.

"My stepsister." Madam Magna spat the word like a foul taste. "Betty Ann Hogg."

"The church organist?" Beau asked, his brow wrinkling. "Judge Hogg's mother? That doesn't make sense. She's too sick to hurt a fly."

"That's what she wants you to believe." There was no

longer any trace of a mysterious Eastern European accent in Magna's down-home twang. "While she's acted frailer than a wilting flower for years, she's gone ahead and laid the foundation for a financial empire stretching across the county. The greatest crime boss in the Low Country."

"That is true. All of it." Pepper nodded slowly. "This situation smelled like a setup job. And who would have the motivation to try to get the judges to turn their backs on Everland? In my observation, the simplest answer is often the right one. In this case all arrows pointed straight to Hogg Jaw. So Rhett and I took ourselves on a reconnaissance drive yesterday. Only one place in that town had an apple tree, Ma Hogg's farm. You could see it from the road—if I stood on Rhett's shoulders and used binoculars. And while we were taking pictures, who do you think came driving up?"

"Me." Madam Magna shuffled forward. "As soon as I caught wind of the Harvest Festival disaster, I suspected Betty Ann's involvement. She's been gunning for Happily Ever After Land for years."

"Why?" Beau frowned. "It's an amusement park. What did it ever do to her?"

"Brought me joy." Madam Magna got a faraway look in her eye. "She wanted payback. See, she's convinced that I stole her suitor when we were girls, and carried that grudge, even though the man went on to marry someone else."

"That guy in question is Doc Valentine," Pepper chimed in. "Rhett's father."

"The catch of the county." Magna's thin shoulders heaved with her dreamy sigh.

"What was it? The bow ties?" Tuesday quipped. Doc was

the type who ate pizza with a fork and knife, hardly a smoldering Casanova.

"Betty Ann was convinced he was her one and only. When he asked me on a date, she never forgave me for accepting. Eventually, he married Virginia, and she threw her lot in with the Hoggs, going so far as to marry a third cousin. But in her heart I think she always believed that Everland thought it was too good for her. And she aimed to prove them wrong. After her husband died, she used his life insurance to start investing. She quietly amassed quite a fortune of power and influence. And all for one goal. To help Hogg Jaw beat Everland."

"One of her neighbors had gotten sick with the norovirus, a man she gets to do yard work. The virus remains highly infectious for days after, so while he was recovering, she paid him triple to pick the apples and transport them to Tuesday's house. He told me the whole story," Pepper said.

"What do we do?" Beau asked. "Call law enforcement?"

Pepper shook her head. "She isn't getting off scot-free. Turns out she got sick in the bargain."

Madam Magna nodded. "Betty Ann's at the Hogg Jaw Community Hospital. She's expected to make a full recovery, but she'll be praying to the porcelain god for forgiveness."

"Buried treasure, poison pies, my, my." Donna shook her head. "This place is certainly exciting."

"That brings me back to why I called you here," Tuesday said. "This treasure has captured the nation's attention. Cedric is right. It belongs in a museum. And what better place to have a museum than right here in Everland?"

Donna gave her chin a musing rub. "It *is* quite the draw card."

"One that will entice people from all over. And while they're here, they'll also shop along our Main Street and, of course, visit Happily Ever After Land. And in conjunction with the museum, we'll be restoring the Roxy Theater. I'm going to write and direct an ongoing production about the Redbeard story. We can continue to roll out Mayor Marino's vision of celebrating what's special about Everland. That it's not and never will be a place that's just like everywhere else."

"She's got that right." Toots gave an emphatic nod.

Donna Summers looked around the room, which burst at the seams with townspeople murmuring their agreement. "Indeed it is not."

"We've got heart." Gil slung his arms around Lettie Sue and Mean Gene's shoulder.

"And a sense of humor," Z-Man piped from the recliner.

"And hope." Beau took Tuesday's hand, holding it like he'd never let go again.

"And that's been obvious all along." Donna clapped her hands, a slow smile creeping across her face. "Which is why it's my great pleasure to inform you that Everland was nominated with unanimous approval by the commission to be a Coastal Jewel."

It was hard to hear the last part of her sentence as the room erupted into cheers.

Chapter Thirty-Six

~

Three months later…

"Has anyone seen my shoes?" Tuesday poked around the cardboard boxes stacked haphazardly along the wall in the Belle Mont master bedroom. The severe monochromatic black-and-white style had been brightened with a bold splash of teal on the walls and included more playful artwork with accents of poppy pink and daffodil yellow. J. K. Growling glanced from a fat goose-down pillow in the center of the four-poster bed with an exasperated snort.

Flick removed her earphones, and Tuesday caught a few lyrics from Hamilton's "The Schuyler Sisters." The kid's burgeoning love affair with Broadway musicals swelled her chest with pride.

"Which of your thirty pairs are today's favorites?" The girl's skinny legs hung off the king-sized mattress, tapering into a chunky pair of purple Doc Martens. She still dressed on the gothic end of the spectrum, but color was slowly creeping into her wardrobe as well.

"First, I only have fourteen. Second, they are all my darlings." She placed a hand next to her mouth, stage whispering over one shoulder, "You know I don't like hurting any of their feelings."

"Um. Yeah. So glad we're pretending shoes are animate objects again."

Tuesday puckered her brows at the girl's dubious reflection in the sunburst mirror over the dresser. Flick responded by poking out her tongue, pulling on her ears, and crossing her eyes.

"Keep making that face, kid, and—"

"It might get stuck that way." The girl giggled and plucked the Sharpie shoved behind her ear, returning to doodling a punk-looking mermaid midthigh on her faded jeans.

After Tuesday had accepted Beau's offer to move in together, there'd hardly been a need for the next discussion. Of course they'd apply to become legal guardians for Flick. Together they felt like a real forever family.

"Did I hear a cry for help?" Beau poked his head in the room, a power drill in one hand. He was finishing the final touches on Flick's new canopy bed, which he'd spent the morning building with his dad. His parents had decided to return to Everland three-quarters time, and lived in a houseboat community at Buccaneer's Marina.

Now their Combat Boot Princess would sleep under a puff of neon pink mosquito netting embossed with lightning bolts—a kick-butt girl who deserved nothing but kick-butt dreams.

"She lost another pair of shoes." Flick didn't glance up from her intricate design.

"Do they happen to be high-heeled and orange?" His

eyes roamed Tuesday's legs, bare beneath her royal-blue midthigh shift dress, with a hunger that made her knees weak.

"Orange?" She managed a huff of mock indignation that didn't fool him one iota. His fleeting but intense grin said he had her number.

"It might be worth asking Karen to schedule you for an optometrist visit because they are coral, thanks very much."

He cleared his throat, a rich male sound, half maddened and half amused. "And it might be worth not storing your favorite shoes in the kitchen pantry. They're shelved next to the steel-cut oats."

"Oh, of course!" She slapped her forehead, falling back on the bed. "I had to kick them off the other night to climb on a stepstool and reach the popcorn for our family movie night. It was actually quite sensible."

"I'll give you that. In a roundabout way." The tender kiss he planted on her forehead made her heart feel fashioned not of muscle and tendons but of moonbeams and summer grass, of rubies forged in the strange wanderings of tectonic plates.

In other words, like magic.

His finger stroked her cheek, tracing the swell of her top lip to press lightly on the indent. "Will you be ready by five thirty?" Tonight Happily Ever After Land would donate all entrance ticket proceeds to the Historic Roxy Theater Redevelopment Campaign. She'd worked day and night for a month to pull this off. Now it was time to reap the rewards.

She pretended to nip him. "Baby, I was born ready."

He moved faster. "Wish I could say the same."

"You're going to do great," Tuesday said firmly. "I believe in you."

Beau made an uneasy sound before retreating.

Flick waited until his footsteps faded back down the hall. "Think he's going to go through with it?"

Tuesday shrugged. "He's been cagey since breakfast. And did you notice how his left eye had a tic? That's a sure giveaway that he's nervous."

"You really know him, huh?"

"I do." A sliver of a smile crooked her lips. "Inside and out. And he knows me."

* * *

"It's so busy tonight, we're going to earn a small fortune." Tuesday hadn't quit gawking at the long line since they'd walked through the park entrance. Not a single ride had a wait of less than twenty minutes—even the clunkers—but incredibly, no one seemed to mind. Instead the air was filled with happy chatter as guests pointed and beamed, posed for selfies and bided their time.

"I ran into Mr. Wilcox at Sweet Brew yesterday and he said visitor numbers are through the roof," Beau confirmed. The pirate treasure museum hasn't even been built, but the news of the find had garnered attention and the GTC had lost no time in making Everland the crown diamond in their Coastal Jewel campaign. They've secured advertising and networked to ensure the find got primo placement in magazine and news articles. Then Cedric sold his book in a preempt to a New York publishing house for a significant deal.

"Here we are." Flick waved her hands at the sign reading THE LOGGER'S REVENGE before grabbing his and Tuesday's. "The moment of truth."

They each pulled her into a hug, an affectionate tug-of-war. "Who is this sweet cake, and what did she do to the Grumpy Gus who was here on that first visit?"

"Eh, I never liked that kid," Flick answered.

"I did. She was brave." Tuesday rested her cheek on top of the girl's head, her eyes seeking Beau's. "Just like you'll be brave enough to sit in the soak seat?"

"The front?" Beau took a quick look at Flick, who had a subtle *Oh shit* eye widening. He made a gravelly sound in his throat before moderating his tone. "That's reserved for you."

"A deal is a deal. Guess you're really keen to pay me back for getting you soaked way back when?"

He searched her face for signs of suspicion, his shoulders relaxing when none were evident. "Something like that."

A log plunged down the chute, and he put his churning stomach on notice.

Buck up, pal.

"We don't have to do this." She touched his cheek. "Good Lord, you look about to pass out."

"Nah. He's going to do great," Flick interrupted, flashing him a secret thumbs-up. *You got this*, she mouthed, before leading them into the line.

When they reached their turn for the log, Tuesday positioned herself between his legs. Little did she know this moment carried a hidden weight, one that kept him anchored to the ground, honed his focus despite the natural panic.

The ride started. They left the loading area and sloshed through scenes where mechanical loggers pretended to chop down trees. Paul Bunyan waved next to Babe the Blue Ox.

"Hurry up already." Flick kneed him low in the kidney, and he let out a startled grunt.

"Oh no, you *are* scared." Tuesday half turned, misinterpreting the pain for a groan of terror. "All I wanted was to help you face your fear—"

"Take my hand?" he asked.

"Of course." She reached and squeezed his fingers as the log began the slow climb. They were higher than the park light posts. It was now or never.

He nodded twice, the signal, and Flick passed him the box she'd been entrusted with, the one he'd gone shopping for last week. There, nestled in the white velvet, was a gold ring, the ribbons of metal entwining around a circular diamond. The look was romantic and stylish, with a bit of show, just like the beautiful woman in front of him.

"I didn't realize how bogged down in fear I was until we met," he said. "At first I was afraid to even talk to you, because I sensed you'd rock my world, roll it off its foundation, the one that I'd cemented with caution, deliberation, and moderation. But sometimes caution needs to be thrown to the wind, and you are a hurricane. We'll have our fair share of big ups and hard downs just like everyone else, but what I'm trying to say is, will you take the plunge and become my wife?"

He slipped the ring on her finger as the log tipped over the edge, and he didn't have time to feel fear, not as she shrieked, "Yesssssssssss."

After the splash, Tuesday threw herself into his lap, her long, wet hair smacking his face as she wrapped her legs around his waist. "Did that just happen?" She squealed. "We're getting married? Oh my God, we're getting married."

He leaned in, slanting his mouth over hers. "We are," he breathed, teasing her lower lip with the tip of his tongue.

"If you kiss me like that, I'm not going to be responsible for what happens next," she purred in his ear.

Heat pooled deep within him. "You're going to spend the rest of my life driving me crazy, aren't you?"

"That's the plan." She grinned, tracing the line of his jaw.

His mouth broke into a wide, unabashed smile. "Can't wait."

As they pulled into the exit, they were met with huge applause. All their friends were there: Cedric, Ginger, Rhett, Pepper, the General and Colonel, Beau's parents, Doc Valentine, Karen, and all the gang from the park.

"You'll never guess what happened!" Tuesday waved her ring in every direction.

"We know." Pepper beamed. "The moment's been immortalized for all time."

Up on the grainy screen in the photo kiosk were the two locking lips as Flick faced the camera, giving a beaming two thumbs-ups. The kid doubled over, clutching her middle, laughing so hard it sounded like any second she'd crack a rib.

Tuesday nuzzled against Beau's neck, breathing in his aftershave. "Best proposal ever."

"Good." He wrapped his arms around her waist, his thumbs rubbing slow circles into her lower back. "Because I mean it to be the only one you ever get." Over her shoulder the sun dropped behind the Happily Ever After Land castle, casting crimson and amber hues across the twilight sky.

"Who'd have ever thought?" Joy husked her tone. "In the middle of ordinary life, I stumbled into my own fairy tale."

"You've been a princess for long enough." He took firm

hold of her hands, pressing them against his heart, and gazed into her eyes with a silent promise that he'd never let go. "From this day forward, forever and always, you'll be treated like nothing less than a queen. I love you more than I can say." And since it was always better to show than tell, he kissed her soft and true, tasting bubble-gum-flavored lip gloss and infinity.

Moving to Everland, Georgia, wasn't *exactly* the career move Pepper Knight was hoping for. So when Rhett Valentine, the town's hot vet, offers her a temporary dog-walking job, she jumps at the chance. But as sparks fly between them, a secret sexy fling might be more than she bargained for...

A excerpt from

It Happened on Love Street

follows

Excerpt from the *Back Fence*:

**Everland News That You
Actually Care About**

Classifieds:

Need a Dog Walker? Got a bored pooch sitting around the house full of energy? Let Ruff Love Pet Walkers throw you a bone. One hour, fast-paced (no jogging) outdoor adventures. Call Norma at 912-555-9867. Discounts available for daily clients.

Snug Cottage for Rent: Sunny, furnished one bedroom, one bathroom bungalow available on Love Street. Quiet neighborhood. Contact Doris Carmichael at 912-555-1700—no texting. Please respond with why this ad sounds attractive to you, and when you'll be able to move in. Do NOT contact me with unsolicited services or offers.

Free Lazy-Boy: Earl don't need two and I want room for my sewing table. It's sitting on the curb. 208 Kissing Ct.

Chapter One

One week later...

Pepper glanced around the cul-de-sac, another bead of sweat trickling down her brow. Sun charred the silvery Spanish moss draping the live oaks while the high-waisted Spanx beneath her pencil skirt compressed her organs into diamonds. Good thing she didn't believe in signs from the universe because this shortcut through Hopes and Dreams Way had turned out to be a dead end. Moisture prickled behind her knees, under her boobs, and between her thighs.

Please, Universe. Don't be a sign.

Her judicial clerkship offer had hinged on an immediate start date. The last week was a blur, packing her Manhattan life into three suitcases. She'd stepped off the Greyhound yesterday afternoon with barely enough time to pick up the keys for her new rental house and visit the local Piggly Wiggly, never mind getting oriented.

The absence of a city skyline or a street grid left her sense of direction as broken as the GPS navigation on her smart phone. She huffed a small sigh, blowing up her bangs.

Everland, Georgia, appeared to be block after block of grandly renovated antebellum homes, all with jasmine-smothered wrought iron fences, rocking chair–lined verandas, and names like Love Street, Forever Boulevard, Hopes and Dreams Way, and Kissing Court.

Better find a dentist. A year surrounded by this much sugary sweetness put her at risk of a cavity (or five).

A glance at her wristwatch revealed that her Human Resources appointment wasn't for another forty-five minutes. Her shoulders relaxed. It paid to be prepared. Dead end or no, she'd left herself ample time to fire Siri and navigate her own route to the courthouse.

The lace curtains in the gingerbread Queen Anne across the street twitched and a blue-rinsed older woman peered through the slit with a frown. Pepper adjusted the strap on her leather computer bag and bit down on the inside of her cheek. First impressions were everything, and a Yankee fish out of water marinating in a pool of her own perspiration wasn't a great one.

Head down, she quickly backtracked, retracing her steps. Homesickness nipped at her heels. Or more accurately...sister-sickness. Tonight there'd be no cuddle fest over Chinese takeout in Tuesday's Hell's Kitchen walkup, no debriefing about her day before her sister performed—in side-splitting detail—impersonations from her latest Broadway casting call. There wasn't time for a check-in, but she could fire off the next entry of their ongoing Ugly Selfie Challenge and let Tuesday know she was in her thoughts.

Pepper paused beneath the Forever Boulevard street sign, stuck out her iPhone, and contorted her face into a hideous, triple-chinned expression.

And that's when it happened.

The menacing growl sluiced icy dread through her insides, numbing her core. She didn't have to turn her head to confirm what her body reacted to on instinct.

Dog, two o'clock.

Collapsing her shoulders in a protective cringe, arms shielding her face, she recoiled in jerky steps as fast as her tight skirt allowed. A white ball of fluff with matching organza ear ribbons sat on a red-bricked walkway in the shade of palmetto fronds—devil's spawn in a lap-dog disguise. It curled back its lips to reveal razor-sharp fangs.

Pug or pit bull, it didn't matter. Man's best friend was her worst nightmare.

The tiny tail twitched. She swallowed a whimper. *Easy, easy now.* The fence separating them was five feet high. Fluffy wasn't going to spring through the air, latch on to her throat, and gnaw her jugular like a corncob. Dogs were statistically more likely to lick a person to death.

By a lot.

By a lot, a lot.

But try telling that to her dry mouth and trembling hands.

The growls crescendoed into shrill yaps. Fluffy reared on hind legs, an eight-pound demon cavorting in the seventh circle of hell.

Pepper's stomach responded with a queasy burble. More yowling rose ahead, a boxer-looking hellbeast tried cramming its fat head through its white picket prison. *Nope.* She veered around a parked minivan and crossed the street, pulse leaping with panic.

"They don't want to hurt me. They don't want to hurt me," she chanted a mantra from Canine Calm, a weekend cognitive therapy clinic she'd shelled out three hundred bucks on after a close encounter with a shih tzu in SoHo last summer left her, well, shit-tzuing her pants.

Blink and breathe. Unravel the negative feelings within before they unravel you. Observe fearful emotions and give them space as they arise, watching them float away like soap bubbles. Blink without judgment. Remember, there is no right way or wrong way to blink. Simply be the blink.

Blink that. She'd dropped out an hour into the nonrefundable session. But now her ears were hot and her jaw tight, all the hallmarks of spiking blood pressure.

She could chant "They don't want to hurt me" all day, but the faint white scars on her cheek, one below her eye, and the other to the side of her nose, the exact match to a Doberman pinscher's mouth, begged to differ. Her nervous system issued a warning: *Imminent threat to life and limb. Take cover.*

Two corgis joined the din, followed by a baritone bow-wow-wow from another backyard.

Which way to go? No direction was safe.

"Is that lady dancing?" a high-pitched voice asked behind her.

"Dunno," another answered.

Pepper turned, and two kids, the girl in a full-skirted pirate getup, the boy in artfully ragged breeches, froze on identical scooters. Their chubby pink-tinged cheeks offset tawny skin, and matching skull-and-crossbones hats perched on top of their thick, black curls.

"Ahoy there, mateys." It sounded like she'd been sucking helium. She cleared her throat, striving for a more natural tone. "Don't you two look cute."

The little girl scratched the side of her nose. "Mama's us-ing us as models—"

"For the Village Pillage ad." The boy fiddled with his eye patch. "She works for Mayor Marino's office, and we gotta beat Hogg Jaw—"

"Village Pillage?" Any distraction from the canine cho-rus was welcome. Even if it meant hanging out with kinder-gartners.

"Memerating Cap'n Redbeard—"

"And Everland's true claim to the lost treasure."

Deciphering hieroglyphics might be easier than under-standing those last sentences. Pepper frowned. "You mean commemorating?"

"And Mama promised us ice cream afterward if we smile real good." The girl bared her teeth in an overwide grin or grimace, hard to say which. "Two scoops of Superman fla-vor for me and mint chip for Will. Daddy said it was bribery, but Mama calls it in-cent-i-vi-zing." She pronounced the last word with careful enunciation.

"Mint chip is one of my favorites, too." Thank God, her ploy worked. The dogs were losing interest the longer they chatted.

"Why do you talk funny?" Caution crept into the little boy's voice, presumably William.

"You mean my accent? Well, see, I'm from Manhattan." A five-year-old had burned her, but who cares? The longer she rambled in the street, the better the chance that awful barking might eventually stop. "Lower East Side. At least that's where I feel that I'm from. I was born in Moose Bottom, Maine, a place even smaller than here, if you can believe that. Located between Podunk and Boondock. No joke. And that's not taking into account Boonie to the south or Timbuktu to the west."

The children's mouths hung open.

Had she spoken too loudly? Too friendly? Too weird? She had no experience chatting up small people. Kids might as well be aliens from the planet Crayon Gobbler, but these two saved her from a public panic attack. She'd had to suck it up and owe them one.

"William John! Katydid!" An elegant black woman appeared on the top step of an ivy-covered house on the corner. Her tailored fuchsia wrap dress popped against her skin's rich bronze, and her long dark hair was pulled into a sleek ponytail. "Get your scrawny behinds back here and brush your teeth. Ah, ah, ah!" She held up a hand, a diamond catching the sunlight. "Don't go telling me that you already did because your toothbrushes aren't wet. Let's go, let's go, we're not going to be late, I'll tell you that much for free."

"Aw, man!"

"Coming, Mama!" The siblings shot Pepper a last lingering look before pushing off on their scooters, whispering as they powered toward the crosswalk.

She gave the woman a *just passing by, I'm a friendly new-in-town stranger who is not trying to kidnap your sweet children* wave. The tentative gesture was met with a distracted smile.

Pepper tucked the corner of her shirt back into her skirt, swallowing an envious lump as the woman reset her Bluetooth earpiece and disappeared inside the magnificent home. Fat chance *she* ate a Pop-Tart for dinner. Imagine having a big house. Cute kids. Effortless fashion sense. The total package.

Must be nice.

Someday she'd meet Mr. Right. One teeny tiny clerkship

in Georgia and she'd be off to bigger and better things back in New York. At this very moment, her true love might be staring out his corner office with sweeping views of the East River as inexplicable longing compresses his chest. "You're out there," he'd mutter, slamming a fist against his open palm. "Out there somewhere. And I shall find you, my dearest darling."

Sooner or later, their gazes would connect in a crowded intersection and boom, a part of her soul would lock into his and that would be it. Cue the balloon drop. Blazing meteoroids. Unicorns dancing the fox trot. Rainbows—make that *double* rainbows—bursting over the cityscape. She'd plan a wedding in the Hamptons, stop hitting snooze on her biological clock, and have her own perfect life.

Yeah.

Someday...

But on the bright side, *right now* she was finally heading in the right direction. A statue of Lady Justice rose from the end of the street, keeping watch over the Scooter B. Merriweather Courthouse, armed with a sword, balance scales, and a fierce resting bitch face. Pepper flashed her a thumbs-up. Ahead, her reflection beamed off the courthouse's glass front door, projecting the image of—

Oh. Schnikey.

Desperate times called for a discreet bang fluff. Taming these frizzy, more-brown-than-blond locks into an A-line bob was a battle at the best of times. Georgia humidity required full-scale war with a leave-in conditioner offensive followed by a barrage of mousse, a wide-toothed comb, professional-grade blow dryer, and straightener.

God as her witness, she refused to sport flyaways on her first day. She smoothed her part, shifting left and right, checking for VSL—visible Spanx lines—a real and present danger as her skirt warped and wrinkled.

Wrenching the door open, she stumbled beneath the rotunda, stifling a relieved moan. Got to credit the South's mastery of the fine art of air-conditioning. The wall directory listed Human Resources on the second floor, down the hall from her new boss, the Honorable Aloysius P. Hogg. Judge Hogg maintained a notorious reputation on the law clerk circuit. Whispers hinted that he didn't interview for a Monday-through-Friday job, but expected seven-day-a-week indentured servitude, including all public holidays.

On her way upstairs, the brass handrail cooled her damp palm. This wasn't a dream job, but no one hired professional cupcake testers. And this year of dues paying in Nowheresville, USA, would land her back in Manhattan with a real shot at making junior partner with Kendall & Kline Associates, an elite corporate law firm with an impressive starting salary and more impressive annual bonus.

Her phone buzzed with a text. Tuesday's image flashed on the screen, her sister's full lips pressed in the ultimate duck face as she did that unsettling trick where she crossed only one eye. The message read: Good luck today! You've come a long way, baby.

Pepper grinned. Her sister was right. This courthouse was a far cry from her family's sugar bush farm in Maine's North Woods.

The sticky truth about the maple syrup business was that people didn't get into it to increase their bank account balance. Yes, there'd always been food on the table (provided coupons were cut), (hand-me-down) clothes on her back, and a (sometimes leaky) roof overhead—although prohibitive heating oil costs meant huddling around a cast-iron stove during the winter months.

Dad boasted they were rich in love, but Mom's parting words before leaving them behind for New Hampshire were tattooed on Pepper's brain. "Whoever said money can't buy happiness must have been poor, honey. Never ever forget that."

And she never ever did.

Dad tried to put a positive spin on the situation: "From now on, girls, we're a trio. Good thing three is my lucky number." But there was no glossing over the fact that Mom had reinvented herself into a far-off Bedford suburb, remarrying a banker and becoming more invested in his stock portfolio than her two girls.

Pepper tried to be a de facto wife to Dad—cooking, cleaning, organizing appointments—and a surrogate mother to Tuesday—nagging her for homework, making lunches, styling her long blond hair before they hurried to catch the school bus.

The more Mom faded from their life, the more Pepper stepped in as Superwoman, self-appointed guardian of the family, and good thing, too. These days Dad was one bad sciatica attack away from being unable to handle the farm's rigorous physical demands, and how long before Tuesday's dreams of Broadway stardom dimmed? Her father and sister were reality escape artists, but someday they'd need her and her pragmatism. Pepper was the third little pig, busily building a sensible future.

Or do you need them to need you?

She lengthened her stride, walking faster than the whisper of doubt. At the end of the hall, Human Resources waited, promising the answers to her prayers. She let out a huge breath, the smallest trace of a smile settling on her lips. *Almost there.* A little routine paperwork and she'd carpe the heck out of this diem.

Chapter Two

~

The hum from the fluorescent lights cut through the examination room's silence. Rhett removed his stethoscope eartips with an inward groan.

"Well? Is he gonna pull through, Doctor?" The redhead in the sunflower sundress hitched her breath. No one gave a performance like Kennedy Day. No wonder she'd done well in all those pageants back in high school.

But the real kudos had to go to Muffin, the bichon frise valiantly playing dead on the stainless steel surgical table. Still, not even expert training could override a strong, healthy heartbeat.

Proper Southern manners dictated a few words of comfort, but his growing migraine crowded out any chivalrous impulses. "He's going to live to lick another day."

Kennedy clapped her hands without a hint of embarrassment. "Aren't you a regular miracle worker?"

And aren't you one hell of a dog trainer?

He reached into his white lab coat pocket and removed a treat. In an instant, Muffin bounded to his feet with a short but definitive yip. "Seems Lazarus here has worked up a healthy appetite."

"Praise the Lord and pass the mashed potatoes. Come to Mama, Muffin Wuffin." Kennedy scooped up the dog and smacked wet kisses on the top of its head.

Muffin stared at him darkly, telecommunicating, *See what I'm dealing with? Be a bro and hand over a Barkie Bite.*

Rhett passed the treat in solidarity.

"Silly me!" Kennedy's shoulders shook with her tinkling laugh. "Before I forget, I brought you something special." She reached into the bedazzled insulated bag beside her chair and removed a cake, as if bearing a fake dead dog and baked goods were normal occurrences.

Everland, his hometown, could be described many different ways, but *normal* wasn't the first adjective that sprang to mind.

The real miracle to this appointment would be shuffling Kennedy out before getting asked around for dinner. She sported that same determined look while wielding a pump-action shotgun on the opening day of turkey season. She might primp into the textbook definition of a Southern belle but had crack-shot aim when a tom was in her sights.

"This right here is the praline Bundt that's won the Everland Fair's Golden Fork five years running." She positioned the cake to make it impossible to miss the caramel glaze or her cleavage. "You do like a nice Bundt, don't you, Dr. Valentine?" She dropped her voice to a purr. "Or are you more of a sour cream pound cake man?

Dessert had never sounded so dirty.

"Rhett," he snapped automatically. "Plain Rhett suits me fine." The words *Dr. Valentine* made him want to check over his shoulder for his father and make a sign to ward off the evil eye. "We graduated a year apart. My dad coached Sailing Club. Your brother Kingston was on my team."

"Of course." She leaned forward with a suggestive wink. "And might I say you've gone from a dingy to a yacht."

Time to hustle her out before things turned dangerous. He didn't want to lead her on. Not when her megawatt smile gave him flash blindness, even as shadows haunted beneath her eyes. Everyone knew last year's divorce had hit her hard. Breakups sucked. He understood. He even sympathized. But at the end of the day, her failed marriage wasn't his circus.

He had his hands full with his own damn monkeys.

"Listen. About the cake." He handed it back and led her toward the door. "My office policy is never to accept gifts from—"

"Gift?" She halted so fast her heels scuffed the linoleum. "Why it's nothing but a harmless little nut cake!"

"Did Lou Ellen put you up to this?" His sister acted like her fourth term as second vice president of the Everland Ladies Quilt Guild was a mandate to nominate him as the town's most eligible bachelor, as if his single status was due to circumstance rather than choice.

Online dating profiles kept popping into his inbox, as

well as invitations to donate a dinner and movie date to the upcoming Village Pillage silent auction, or meet so-and-so's third cousin, niece, dental hygienist, or belly-dance instructor. If he dared to smile at a woman at the post office, the local gossip blog, the *Back Fence*, posted a poll about wedding cake flavors by sundown.

He'd rather lick one of his waiting room chairs than date under that kind of scrutiny. Besides, bachelorhood came with undeniable perks:

He never woke without the covers.

Never got an arm ache from spooning.

Never had to fake laugh at a chick flick.

And when blue balls struck, well, his right hand had him covered.

Yep, all a man needed was a cold beer, a boat, and a couple of dogs.

And if he ever hit his head hard enough to climb back on the relationship horse, it would be to a low-maintenance country girl who made up for a lack of drama with a love of big bird dogs. Labs would work. Or Chesapeake Bay retrievers.

"Weeeeell, I *did* run into Lou Ellen last week at the club." Kennedy's cheeks tinged pink as he opened the exam room door. "And she may have let slip that you were in need of a little female companionship. After all, it has been a long time since...well..."

Ah. And there it was. His own personal elephant in its own personal corner.

He reached for the knob, careful not to grind his molars, at least not audibly. If there were a better way to deal with references to that one time he was left at the altar...he hadn't found it.

Once, just once, it would be nice to make it a goddamn week without some reference to Birdie.

"Remember this, Rhett Valentine." Kennedy squeezed his bicep, her thick gardenia perfume exacerbating his headache. "There's no *I* in happiness."

"Come again?"

She screwed her nose like he'd come up a few Bradys short of a bunch. "H-a-p-p-y-n-e-s-s?"

He took a deep breath. She had to go. Now. Before he said something he regretted.

He ushered her and Muffin into the foyer. "Don't forget to grab a Milk-Bone in the bowl by the magazine rack." He shut the door, the loud snick cutting her off midprotest.

He scrubbed his jaw, eying the locked cabinet that stored the horse tranquilizers. Lou Ellen was going to raise hell once she caught wind of this snub.

Tempting, but nah. "Suck it up, Buttercup," he muttered. If the biggest problem in his life was a bossy big sister determined to sail him off into a happy-ever-after sunset, he should be grateful that things were looking up.

Or at least not facedown in the gutter.

Was he happy? Well-meaning busybodies pestered him with the question, but no one ever quit talking long enough to hear his answer.

Yeah. He was. Happy enough anyway.

He didn't return to his office until Kennedy's Miata convertible screeched from the parking lot. His three golden getrievers, Faulkner, Steinbeck, and Fitzgerald, dozed on their respective pillows and didn't flinch when his desk phone rang.

"Valentine Veterinary," he answered.

"The council work session got postponed to next Thursday," Beau Marino drawled in his deep, no-nonsense tone. He was Everland's youngest mayor in a century, son of a Bermudan bartender and local blueblood, and Rhett's best friend since kindergarten. "Weather service predicts it'll be blowing seventeen this afternoon with gusts to twenty."

"Sounds good." Rhett broke into a grin. They jointly owned the *Calypso*, a bachelor pad in the form of a coastal cruiser moored at Buccaneers Marina. "I don't have an appointment for an hour. I'll swing by home for the marina key and pick you up after work."

"You know where to find me." Beau lived in Belle Mont Manor, the biggest house in the county, but he called city hall home. Worked around the clock.

Rhett hung up and drummed his fingers on the desktop, shedding the irritation from Kennedy's appointment like an onionskin. An evening sail should screw his head on straight. Always did.

As his headache faded, the wall clock chimed ten o'clock. Outside the street-facing window, a silver-haired man in a seersucker suit led a Maltese whose lavender ribbons matched his bow tie. Doc passed the same time each day, a warm and cozy thirty seconds carefully orchestrated to make his only son feel like shit.

And the gambit worked.

Migraine roaring back, Rhett opened his top drawer, shook two ibuprofen from the bottle, and chased the pills with a swallow from the cold coffee in the mug next to his keyboard.

What masqueraded for an innocent pleasure stroll was,

in point of fact, a one-man protest against Valentine Veterinary. Doc had made good on his long-ago vow never to darken the door to Rhett's office—going so far as to drive to TLC Pet Hospital in Hogg Jaw for Marie Claire's care— a dick move, but it proved the saying about Valentine men. They did stay true.

Even if it was to words spoken in anger.

Rhett was groomed to study family or internal medicine at Duke and join his dad's practice, not bolt to UGA and become a doctor of *veterinary* medicine.

Mama's death had sent them both to hell, but they dealt with different devils. Seemed his old man was bent on sailing into his final years on a bitter ship.

God-fucking-speed.

As for him, Rhett had his dogs, a growing practice, and low tolerance for bullshit. He was sick and tired of being the bad son for having a different vision of his future. He sank into his leather office chair, shoved his glasses up his forehead, and exhaled.

Next to his computer perched a brass-framed black-and-white photograph of a laughing woman surrounded by two Labs, a Siamese cat, lop-eared rabbits, lovebirds, and three guinea pigs.

He grabbed the picture and ran his thumb over the glass. To live with Ginny Valentine meant to love loudly, indiscriminately, and with gusto. Doc tolerated the chaos because it made his wife happy, and she was his sun, the light in all their lives. Rhett's core constricted as if an invisible screwdriver tightened his solar plexus. Did Mama watch over them? He set the frame back down. There'd never been a single sign after her death. No visitation dreams. No soft shift to the air as he turned his shoulder muscles to jelly beating on the speed bag in his tool shed or sanded cedar planks for the fishing skiff he was building in his backyard.

Nothing. Not even during the whole bad business with Birdie.

With any luck, Mama was up there plenty distracted by drinking gin with Margaret Mitchell, her favorite author. Or flying. She always said that's the one thing she wished she could do, fly wild and free like one of the storm petrels that haunted the coast.

His gut twisted knowing how much she'd hate the way her beloved family had grown apart in her absence. Lou Lou smothered everyone in her path, relentless as a weedy vine. Dad sheathed himself in a thick shell, gnarled and bitter as a walnut casing. And Rhett, well, he grew long "keep your fucking distance" spines like a prickly pear cactus.

He couldn't fix any of that, but so help him, he'd give Mama a fitting legacy—a rescue shelter that bore her name. The Virginia Valentine Memorial Shelter would be her real monument, not that cold slab of ornate granite nestled beneath a dogwood in the Everland cemetery. Her love and compassion for any animal great or small deserved to be made permanent through bricks and mortar.

Or do you want to atone? He rubbed the lines between his brow as if the gesture would erase the gnawing question.

If Mama was a saint, he was another simple sinner who kept on trying.

Word from the Low Country Community Foundation was that the construction loan was as good as wrapped up. The last obstacle before being deemed "shovel ready" was persuading Doc to donate the land. The shelter deserved to be built on the spot where Mama used to take them to play as children, the small rise where live oaks rang with katydids and tree frogs, herons silently stalked the tidal marsh at the bottom, and in the distance the ocean unfurled across the horizon like one of those bright blue ribbons Mama wore in her hair.

He drained the rest of the coffee, grimacing at the final acidic swallow. *Shit.* He'd put off the request long enough, but for better or worse, Doc was his dad. The guy who'd walked him around the back patio on his feet, taught him how to trim a sail, and helped him win third in the state science fair with his stem cell research project.

The guy who'd championed him.

Rhett's gaze tracked the ceiling fan in mute outrage. What the hell? Maybe Doc deserved a thank-you, because nothing ever made Rhett want to succeed at his clinic like the fact his father openly rooted for his failure.

"All right. Let's get this over with," he announced to the dogs. They scrambled to attention as he stood and grabbed the three leashes dangling off the hook by the door.

Doc was a creature of habit. Not only could Rhett set a clock by his dad's morning walk, but the man had a sweet tooth. Right now he must be stopping into the What-a-Treat Candy Boutique for his daily Charleston Chew before joining the Scrabble game at the dog park. With a little hustle, Rhett could catch him by the courthouse.

He shoved on his glasses and adjusted the frames. This conversation was going to be as fun as a poke in the eye with a sharp stick.

But nothing good ever came easy.

ABOUT THE AUTHOR

Lia Riley is a contemporary romance author. *USA Today* describes her as "refreshing," and *RT Book Reviews* calls her books "sizzling and heartfelt." She loves her husband, her three kids, wandering redwood forests, and a perfect pour-over coffee. She is 25 percent sarcastic, 54 percent optimistic, and 122 percent bad at math (good thing she writes happy endings for a living). She and her family live mostly in Northern California.

You can learn more at:
LiaRiley.com
Twitter @LiaRileyWrites
Facebook.com/AuthorLiaRiley

Fall in Love with Forever Romance

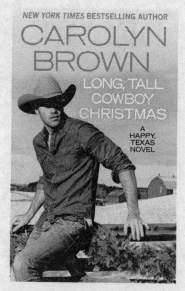

LONG, TALL COWBOY CHRISTMAS
By Carolyn Brown

A heartwarming holiday read from *USA Today* bestselling author Carolyn Brown. Nash Lamont is a man about as solitary as they come. So what the heck is he doing letting a beautiful widow and her three rambunctious children temporarily move in at Christmas?

Kasey Dawson thought she'd never get over the death of her husband. But her kids have a plan of their own: Nothing will keep them from having a real family again—even if it takes a little help from Santa himself.

Fall in Love with Forever Romance

THE TROUBLE WITH CHRISTMAS
By Debbie Mason

The Trouble with Christmas is the first book in the *USA Today* bestselling Christmas, Colorado series by Debbie Mason. This special reissue edition will feature bonus content never before in print! Resort developer Madison Lane is trying to turn Christmas, Colorado, into a tourist's winter wonderland. But Sheriff Gage McBride is tasked with stopping her from destroying his town. After meeting Madison, he can't decide if she's naughty or nice, but one thing is for certain—Christmas will never be the same again.

Fall in Love with Forever Romance

MAYBE THIS CHRISTMAS
By Jennifer Snow

One more game is all that stands between hockey star Asher Westmore and a major career milestone. But when an injury sidelines him for months, the only bright spot is his best friend and physical therapist, Emma Callaway, whose workouts improve his body *and* his spirit… Fans of Lori Wilde will love the latest from Jennifer Snow!

Fall in Love with Forever Romance

TOO BEAUTIFUL TO BREAK
By Tessa Bailey

Losing Sage Alexander is not an option for Belmont Clarkson. His heart is hers, has always been hers. He knows she's hiding something from him, but nothing will stand in his way of telling her just how much she means to him—even if saving her from her past ends up costing him everything. Don't miss the final book in Tessa Bailey's Romancing the Clarksons series!

THE CORNER OF FOREVER AND ALWAYS
By Lia Riley

Perfect for readers of Kristan Higgins, Jill Shalvis, and Marina Adair. When princess impersonator Tuesday Knight faces off against Everland mayor Beau Marino to save her theme park from demolition, sparks fly. Will she save Happily Ever After Land only to lose her own happy ever after?